BETWEEN THERE
VOLUME 1

BETWEEN THERE
VOLUME 1

Anthony S. Buoni
editor

Stay Spooky
Anthony Buoni
To Jeff
11/9/2012

Pulpwood Press
Panama City, FL

TABLE OF CONTENTS

The Harbinger   Anthony S. Buoni   11

Cold Spot   Lynn Wallace   15

I live with the dead   Nathan Simmons   21

The Scribuline   Joni N. Scott (LeCompte)   23

Soul Spheres part 1   Conrad Young   33

Into the Dark   Buoni & Lamoureux   63

Whiteblood   W. Adam Burdeshaw   157

Promise   Toby Union   195

Café Elysium   Anthony S. Buoni   198

Space Oddity   Tony Simmons   259

Friend to Darkness   Lynn Wallace   263

Where Shadows Crept   Anthony S. Bunoi   269

ACKNOWLEDGEMENTS

There are many between the here and the there I owe thanks, but these cats helped and haunted me through this adventure and deserve special mention:

Mom and Dad for living with a haunted writer. Fallon for making life interesting, Michael Lister for making this dream become reality. Adelle Davis for synchronicity. The contributors to this anthology for believing this idea, themselves, and working together to make a damn fine book. The MEOWs for fearlessly sharing this creative life with me and the world—you know who you cats are. Tony Viejo II for haunted holidays. Aaron Bearden for music. Erich Pupala for European ghost stories. Hemant Patel for waxing poetic at dawn. Kami Jo Tassin for full moon texts. Joe Hill for philosophy. Chris Porter for haunting us still. Kim Renfroe for the patient ear. Eryn Barker for my first cat ears. Amber Mattson for porch drinks. Paige Hudson for fliers. Amanda Harcrow for not just ghost stories, but hanging out with real ghosts. A.J. Englehardt for being so close and so far. Dan Fennell for Christmas Chess. Wade and Frankie Kennington for Sookie shots. The crew of the Newby's establishments for letting me write in peace all these years. Bay County (Florida's Twin Peaks) for being scary underneath the warm and sunny surface. The city of New Orleans (need I say more?). Puddle of Mudd for filling my jar. All the bars and nightclubs that allow the paranormal to unfold over phantasmal conversation.

And to the Children of the Night, what music they make: The Damned, The Cure, The Cruxshadows, The Doors, Nick Cave, NIN, The Smiths, Tim Booth and James, Ween, Primus, The Feeding Fingers, Peter Murphy, Aaron Bearden. Pig Chicken Suicide, Joy Division, Siouxsie and the Banshees, Tiesto, Pink Floyd, David Bowie, the Rat Pack, Cory Branan, The Hold Steady, Alice Cooper, Death Before Dying, Disco Vato, and all the DJs that stay up late with the phantoms.

INTRODUCTION

Do you believe in ghosts?

I noticed whenever I mentioned this project to friends and strangers alike, everyone had a story. Phantom encounters in old houses, eerie sounds in the woods, shadow people lurking in dark corners—I was surprised at how many sane, respectable people have been touched by the unknown. In an age of incredible technology, rational thought, and a prevailing *I'll-believe-it-when-I-see-it* attitude, the notion of apparitions is still very much alive.

It seems ghosts and other supernatural ideas have saturated our culture. Many cable stations have shows dedicated to ghost hunting. Cities offer haunted walking tours, and visitors shell out big bucks in hopes of catching a glimpse of living death. Teen novels present unearthly creatures living harmoniously with humanity, just underneath the surface of everyday life. It is almost impossible to turn on the television, open a book, go to the movies, or even play video games without finding paranormal themes. Sometimes these images and ideas are terrifying. Other times, they are silly. But where do these stories come from?

Are ghosts simply our desire to validate life after death, or do they prove there is more to this existence than what we can see, hear, feel? Maybe they are the product of overactive imaginations, our fears manifested into something tangible. Maybe they are just stories to scare children, morality tales forcing us to inspect the way we conduct our lives. Or maybe, just maybe, whether horrible or angelic, they do exist, and our brains, technology, and collective consciousness are not evolved enough to comprehend them.

This collection is home to many types of specters. Some are benign, even helping us during our journey. Others… well, you'll see. I am pleased to present *Between There, Volume 1*. Light a candle, turn off the lights, and enjoy these amazing stories by some equally remarkable writers. If you should happen to find your heart racing, or there are strange sounds coming from the other room, remember: these are only stories…right?

Anthony S. Buoni
Panama City Beach

5 May 2011

THE HARBINGER

Red flashes across a portrait of a couple standing in their wedding attire—the bride in white and the groom a penguin. Red to blue, dancing on a framed photo of a toddler chasing a white and brown duck by the shores of some ancient Florida lake. With a burst of white, the cycle begins again...

Pushing a toy police car down the darkened hallway, Hugo made siren sounds as he approached his parents' closed bedroom door. The car's tires snagged the brown carpet, pulling at the black and white, but Hugo pressed on, the lights blinking to the ceiling. Mom was folding laundry in the other end of the house, granting space to let his imagination wander.

"Officer Smith, we're near the great door. Turn back—turn back," Hugo said in the roughest voice his five years would manage.

He began to turn the toy when the bedroom door popped open and creaked softly, widening enough to peek in. Hugo paused, and the lights on top of the car stopped flashing; the hallway became dark and quiet. Hugo set the car down and crept towards the open door, peering in.

His parents' room had thick curtains covering their window, and the heavy material allowed only muffled light to penetrate. The bed, the TV, the dresser, Mom's vanity, the nightstands—ominous, shadowy forms.

Hugo looked over his shoulder. His pulse quickened—if he was caught playing in her bedroom, it would be in the corner or straight to bed with no supper. His parents established from the beginning that their lair was not for Hugo's inquisitive eyes, making it an irresistible longing to the knowledge-hungry boy. Looking back into the room, the sound of distant thunder tickled his ears.

Hugo reached up to pull the door shut when soft humming floated from the corner of the room. It was a beautiful voice—the mesmerizing melody was mysterious and dreamy. The music grew louder, and Hugo could no longer remain outside. With another glance towards the living room, Hugo pushed the door open.

As Hugo entered his parents' room, the honey-like humming circled his heart and pulled him deeper into the darkened chamber. Hugo swallowed hard, failing to see the music's source. Defenseless against the tune, he was breaking one of Mother's scarce but firm rules. He began for the door but stopped in front of the vanity.

Where once had only been shadow, a woman sat radiating eerie white, wearing a flowing gown. Her hair, also white, tangled within a breeze, obscuring her face. She continued the melody while working her hands in the gown's folds.

"Hello," whispered Hugo, "that's a pretty song, miss." Never glancing up, the woman's hidden hands worked out of view. "Who are you? Does my mom know you're here?"

She looked up from her work. Where her eyes should have been stared two black, almond-shaped sockets. The wind surrounding her increased, tossing her hair and waving her dress. Hugo stepped back and gasped. She extended an arm outward as if to embrace the boy, still hiding what she was doing within her dress's folds. Hugo looked into the recesses that should have been her eyes and fell into their abyss...

Hugo's mom entered the bedroom, flicking on the light.

"What have I told you about playing in here, Hugo?" Her voice was angry, and she folded her arms across her chest. "You're in deep trouble, young man."

"But, Mom," pleaded Hugo, "there was this lady in here. She was singing to me and—

"That's enough, Hugo. I don't know where you come up with these ideas. Come and help me fold the laundry before your father comes home. You know how he likes all the chores to be done."

Hugo stared at the now vacant seat. On the floor beside the chair laid a crumpled handkerchief, and Hugo snatched it up, careful not to arouse Mom's attention. He could feel her burning glare as he headed towards the door.

Hugo sighed and when he exited the door, he picked up the toy cop car and pressed the button that made the lights whirl round and round. Mom shut the door behind him and returned towards the laundry room. He let her get ahead of him before he pulled out the handkerchief and turned it over in his fingers, examining what she left behind. Covered with intricate spirals, the cloth was the most beautiful thing Hugo had ever seen. He stuffed it deep in his pocket. He knew the visitor would be back, and he couldn't wait to see her again…

ANTHONY S. BUONI

COLD SPOT

There I was, in a hurry, traveling too close behind a Suburban, of all things, much too close just as I was clearing the high point of Hathaway Bridge, heading east. That's when I had a moment of panic. Ahead of me, all these brake lights start flashing red, almost in perfect sequence, starting about a hundred yards down the incline of the bridge. So instead of tapping my brakes and maybe even easing over into the safety lane, I ram right into the backside of a Suburban.

Oddly enough, my airbag doesn't deploy, but I bang into the Suburban pretty good. My head whacks something, my steering wheel, I guess, but I don't see how. Still, as the Suburban and I pull over into the safety lane and everyone else moves on past us, I feel this stinging spot in the middle of my forehead. I rub it, but it just stays there.

I release my seat belt and harness and get out of the car, waiting on the driver of the Suburban. I check out the front of my Camry, which has a crease across the front, one smashed headlight. "Damn!" But at least the radiator seems okay. The driver still hasn't moved, so I start to walk up to the driver's side door. Suddenly the Suburban takes off, pulling back into the traffic lane, quickly losing itself in traffic. Probably an uninsured driver, or suspended license. Just as well, I think, because I already have 4 points this year, have suffered through one of those dumb-ass online traffic schools, and my insurance is just itching to double. I don't need that. I can get this front end fixed. Cheaper by far. Plus, I have five minutes to get to work.

So I breathe a sigh of relief, again vow not to tailgate, and generally promise myself that all this rush, rush, rush has to change.

The spot on my forehead doesn't sting as much now, but it's sort of numb. I can't for the life of me figure out how anything could have whacked me in the forehead. As I'm driving, I lean forward as far as I can. No way my head could have hit the steering wheel. It's got me stumped, but anyway, another narrow escape, I'm thinking.

I pull into Simm's Auto Parts just in time, leap out of the car, and sling myself through the door. Old man Warren looks up. "Not a moment to spare, Turk." He calls me Turk because I'm pretty dark-skinned from all the fishing, I'm tall and have dark hair. Why "Turk" rather than some other damn thing, though, I can't say. That's the way it is and it's stuck, so now everyone's calling me "Turk."

I start with some inventory, checking in a Mopar shipment till the alpha-numeric codes start to go fuzzy. I feel my forehead, and it's cold, not the whole forehead, just the spot from before, the place where nothing on earth could have possibly hit me.

Still, there it was, a cold spot about the size of a silver dollar, colder'n fuck. So I rub it, and that doesn't seem to make any difference. It just stays cold. Doesn't hurt or nothing, just cold.

Then, for some reason, I look up through the parts aisle. I just know I need to look up that way. There's Ol' Warren, silhouetted, and suddenly he turns around, looking back at me. "Turk," he yells.

I walk up his way. He looks at me curiously, scrunching up his left eye, and rubbing a hand over his gray stubble. "You just sitting back there waitin' on me ta call you or something?"

"No, just checking in that Mopar shit."

He hands me about eight pulley belts partly sticking out of a bag—"Look, I need you to take these here belts over 'that place on Joyce Avenue. What's the name of it?"

"Perkins," I say.

"That's it. Perkins. Receipt's in the bag. No check, Turk. Only take cash, ya hear?"

"Right, cash only." I stand there a minute.

"Well, what's the holdup?"

"I gotta cross that bridge again?"

"I'm not paying for you to go Lynn Haven, Southport, Ebro, 79."

So I take the belts and head on out, back in the sunlight, back to my Camry with the creased front end.

I head on out. Car starts up fine. That's good.

I'm making good time on 98, sliding under one yellow light at Beck and another at Michigan, but no luck at the bottleneck near the college. Traffic's backed up a bit.

For some reason, I notice my forehead again. It feels even colder, if that's possible. And I look over to my left. There's a brown-haired girl, young, maybe college age, behind the wheel of a kind of van, and she's just bawling. I mean, I can see the wet streaks lining the side of her face. I can't remember seeing anyone in public looking so miserable. Well, it's not really public. She's in the thin privacy of her car. She's so thoroughly sad. It's heartbreaking, really. She found out she's pregnant. Her fiance's dead in Iraq. Her mother has cancer. I can't imagine what.

Traffic moves on, more for my lane than for hers, so she drops back behind me. I check my rearview. I could swear it's another Suburban, but I've got Suburban on the brain now. I keep looking for her as her traffic lane picks up and even catching up and passing mine, but I never see her. I start paying attention to my own driving, especially as I near the bridge, even catching myself white-knuckling the steering wheel.

Lighten up, I tell myself.

Traffic this way over the bridge isn't as bad as I thought. I keep my distance, but I'm the only one who is. Some guy with Georgia plates gives me the finger, whipping around me. I just tell him to go fuck himself. Sorry if I'm not in a hurry, you stupid fuck.

In a few minutes, I'm at Perkins. I have to insist on cash even
though the owner, an Italian guy, Peretti, Perinni, something like that,
has already whipped out the business checkbook. He gives me a
pained look that I swear I can feel in my forehead.

"What wrong with you, anyway?" he asks.

"Nothing," I say. "I was just told to get cash."

"My check's not good for Warren?" He stares at me for a moment.

"You know how it is. Business is slow. He probably needs to
liquidate some inventory."

"Yeah," the owner says with a sneer. "I know how it is."

He counts out the cash from the till. I take it in a little paper bag
and leave.

Now, I have to face the traffic again, past Zoo World, WMBB,
then the Thomas Drive exchange at the Navy base, and the long
incline up Hathaway again.

I happen to glance at my gas gauge. "Damn." It's on empty, and
I filled up two days ago. No way. Maybe my accident earlier knocked
something loose and I'm leaking fuel. I just want to make it over the
bridge.

Sure enough, though, the car starts lugging, not drawing enough
fuel just as I'm easing up the hump. Then there's nothing, so I coast
over to the side, again moving into the no-traffic lane. My forehead
stings like I've put an ice cube on it, aching for real now. All the traffic starts slowing, moving past me, some people smiling at me, shaking their heads. Real sympathetic fuckers.

Behind me, someone slams on brakes and someone else does the
same. A flash of someone swerving over toward me catches my eye,
and I just throw myself out of the way. Metal screeches, and this
behemoth van launches itself up the back of my Camry and climbs
over the roof, landing on the outer rail of the bridge.

There's a girl inside screaming. I swear to God, it the same girl
I saw earlier. She's looking over at me, this horrified look in her

eyes, her vehicle teetering on the rail, hanging out over the bay. She's ripping at her seat belt, mouthing something, "Help me!" looking straight at me.

I get up and move toward her. Several people have pulled over and gotten out of their cars.

One guy says, "Get her out of there," so I reach up to her door handle and begin tugging on it, but the car seems to be inching away from me, and the door won't budge. She has climbed into the back seat now and is kicking at the passenger door. I try to open that door. The car is sliding away from me. It's going over.

Her door slings open, and she's right there three feet away from me, her eyes as large as moons, the car dropping over the railing. I reach for her, and she launches herself. It's like she's kicking into air, though, and she's just suspended there for a second as the car drops away beneath her. She claws for the railing, for me. I brace myself against the railing as I reach for her, only to see her eyes begging me, longing for me, her lips moving but no sound coming out as she drops helplessly toward the bay.

The car crashes into the water below, and she plummets toward the same spot, the whole time facing me, her eyes boring into my eyes, into my forehead.

*   *   *

I'm in my little skip, the dark shadowy water around the central pillars of Hathaway lapping my boat. I've got poles to make it look like I'm fishing, but I haven't fished for a year. I haven't done anything for a year.

I'm leaning over the side looking into the water while traffic hums overhead.

I'm looking for any sign. I place a couple of fingertips against my forehead, and my lips move, but I have no ideas what I'm saying. I'm not saying anything. My lips are just moving, that's all. No one can help me with that.

A Florida FWC patrolboat comes motoring up.

One uniformed guy in dark sunshades gaffs over to my boat.

"Hey, you can't fish here, buddy."

"Yeah, I know," I say.

"Then why you here?"

"Just looking."

The one FWC officer glances over to the other officer behind the wheel.

"We're gonna tow you outta here," the first one says.

"Just let me look a little longer," I say.

The officer casts another look at the officer behind the wheel and shakes his head.

I look over the side again. It's cold down there. I look at the deep reflection. Only there's a bit of white right in the middle of a forehead. Otherwise, it's a dark wavy pattern of a face. It's not me at all. I see a tear-streaked face, lips moving, saying something to me, and I'm feeling really, really cold.

LYNN WALLACE

I LIVE WITH THE DEAD

I'm listening to countless tales
Of sexual depravity
While all my spoons and forks and knives
Seem to defy gravity
He acts like he's better than me
His wit is lightning quick
Oscar Wilde haunts my kitchen drawers
And, man he is a dick

Perhaps I should back up a bit
And mention how this started
My realtor warned me when I signed,
"It's full of the departed!"
You sure you wouldn't like to see
Another place, instead?"
But I filled the papers out
Now I live with the dead

But if I'm to be honest with you
And do the actual math

My kitchen has two ghosts inside
The other's Sylvia Plath
She starts to panic, begins to cry
When I turn my oven on
She says, "It's time," and I say to wait
Until my potpie is done

I make my way into the den
Where John Holmes is getting freaky
The blonde chick swore they broke it off
(That's Marilyn, she's sneaky.)
Brando sinks to the stained floor
And begins to bellow "Stella!"
While James Dean cradles a broken neck
I'm creeped out by that fella

A fetus limps across the floor
And says she's got it sorted
She stood in her mom's career's way
THAT'S why she was aborted!
Who knows what fame she could have known
Whose child she could have been
But at least she didn't turn out like
The assholes in my apartment

Perhaps one day I'll move away
And leave these shades behind
Till then, I'll do the moonwalk
MJ says I should unwind

NATHAN SIMMONS

THE SCRIBULINE

March 2005

The music was loud; the cadence was low. The spirit that called herself Miria kept it that way. She could chance nothing to interrupt her.

It was another Spring Break party on Panama City Beach, Florida. The college flops were drunk and numerous. The alcohol flowed like rivers, and there was such a myriad of mind-altering substances that one could get lost just in the choices. They really made it too easy for her. Miria could linger among them, biding her time, savoring the scene before she would find him. The room held utter bedlam. She was close enough, and it was only a matter of tastes.

October 1969

She went about her business, pretending not to notice the clock. She knew he would come soon enough; he was faithful in that way. She lit a stick of patchouli incense and with the same flame lit a joint, savoring the sweet pungency of the herb while extinguishing the match.

Admiring her slender frame and long flowing blond locks in the mirror once more, she reflected on the gig she had just finished at the club with her band Cherry Dream. She had been radiant and they had gravitated to her. It was more than the LSD she and her band mates had taken before the show. She knew it all too well. She had been calling to them in her words, in her voice. She called to them and her flock had come. What a musical orgy tonight had been, and she, Sarah McCory, had held its sway.

Rather than join her friends for the after concert festivities, she had retired to her apartment near downtown Harrison Avenue in Panama City, Florida. She wanted to be ready for a meeting she knew would come. Now standing at her window, listening to the night's furtive sounds, aware the witching hour was near, she couldn't help an inward grin.

> "She turns
> and the night forgets
> her promise
> and her hush
> whispers on the wind
> begging for the…"

Her smile deepened. She had been aware that he let himself in and had stepped up behind her. He knew he was welcome there, so he never bothered to knock.

Sarah turned to him, soaking in his tall slender and muscular frame, deep blond hair, and deeper grey eyes—enjoying the poetry he continually entered with. It was all linked, a new stanza each time that seemed to further the thought of the last.

Receiving his proffered bottle of wine in exchange for the joint, she smiled at him this time, "On time as usual I see."

"Would you have it any other way?"

"Of course not. Let me chill this." Sara swayed the bottle in indication and went to the kitchen.

When she returned she found him settled on the couch, so she went to join him. His eyes followed her, taking in her easy grace.

"And now before we get on with the rest of the night, I have another present for you."

He pulled out the small package, opened it and placed a sugar cube marinated with liquid acid on her tongue. Sarah let the cube melt in her mouth as her own saliva rose up to greet it and soak it in. She was still on the fringes of the trip she had taken earlier. This would be a welcome addition.

"You smell electric tonight." He leaned over and kissed her, sensuously subtle, teasing her lips. She returned the affection, knowing it was not time—not yet. He knew it as well and made the contact brief, but not without letting his hands roam slowly down the front of her blouse. She smiled as she broke contact in reply to the tease, getting up from the couch.

Sarah moved to light the various candles placed specifically about the room. They made more small talk. There always seemed to be a play between them of unspoken thoughts. She continually had a sense of meaning and nuances hidden just below the surface. Their game of words never exhausted her.

"I didn't see you there tonight." Sarah lit another candle.

"I'm sorry. I...had been tied up."

He let the lack of explanation fall whimsically. What a tease.

"I'm sure you'll be at the next show then. You should have seen me tonight. It was..." her voice slipped lower, "...magical."

"Perhaps I will then." He let a coy smile slip out, the twinkle in his eyes explaining that he would reveal nothing.

Sarah gave off a knowing smile, playing the game. "Oh fine, have it your way." She sat down on the floor within the designated sacred circle they used for their ritual. He rose from the couch and joined her.

This time, he kissed her deeply. They both know it was time to initiate a rite so ancient there were no words to record the beginning deed.

Sarah closed her eyes; the swimming sensation of the drug taking over her, she had one final thought on the way to this night's trip. He would make her the immortal goddess she deserved to be, the goddess she already was.

March 2005

Ian was too buzzed to know, never mind care. So Carley had skipped out on him tonight. She'd been acting off the last couple of weeks anyway. She seemed more distant and argumentative. Ian knew Carley was trying to break up with him and just didn't know how to say it.

At first it had bothered him, but as time and classes rolled on at Florida State University in Tallahassee, he realized it didn't matter as much to him as he thought it did. He liked Carley well enough, but he knew he didn't love her. It was more the ideal of her—young, stylishly pretty, and on the college cheerleading squad. He would have never had a chance with a girl like that in high school. He was no dork, but he was no jock either.

Well, fuck her. There were plenty of other eligible young women. He didn't need her after all.

Now standing near the keg at this raging Spring Break party, Ian had long ago worked on putting Carley behind him and was focusing on finding some other hot thing to have some fun with. So far, no takers.

Ian downed the rest of his beer and went for another. Maybe he would hit Mark up for some more coke. It had been more than ten minutes since he'd done those last three lines. Maybe some more would do the trick.

Ian couldn't see why he wasn't having any luck. He was hot enough; he wasn't devilishly handsome, but he worked out at the school gym. He was toned and held a decent image. He wasn't sweating "fuck me, I'm beautiful," but as trashed as all these people seemed to be, it shouldn't have mattered.

Maybe this party wasn't for him. He never had this much trouble at keg parties before. Ian was beginning to think he might take his ass down to Club LaVela next to the high rise condo where the party was kicking. It sounded like more fun anyway.

Ian was scanning the room for Mark or his other buddies when he spotted a young woman staring at him. She noticed that he was looking at her so she gave him a ravenous smile. Not one to be outdone, and to show his own interest, he attempted to give her his bad boy smile, pulling out all the charm he could muster in his severely altered state. He tried to stand up straighter without falling over, no small task.

She was making her way towards him. Wow, she was beautiful—completely alluring. Everything had been starting to go a little blurry around him, but as he approached, she seemed to get clearer, though not painfully so. He was drunker than he'd thought; he would have to work on playing it cool.

Maybe this party is for me after all.

Miria watched the young college boy from across the room. He was flirting with every woman in sight, an interesting endeavor considering how strung out he was.

He just thinks all women are made for him.

Miria smirked as she strode coolly toward her prey.

The young man had been finishing his 14th beer when she made her approach. The look on his face said all she needed.

He waited until the lights went on in the apartment. He could almost smell the patchouli's aroma from where he stood in the alley. What a lovely catch this woman was. He decided he would certainly pleasure her tonight. She had earned that much. He might even grant her wish, who knew? He chuckled beneath his ancient breath. With a bottle of wine in hand (1842 chardonnay, no less), Aaron strode up to the apartment. The appropriate lines would be necessary. After all, a gentleman always knocks—even if doesn't use the front door.

She acknowledged his presence as he knew she would. He knew she wanted immortality. She knew he could grant it—If he so desired. There was a mutual acceptance between the two of them that went beyond this bargain that they were both aware of. He couldn't help but admire her for that. She was going to cheat him of his own game. They were both aware of what was at stake. Looking at her now, Aaron decided it was time to end the game before it got out of control. Tonight.

They had begun the ritual—he, summoning his ethereal scribuline and then calling to hers. Sarah's scribuline was there quickly, arriving brighter than Aaron had ever experienced from her. Where hers had usually taken several minutes to take shape in its arcing light within and around her—enhancing every feature—it had only taken seconds this time. Aaron was almost not ready for it, and it took him a few moments to gain control of it. If he was going to guide them and fulfill their (and his real) purpose, he would need full access to her throughout the whole ritual.

This was definitely the night. He could not wait any longer and risk her becoming any stronger. Sarah was already more vivid and dense than all of his other victims. He had played around with her too long. Damn the seductive bitch. Her soul was his—all he had to do was completely separate Sarah and her soul from her scribuline.

The ancient guardian of the soul, or scribuline, could be gotten rid of if one could tease it out far enough away from the soul's host body. It was a delicate process but one Aaron had performed for countless ages. Primal sexual influences used to make the ritual much easier, but as humans became more sophisticated, more intricate and lengthy phases of seduction became necessary. Yet once the scribuline was separated, and therefore disoriented by existence without its host, the soul was his. He had also been aided greatly by the great disconnect of humans from their own nature by becoming more complex. Aaron would see to it that tonight would prove no different.

Aaron had just grasped control of Sarah's scribuline when he began to notice two new circumstances arising.

Sarah felt the LSD coursing through her, but she also felt an inner sense of elation as she began the rites of initiation with him. She was empowered as never before. Sarah had been paying attention to the rituals over the past several weeks since their courtship had begun. She had an idea of what he really was about, and had been practicing some of the rituals on her own. Sarah had worked on calling up her scribuline, and although she had greatly struggled in keeping it present and structured, she believed she was starting to get a better grasp on it. Sarah also knew his story about the scribuline—after working the ritual on her own—being the first gate to her soul was only a half truth. She had sensed the two entities working separately several times and was ready to try and take matters in her own hands.

She felt the familiar pull in her upper abdomen that accompanied his calling of her scribuline. The ethereal form issued easily as Sarah began to feel strain from him. She felt him working his thought all over her being, probing her as waves work their way with grains of sand. Sarah allowed the scribuline to take strength in its own light— growing more pronounced while still allowing for his ethereal grip. It was then she realized what he really wanted. The scribuline was nothing. He was going for the one ideal he had sold her on—Immortality. Her immortality.

Sarah decided it was time to protect it.

Aaron noticed the light begin to shift in the room. Where it had been white hot before, it was now a colder haze. He also noticed the pull he had on Sarah was becoming a vacuum. Aaron worked hastily to detach his scribuline from hers, knowing he had only moments. Cursing himself for playing with prey too long, he pulled all of his scribuline within. He barely escaped the suction from the writhing body across from his.

Aaron had developed his scribuline and had achieved the ultimate—Immortality. He had continued to advance his skills but had discovered that the only way to maintain immortality was to keep the souls coming. Once a soul was without its scribuline, it would wither and fade out of existence. He had dealt with his own near misses in the beginning, where his scribuline would be momentarily disoriented and would automatically seek to protect the soul it was guarding. To anyone who did not know how to call the scribuline back, the next steps would be what was unfolding for Sarah now.

The scribuline protects the soul—not its host. Aaron had seen it before knew what would come next for her. He wanted to have their soul before this and he knew he was to blame. He also knew he would have to vacate her apartment quickly. She would still be attracted by his scribuline, and the longer he lingered, the worse it would be for both.

March 2009

Ian made his move to approach her as the crowd mingled. Ian couldn't shake the blurriness. If this chick wasn't willing, then he was just going to crash. No party is worth the crap he was going through here.

Ian jostled with shoulders and faces and almost lost sight of the woman once. He had spotted her over by the fish tank near the window so he made for that direction. Ian was almost there and had thought he'd lost her when he spotted her by the sliding glass doors. She glanced over and gave a radiant smile, opened the door, and moved out onto the balcony.

Ian moved towards the sliding doors and made his way to the doors. His head felt itself under a serious fog by then, but this was a party. Fuck it.

He opened the door and walked out on the balcony ready. The quiet hiss of wind threw him off after the noise of the party. But there she was, leaning her elbows backward on the rail and looking at him with a smile worth a thousand hard-ons. Ian stumbled as gracefully as he could forward until he managed the railing.

Ian leaned into the railing while aiming for the woman's ear.

"I saw you looking."

She let out a giggle and looked up at him, smiling flirtatiously. "I saw you."

He moved himself in for the kiss and she let him.

"It's cold out here." She moved herself with hers hands on the balcony so now she was sitting. "There is a Jacuzzi two flights up." She giggled with mischievous fun. "Are you ready? Come on."

Ian couldn't resist. A rooftop Jacuzzi with this fun chick; fuck the rest of this night—he would make the most of this, with a little daring in getting there.

Ian was almost up the next story when the chick disappeared. She must have reached the top already. Ian was feeling both left behind and cushion-headed. When he looked up, the woman was not standing on the ledge waiting, but hovering formless above. She began to float down on top of him. His fingers slipped as he tried to shield himself, and Ian knew his new reality only a few seconds.

Twelve stories down there was a sharp, sickening crack on the pavement two feet away from a couple of partiers returning from the club.

The spirit who called herself Maria watched the crowd gather below, and called to the scribuline as it rose up from the sidewalk to follow her. She was not afraid of being seen. Ever since that night in 1969 when she had been robbed of her body, Sarah had decided to become Maria, and start her own following. As long as there were men who thought they could seduce and use women, she would be ready to dislodge their wretched souls and claim them for her own. This was not the first Spring Break on Panama City Beach, and it would not be the last.

JONI N. SCOTT (LeCOMPTE)

SOULS SPHERE PART I

Simon awoke in his car. His ride was wrecked and so was he. Lynn Haven sunshine glared murderously through the spider webbings of his windshield. He felt like his guts were cooking.

"Not again," he said aloud, "no fucking way."

His eyes struggled to focus on the interior of his freshly crushed car. Glass, blood, beer cans, and assorted rubbish had exploded from every cranny in his vehicle when he hit the ditch. Now much of it sat in his lap. Considering the temperature, it was easy for him to imagine himself as a heap of garbage being incinerated.

This situation was all too familiar. He knew he still had booze in his system, but that could not account for the eerie realization that began to creep into his psyche. Like an octopus struggling to open a mason jar, his thoughts wrapped around themselves and began to tighten up. Did he hit the same ditch again? He looked out his busted driver's side window. Green algae sat atop murky, stagnant water. His car sat nose down in the ten-foot decline on the side of the road, damn near rolling over sideways. He woke up the same way the last two days. Exactly the same way. The angle of the shattered world outside the car was precisely as he remembered it.

"That's got to be impossible," he said to himself in a half-hearted attempt at reassurance. "How the hell can this be happening?"

The answer glared menacingly at him from the passenger's side floorboard. An open bottle of Jim Beam Black sat upright like an angry serpent poised for strike. He struggled for memory. He didn't remember crashing his car but after regaining consciousness, every moment that passed felt like a recent memory relived. It was as if he had been to a dress rehearsal but failed to pay attention. He closed his eyes and used his palm to apply pressure to his forehead. The bridge of his nose was swollen. Probably broken again. That was the least of his problems. He was playing spin the bottle with Death. Against his better judgment, he gripped his accomplice 'round the neck and turned the bottle up without opening his eyes.

He regretted this action before he was finished swallowing. A bloated, soggy cigarette butt had spent the night in that bottle and was ready for liberation. He imagined it took great pleasure in splatting against his uvula and causing instantaneous vomit. The stuff came in blistering waves. His eyes bulged, capillaries in his face busted, and he may have shit himself a little bit. He didn't bother checking. The flavor of bile and sour mash tray washed over his senses. The smell was tremendous. He had to escape.

His immediate instinct was to smash the driver's side window and flee, but he caught himself. Instead he pulled the interior handle of the passenger door and propped his feet on the driver's seat. Using his legs to lift the door, he was sure to keep grip on the handle to avoid getting concussed on the way out.

He pulled himself atop the side of the car and surveyed his wreckage. He scanned the streets for onlookers. There was only one, a familiar looking man with a bushy goatee and well-pointed eyebrows. Panama City was a small town and he was sure that he had seen him before. It was late night at some bar, and they hit it off. They played music on the jukebox and talked about something. He did not remember the intoxicated conversation. There was a lot he didn't remember.

The guy wore the look of a deliberate scoundrel. He looked to be in his early thirties, but he had the timeless look of a thuggish dope fiend, classic street noir complete with black fingerless gloves. His grey trench coat was fashionably stained with a pigment of unknown origin. His smile was equal parts disturbing and endearing. His grin gave off an air of perverse confidence usually unseen outside swinger's club parties. Aviator glasses hid his eyes. Simon was relieved by this fact. He was afraid of what he might see in those eyes. Or what they would see in him.

"Yo," he yelled across the gap between his heap of a car and the embankment.

The figure gave a nod accompanied by a vacant wave of his hand. He was beckoning Simon to the roadside. Simon leapt to the bank without hesitation. He didn't even realize what he was doing until he landed on the spongy, ragged clumps of grass and roots that bordered the odorous water. He wasn't the type to approach a beckoning stranger, even after a collision. New Orleans had taught him that. He knew this was no chance encounter. And the longer he looked at the man, the less he thought of him as a stranger.

He dug his hands into the side of the ditch and began clawing his way up but found unexpected difficulty. His feet had a hard time finding traction and clumps of ditch grass came off in his hands. It was like wrestling Swamp Thing. The man extended his hand and pulled Simon up effortlessly. He still had that shit-eating grin. Simon was grateful but far from amused.

"Good job," said the stranger.

"No need to be facetious," replied Simon. "I appreciate the help but you don't have to rub it in."

"I'm not," he replied, taking off his glasses. His eyes radiated serious intensity. "I meant good job not falling in the water this time."

Simon leered at him, a puzzled look of horror smeared across his face. Fleeting memories flashed before him. Puking cigarettes, breaking windows, tumbling into the rancid ditch, over and over. Variations of the same mistakes presented themselves like high-speed

celluloid with extra frames inserted by a delinquent projectionist.
The stranger's laughter was present through all of those mistakes.
But it was not all pathetic, bloody slapstick to him. He seemed
concerned through his crass, mysterious words of encouragement.
He preached enlightenment. They had stood on this shore more
than once. His mind raced, trying desperately to process the barrage
of information overrunning his consciousness. The world waved
around him and then stuttered to a halt. He felt that clarity danced
just outside his peripheral vision, always one step ahead.

"You're figuring it out," said the familiar man, his deviant smile
in place. "I knew you would catch on sooner or later. Otherwise, I'd
leave you in that sludge pit. Now look at you, all high and dry."

"Figuring it out? What are you talking about?"

"Picking up where we left off," was the reply he did not want to
hear.

"Ok, now that's just creepy," Simon insisted. "What the hell is
going on?"

"You tell me," the man replied.

"Come the fuck on, man," Simon snapped.

"I'm not trying to be rude," said the man, "but I didn't crash your
car. And now you have approached me. So why don't you tell me
what's been going on."

Simon looked down at his shoes, a little embarrassed. He did just
wake up from a drunken coma in the front seat of a car that looked
like a stepped on beer can. He could have easily gotten killed in a
wreck like that. He was disoriented.

"Well, I woke up in my car again. I know I have been fucking up
lately. I have been drinking a lot. I've wrecked my car repeatedly. I
don't know how many times it's happened now. It's like I'm in that
movie "Groundhog Day," you know the one with Bill Murray. My
first few moments are the same, but after that I feel like a million different things have happened. So many that I cannot count or recall
them. I know you from somewhere. I feel like we have had intimate

discussions that I cannot remember, and it's fucking with my head. I probably just hit my head in that crash."

"Yes," replied the man.

"Yes what?" asked Simon.

"I understand and so do you," said the man.

"No I don't, I don't have any fucking clue what's going on," shouted Simon, hoping he was telling the truth.

"You have the information," he replied. "I gave it to you. Apparently, I have to give it to you again. Such a pity"

"Was that when you preached to me about enlightenment?" Simon asked.

"I never preached to you, merely offered some friendly advice," the man replied.

"So we have met before?" asked Simon.

"Why do you keep asking me questions you already know the answers to?" The preacher's tone was serious, almost cold. "You have the information, now access it." This was not a suggestion. This was a command.

Simon felt like his brain was being electrocuted. His vision tunneled as he look around, seeing himself again in the water. He remembered being hoisted ashore and scolded by this prick with questionable intentions. He had gotten angry and combative with this man who helped him. He was told things that he didn't want to know but needed to hear. His whole belief system had been called into question, and he lashed out in an attempt to suppress this. How many times had that happened? Ten, twenty, twenty thousand? His estimate was infinite.

"I don't know," said Simon sheepishly. "Countless times?"

"YES," the man's eyes beamed. "You are figuring it out. Now tell me my name."

Simon raised a brow.

"Quit looking so God damned bewildered and concentrate," barked the stranger, his playful hostility inspiring a strange confidence in Simon.

"Christopher," he replied without thinking.

"Christopher what?"

"Christopher Lee," Simon returned.

"Correct," said Christopher, his eyes widening with glee at this response.

Simon stood there stunned. He struggled to understand. How did he know this? The answer seemed to be "through experience," but he had a hard time wrapping his head around that. What detail was he leaving out? How could he have relived the same scenario so many times? Was he dreaming?

"You are not dreaming," said Christopher, "and no I don't read minds. My memory is just sharper than yours."

Simon shut his mouth. Those questions were about to succeed one another. He had to be dreaming. But this felt as real as anything he had ever experienced. He already remembered more than he could recall in any dream. Unreality was easier to navigate than this. His mind began formulating new questions. He allowed his mind to submerge in concentration and let the questions form themselves.

"Then what plane of consciousness am I on?" asked Simon a little more confident.

"Finally," exploded Chris, "a new question! You have no idea how happy this makes me."

"So, answer it," demanded Simon.

"Post Mortal. The land beyond the flesh," said Christopher, satisfaction ringing from his words.

Simon blinked and then fixed his gaze to Christopher's. He was beginning to catch on.

"That's right," said Christopher. "You are dead."

"And this is the afterlife?" asked Simon unsurely.

"No, I don't call it that," responded Chris. "Consciousness after the mortal experience is what you make of it. 'Life' is a word I don't even understand yet. I prefer to call my trip 'the after party.'"

"But this is life after death," persisted Simon.

"I guess it depends upon how you define that word. In the clinical sense, you literally don't have a leg to stand on," he chuckled and then paused. "But I understand your point, so for argument's sake I shall concede. This is your afterlife, Simon. If you believe it, then it is real. It is truth."

"Ok," said Simon, "then why the repetition of events?"

"Because you refused to believe what was happening to you. My previous attempts at helping you figure out your situation have all ended poorly. Over and over you would lash out and run away. Your refusal to believe in the world around you made you keep retreating to your last known mortal reference point," said Chris.

"But how?" Simon asked.

"Without physics or a body to hold you back, your experience truly is your perception. You are Post Mortal. If you can accept that fact and embrace it, then you can do anything. Not in the figurative sense that people push on you as a kid. I don't mean you have the opportunity to do anything. I mean you can do it. The power of belief is as powerful as any force of nature. To the believer, sometimes more. You can harness that power," Christopher continued, "or that same force can keep you stuck in the same mundane pattern for eternity."

"Purgatory?" said Simon.

"Something like that, I guess if you spun it that way," said Chris. "In Christian context, I'm sure you're right on the money. But I didn't think you believed that way."

"I don't know what to believe," said Simon.

"Then figure it out. I can help you by passing on some of what I have learned but what you truly believe will have a huge bearing on your 'afterlife,'" said Chris.

He still wore the smile, but his eyes were stern. "Keep an open mind. Pay attention to what is going on around you. Soak it all up. Never retreat. You don't want to wake up back here again, do you?"

"Not really," Simon answered.

"Good," replied Chris. "Now that you are retaining information, we have a LOT of conversing to do. Let's get you into a more comfortable environment and talk further about this. Today is your day to break those chains of denial."

"What day is it, anyway?" asked Simon.

"Every day," said Chris jovially. "Call it Saturday if it makes you feel better, but I gave up on that kind of thing a long time ago. I suggest you do the same. Now let's go."

"Where are we going?" inquired Simon.

"Strip Club," replied Chris.

"You know actually I'm not really big on…"

"Strip club," said Chris again.

"It's too early for that shit," said Simon anxiously. "The sun is still up, way up. Nobody goes to a strip club in the middle of the day."

"Is that the problem?" Chris arched a brow. "Then, pray tell, what time is it Simon?"

"I don't know but it's…" Simon worlds trailed off into the darkness around him.

He looked up at the sky and her new black dress. A previously unseen shade of night. The true color of absent light. His eyes darted around wildly, expecting to find the edge of a Hollywood soundstage just beyond some bushes. A beret headed director would certainly shout "CUT," at any moment. Camera men would reposition themselves for the next shot. Boom mikes would be conveniently overhead. But this was no motion picture production. He was not a movie patron observing special effects from the safety of a dimly lit theater. He was certainly no actor paid to regurgitate lines in stage makeup one minute and retire to the safety of a personal trailer full of goodies and personal assistants. Reality had rapidly become stranger than any dream.

He could barely muster his words enough to manage a mumbled "How… did… you…"

Chris laughed. "Because I know what time it is. Your reliance on numbers will get you nowhere. You are in the mindset of being a slave to time, to reacting to your environment. I prefer to influence the world around me. I make time."

Simon was astonished. What if all of this was true? Was he a soul trapped in Purgatory? Was it really possible to achieve enlightenment after death? He wanted to believe so. He didn't come anywhere close in life. He lived reacting to the world around him without observing much. He worked to pay bills his whole fucking life and then he died. And if what Christopher said was true, then it might not be all that bad. With that moment of introspection, an idea was born and, like a baby calf, began to awkwardly raise itself upon spindly legs.

"I guess I can't argue with that," said Simon.

He was tired of reacting, tired of being confused, and tired of waking up in that fucking car. He didn't know how many times it happened but he was determined to make sure that it never happened again. And if it did then he would be ready. He decided to drop his guard. He had been in a car crash. He was either dead or in a dream state due to coma and would soon be dead. He decided to let go of his reservations and suspend disbelief. Wherever he was, the normal rules did not apply here. He had seen a man turn day to night. He didn't know what he might see next, but he was ready to see something besides this lonely street.

"I could use a change of scenery," admitted Simon. "Plus I am kinda thirsty. May as well have some hair of the dog that killed me."

"Great," said Chris. "Let's get going."

They walked to the road. Chris stood on the corner and held his right hand up, as if he was hailing a cab. Simon pulled out a cigarette from his crumpled pack and lit it with his Zippo. He snapped the cap back into place and put it back in his pocket. As Simon took a deep breath of his smoke, Chris produced a lit cigarette from the palm of his hand and placed it between his lips. No doubt another one of his tricks to show Simon how different things could be. A white Cadillac pulled up next to them. Chris opened the driver's side door. The car was empty. Simon was not surprised. He understood he was in a place unlike any he had seen before. More strange happenings were on the way, and he was comfortable with that.

Simon wondered what strip club Christopher was taking him. None stood on Panama City Beach, and their options in town were limited. Bambi's was out of the question. He wouldn't be seen at Dock Strutters even if he WAS dead. Maybe he'd come back later, just to see what kind of things might lurk behind those walls. He decided to save that for another adventure.

He figured they were either going to the Limb Box or the Yellow Ball. Most people preferred the Ball, but sometimes it got so packed, you had no choice but hit the Box to see some nudes with more than six teeth. He did have a bit of a soft spot for the Eastern European girls who cycled through there with shocking regularity. Euro girls were good; maybe he'd luck out and be treated with a trip to Slammy's. It was over in Destin, but well worth the drive for the quality and work ethic of the girls.

They were close to none of the clubs he had just rattled off in his head. They appeared to be headed for MLK.

"This traffic is ghastly," said Chris. "There wouldn't be traffic like this if more people could pull their heads out of the sand."

"So these are," started Simon.

"All ghost cars, yes. We share the same impression of the physical plane we remember. All of what you see is Post Mortal. You will not see a car driven by the living. The only time you will see the living is through water. Even then, all you are apt to see is a reflection. I'll touch more on that later. Right now, I'll focus on not smashing my awesome ghost car into these Darkies," said Chris with that threatening grin adding an inflection of morbid humor.

"Darkies?" said Simon a little puzzled as he looked out the window to see the night and the ghosts on the side of the road had gotten darker.

"BWAHAHA" roared Chris. "Not that kind of Darkies. I am talking about the dead who are so closed-minded they don't realize that they have passed on. The majority of Post Mortals are in deep denial. If they are never confronted or never find some personal catalyst of change then they stay stuck in their daily life routine FOREVER. You evolve when you drop the meat and leave your old vessel behind. The journey changes like a chartreuse moth. Your spirit unbridled, you can do anything. But without realization it can be a curse. Monotony, drone work forever. Lost in the machine, blinded by disbelief, turning the gears for some great unknown. A lot of people call them 'Dim,' but I prefer 'Darkies,' because of the reaction it gets. Either way most of these cars are just driving around in the dark. They are on the way to and from work indefinitely. They usually drive for shit too. Fucking Darkies."

Christopher's brashness was growing on him. He considered himself somewhat intelligent, and he could relate to frustration with stupidity. Simon was loosening up. He even allowed himself a laugh at the Darkie bit. He may as well, right? If he was dead, it wouldn't get much worse. If he was dreaming, he would wake up, hopefully not in a car. If he was in a coma, he'd either die or wake up with brain damage and wish he was dead. He was having another recurring train of thoughts. Beautiful women, flashing lights, money, drugs, gasoline, walking mutilation. The images and impressions blasted him like a sandstorm. He gripped the arms of the car seat and felt like his hair was blowing back. The guy from old Maxell ads came to mind.

Simon was breathing heavy. He thought it was funny that he still did this. Then again, if what Chris said was accurate, humans were creatures of habit. He decided to hold his breath for as long as he could.

"You OK over there?" asked Chris, sounding genuinely concerned.

"Just more crazy pictures flashing through my head," replied Simon.

"I call those 'Quantum Memories,'" announced Chris.

"I call them frustrating indecipherable nightmares," said Simon with a squint. "I wondered how I could possibly have so many memories. How long have I even been dead?"

"Only for a moment," said Chris reassuringly. "One of those Forever Moments."

The car was slowing down to stop at a corner by a seedy looking liquor store with bused out windows. Somehow, Simon had gotten so into their conversation that he failed to notice they had slipped into a previously uncharted patch of ghetto. He did not remember Panama City having these spray painted tenements. There was more graffiti in this neighborhood than he had seen in his entire life. Amazing feats of spray paint magic covered almost every building surface. Large-scale depictions of graphic violence burst from the brick wall canvas including a zombie Jesus and a bludgeoned Virgin Mary. High barbed wire fences bordered eight blocks surrounding the forgotten tenements.

"So, the moment of death lasts forever," concluded Simon. "Why are we stopping here?"

A busted up looking hooker spotted them, perked up and started limping towards the car. Chris rolled down his window and waved. Simon looked at Christopher like he was insane. Christopher went right on with his Post Mortal explanations like nothing was happening.

"Quantum Theory states that time essentially does not exist. All things that have happened or will happen are happening right now." Chris was clearly enjoying this. "In life, we only have the perception to see one facet of our mirror ball multi-verse. Players like me find new angles all the time, and the Pros learn to work those angles. Inklings like yourself can see more than those stupid Darkies. Lord only knows what the Shambles can see. Some of them don't even have eyes, yet their insight is profound."

"Shambles?" asked Simon. "Who are the Shambles?"

"These guys," he replied, gesturing to what looked like bums on the side of the road. "Welcome to Tatter Town."

Christopher rolled down all of the windows. These were not ordinary bums. They looked more like reanimated corpses. Not just any corpses, but mangled corpses. No doubt, the products of car crashes, industrial accidents, and whatever kinds of fates that result in extreme disfigurement. A man whose head had been reduced to a fraction of a bottom jaw with a chunk of matted beard attached caught Simon's eye. He sat on the corner, pouring Night Train down his neck hole. Wine dribbled down the chunk of coagulated blood and facial hair and combined to make a new kind of disgusting. These were the dead who looked dead. These were the zombies from his tangled memories.

As the girl shuffled closer to the car, Christopher opened the glove box and produced a brown paper bag the size of a magazine. He got out and approached the ragged prostitute. Simon opted to stay in the car. He couldn't help but stare at her for a lingering moment. Half of her face was smashed and looked like raw steak hit with a weed whacker. The other side wasn't all bad despite the awful showgirl makeup and random spatters of blood. She was probably pretty once. Her pink elastic mini skirt hugged her firm buttocks and revealed a bruised but well-shaped leg. The other one hung sideways, apparently broken at the femur. This accounted for her awkward gait.

Chris handed her the bag and she gave him something which went directly into his pocket. Simon could not see what it was and figured it best not to ask. Whatever deal he had going on with this zombie prostitute was none of Simon's business. He saw a jogger with the flattest stomach he had ever seen. The man must have been run over by a truck. His midsection had been smashed perfectly flat, complete with a cartoonish-looking tire tread print. A woman with a large gunshot wound in her neck bled profusely while pushing a baby carriage that was on fire and billowing smoke.

Other Shambles were going about their normal business. He saw
a couple of guys shooting dice behind the liquor store. One man
had a crowbar protruding from his head. It was buried deep. Simon
noticed he moved his shoulders every time he moved his head. That
thing was jammed in there good. The other guy had no legs and one
arm. Blood flowed steadily from his massive open wounds. With his
one good hand, he scooped up the dice, blew on them for luck, and
tossed them onto the bloodstained pavement. He shouted something
and scooped some cash up off the ground. The money was red too.

"See you later, Corpy," Chris said, waving to the girl, "and thank
you."

He sat down in the driver's seat, and they slowly made their way out
of the hood, being careful not to further disfigure any tattered children. He was sure he wasn't dreaming now. The things he just saw
would turn any dream into a nightmare. Simon wasn't scared at all
though. He was intrigued by what saw. These were walking em-
bodiments of lethal physical injury. He felt bad for them more than
anything. Was that the fate of all the poor devils who met less than
aesthetically pleasing ends?

They sat in silence for a minute before Chris turned on the radio.
Simon was bursting with questions now. He sat through half of Roy
Orbison's "Runnin' Scared" before he could take it no longer.

"That was fucking crazy," said Simon. "Death has turned those
poor people into monsters."

"Not monsters," replied Christopher, "Shambles. And most of
them are perfectly happy."

"Is that what happens to people who die violent deaths?" asked
Simon. "If my wreck was worse would I have turned out that way?"

"Looks like you came pretty close," replied Christopher.

"What do you mean?" asked Simon as horrible images of disfigurement assailed his mind's eye.

"You certainly did not come out unscathed," Chris replied in his
distinct matter-of-fact way.

The thought occurred to him that he had somehow avoided his reflection thus far. Fearing the worst, he turned the rear view mirror to observe his face. He was fucked up all right. Apparently, he died of a head injury. His forehead looked like a lump of clay with an indentation the size of a soft ball. His entire left eye socket was displaced. He almost favored the Toxic Avenger. Was Chris dumping him here with the rest of the derelicts?

"Oh shit," cried Simon, "am I a fucking..."

"No, silly," Chris cut him off, "and I know what you're thinking. Don't worry. I am confident that this is not your destiny. Let's see." Chris put his hands on Simon's head and face. He began massaging Simon's wounds.

"Now relax and concentrate on how you looked, pre-injury," Chris said. "Think of how badly you do not want to stay here and live among the deformed. You can fix it. Fix it."

Chris took his hands away. Simon rubbed his eyes. His face felt all right. He looked in the rear view mirror in disbelief. He was back to normal. No longer a face crushed monstrosity, he was elated.

"We did it," said Simon with pride.

"No," Chris responded, "you did it. You passed the test."

"Test?" asked Simon. "What do you mean, test?"

"I had to see if you could handle the truth and use that belief to affect change without my actual assistance. All I did was suggest a course of action, and you followed it. You'll make a formidable spook and a powerful Player in your own time," responded Chris with pride. "Change your face and you can change the world."

"And those who cannot change their faces become Shambles?" asked Simon.

"For the most part," said Chris, "but not always. Some of them are Darkies who died in gruesome fashion. The last thing they saw was their own reflection, so they know they got fucked up. For some reason they can't even figure out that they are dead even though they are walking heaps of gore. Maybe they get brain damage before they die, so the impression of their disfigurement is more profound. I don't know. Some of them are well aware of their situation and choose not to do anything about it for personal reasons. Others get splayed after death and banished to Tatter Town."

"That's all very confusing," said Simon.

"You're telling me," said Chris. "I am a great communicator, and I can't get the answers I want out of these people."

"Why would people get banished to Tatter Town?" asked Simon.

"It all comes back to the power of denial." Chris explained, "Shambles are not allowed to interact with unenlightened souls. If you get bisected and can't pull yourself back together you are labeled a Shamble and made to live in the Forgotten Tenements."

"But why are they separated from Post Mortal society?" asked Simon.

"Let's just say that there are certain entities who benefit from the Darkies." Chris looked perturbed by this. "They are in the business of protecting that interest. Nothing will send a Dim motherfucker into shock like coming face-to-face with the embodiment of violent demise. Certain entities do not want people, to wake up, retreat or break their cycles in general. At one point, there was even a 'Zombie War,' to reroute the Darkies beliefs. Apparently for those in denial, it's easier to swallow the concept of reanimated corpses coming to life than to understand that they are dead and evolved to a higher consciousness."

"Whoa," said Simon, "get into conspiracy theories much?"

"Laugh it off," said Chris, "but shit gets complicated after you die. Loss of life does not quench Man's thirst for power. You'll see for yourself one day."

"What do you mean?" asked Simon.

"You are a rare beast, Simon," replied Chris, "you have a clue. Only a small percentage of people you come across will ever figure out as much as you have already. You have the potential to be a Power Player, like me, and I am not the only one who has noticed that."

Simon's Quantum Memories started acting up again. Chris was not the only person he had spoken to in the afterlife. There was a woman, a gorgeous red head at that. Also another man had approached him on the street and spoken with him. This was before his talks with Chris. Once again, the details were blurry. He could not remember the conversation. He had offered to take Simon somewhere, but Simon did not go with him. Simon wondered when he would turn up again. He tried not to worry about it.

"I'm definitely ready for a drink now," said Simon.

They were nearing the Hathaway Bridge, headed towards the beach.

"Where are we going anyways?" asked Simon.

"You'll see," replied Chris.

"Well if we are going to Destin or Ft. Walton, I want to go ahead and recommend Slammy's," suggested Simon.

"We're not going there," said Chris flatly.

"Well then which one?" asked Simon. "The Singapore Tree is good."

"Don't worry," said Chris. "You'll like this place."

To Simon's surprise, they took a left turn onto Thomas Drive instead of going straight down Back Beach to head west. The roads were pretty much the same as Simon remembered, but a lot of businesses were different. Some were not there. He did notice that Wal-Mart was back in business. Movie Gallery was there in the afterlife too. He decided to do some browsing later for nostalgia's sake. They rounded the Curve, which was back to being a Strip Club again. To his surprise they didn't turn in the parking lot.

Chris drove them a few more blocks down and pulled up at the Show n' Tail. Having burned down years before, it was the last place Simon expected. The familiar pink marquee cast an alluring glow over the white Cadillac. Simon had not been there in years. It was kind of comforting to see a familiar place which also happened to be the best strip club on the beach. Christopher walked ahead of him and pulled open the heavily tinted glass door. Simon followed, smiling for the first time in what seemed like an eternity.

The air hung like Spanish moss heavy with the aroma of smoke, sweat, alcohol, and just a little burning meth. Standing at parade rest just inside the door was a massively bored looking bouncer. Living or dead, this man was a spectacle. He was at least six-and-a-half feet tall. His handlebar mustache was immaculately waxed and damn near up to his eyeballs. His goatee was a foot long, burly and red. Every inch of exposed flesh was covered in artwork. Even his shaved head was adorned with a large tattoo of a skeletal crocodile.

"Oi, Luger!" shouted Chris.

"If it isn't the nefarious Dr. Christopherious," boomed Luther in voice that any radio DJ would sell their whole family to possess.

Chris reached out and shook the hook that Luger kept as a right hand. Simon's eyes fixed on it. More memories bubbled to the surface. They had been to this bar together before. Simon had met Luther and witnessed him turning a mouthy patron into a Shamble with that hook. The big man was no lummox despite his looking like a cross between Captain Hook and a member of the Hell's Angels biker gang. His appearance was not that of a great thinker, and he played into that role sometimes. Simon easily saw past that. Luther was extremely observant. Even when nothing seemed to be going on those razor sharp eyes were ready. They were fixed dead on Simon.

"Checkin' out the hook, huh?" inquired Luther.

"Yeah, you got me," replied Simon.

"You like it?" said Luther, extending the hook in greeting.

"Yeah, it's great," said Simon with as much enthusiasm as he could muster. He shook the cold metal hook.

"It's good for yankin' fuckers out of here in a hurry, I tell you that," confessed Luger with a wink. "Let's not make you one of them."

"Forgive me for my lack of manners," said Chris. "Luther this is my new friend, Simon."

"He catching on?" asked Luther.

"Like a fucking hang nail," said Chris proudly.

"Good," said Luther, "then you already know I'm Luther, and my word is law in this club. Keep that in mind, and we'll be best friends. Break my law and not even this grinning bastard can save you, not in these walls."

Simon looked to Chris for assurance. Chris gave a nod to assure him that Luther was dead serious.

"Well, alright then," said Simon casually, "I'll be a model citizen while I'm in your strip club, sheriff."

"This guy is kind of a dick, huh?" said Luther. "I like him. Alright boys, enjoy your stay and don't touch the girls. I'll make sure you get your regular table, Chris."

Chris gave Luther a nod and pulled a lit cigar from his coat pocket. Luther shook his head in mock disdain and smiled. He reached out with his hook and Christopher balanced the stogie precariously at the tip. Luther brought it to his mouth effortlessly. The cigar held in place. Simon imagined spectral fingers securing the smoke and carrying it up to the giant's face. He tried not to gawk. The magic of will power was going to take some getting used to. It was time to break down some psychic blockades and loosen up a bit.

Chris led Simon around the dance floor. They walked between some tables crowded with ghostly patrons. The lighting was no more deceptive than that of a mortal strip club. The crowd was a mix of nicely dressed career criminal looking types along with relatively normal looking beach service industry people. He even recognized a few faces of the recently deceased. When he used to go to this club, he knew most of the people there. This crowd was different and largely unfamiliar. Probably because most of them were dead by the time he reached drinking age. Damn, he was dead at twenty-eight. He had not allowed himself time to think about what that meant. He decided to address that disturbing little fact later. This was not the time for deep introspection.

They made their way to a particularly dark booth in the corner of the room. The half wall that lined the dance floor capped off one

end of the booth. Chris sat with his back against the wall and peered
over the half wall at the stage. Simon recognized the strategy in this
seating arrangement as an old mafia trick. Nobody could sneak up
on Chris at this table. It was the only one set up like this. Christopher carried some weight in this bar. At least he was in good company. The girls on duty weren't bad looking either.

Simon sat in the booth across from Chris. A cocktail waitress with
voluptuous curves swished her way across the floor and deposited
two cups of whisky on their table. Her thigh high boots were made
of reflective vinyl perched atop six-inch stiletto heels. Simon caught
a whiff of her perfume as she dangled her ample breasts temptingly
close to his face. It was nice to look at a woman without blood coming out of her. A smiling Chris slid the ashtray to the center of the
table and produced another lit cigarette from nowhere. Simon pulled
one of his Camels out and lit it the old-fashioned way.

Two girls gyrated to the music on opposite sides of the stage.
Their dancing skills were well honed and downright acrobatic. They
clearly had plenty of time to practice. The girl on the left was a svelte
blonde with the Eastern European features that Simon loved so well.
The dancer's waist length platinum bleached hair and neon purple
fishnet hose glowed under the black lights on her side of the stage.
Her purple pleather vest was being slowly unbuttoned. The avant-
garde lighting made him have to stare extra hard to see the shape
of her nipples, but her tanned bosom was glorious to behold. He
wished he could be holding that bosom.

Then his eyes fell upon the girl of his quantum dreams. On the
right side of the stage, slowly writhing to her own song was the most
beautiful woman he had seen in his afterlife. An explosion of natural
red hair cascaded down her back. She was sculpted perfectly, a ginger
goddess with curves. As she turned around, he saw the wall of scars.
It looked as if a freighter set ablaze had traversed the ocean of her
backside. From the waist up, the back of her arms were charred to
a Freddy Kruger-like mess of skin. Her deformity made her all the
more alluring. Maybe it was because of the way he empathized with

the Shambles. Her immense beauty kept her out of Tatter Town, but
her blight was sizeable.

"I see you looking," said Chris. "You can have her, you know?"

"Yeah?" asked Simon in disbelief.

"Oh yeah," said Chris. "For one, she's a stripper. For two, I am a
'silent partner' in this place, and they would probably shut down and
retile the bathrooms if I asked them to."

Simon let his eyes keep wandering. There were a couple more
cocktail waitresses on the floor. Each had the slutty hot look that
Simon had favored in his younger years. All three of them wore
sheer tops and g-string bottoms. The unknown man from Simon's
ragged memories stood directly in front of the stage, chatting with
one of the waitresses. He saw Simon notice him and nodded. Simon
slammed his beverage in one gulp. He didn't care when some booze
and a piece of ice slipped from the corner of his mouth and landed
in his lap. Chris puffed his cigarette and smiled.

"I knew you needed a drink," said Chris. "You look a little anx-
ious. Have another."

Simon raised his hand for a waitress. Chris lowered it back down
with a mere look. He slid his glass over to Simon and produced another from beneath the table. A fresh drink from nowhere, complete
with ice…miraculous. Simon sipped at his beverage this time. He
raised a brow as he looked at Chris.

"What?" asked Christopher.

"Well," said Simon, "I was just wondering how you keep produc-
ing lit cigarettes and full drinks out of nowhere. And if you can do
that, why do you bother buying drinks and exchanging money?"

"I already told you I am a Player, Simon," said Chris. "Let's just
say it's all part of the game."

"But how does money work?" asked Simon.

"For Darkies, it's just like on the material plane," Chris explained.
"For people like me, and soon you, it is meaningless. You can literally
pull it out of your ass, or pockets, or wallet or wherever you choose
to keep the stuff. Once you figure it out, you'll have as much as you'll

ever need to deal with those imbeciles. Think about it, an infinite supply of petty cash backed only by the power of belief. Too bad you can't use it to buy anything of real worth. Enlightened souls deal in matters more valuable than material. We exchange ideas, information, strategies and other things useful to those of us who have experienced brain death without losing our minds."

"So what's it going to take to get me pulling off some of these useful tricks?" asked Simon.

"Belief, concentration, persistence, and a little bit of knowledge doesn't hurt," replied Christopher.

"Ok then," said Simon, "you told me earlier that time is meaningless and that the old rules of physics no longer apply, yes?"

"Yes," responded Chris, nodding.

"So, I guess what I am asking is what can I get away with?" admitted Simon.

"I like the way you think," said Chris. "I am glad we found each other."

"Did we find each other or did you find me?" asked Simon.

"I am certain it was a mutual destiny kind of thing," replied Christopher. "Why do you ask?"

"Well, I was thinking," said Simon, "this other guy came up in my Quantum Memories. He talked to me and for the un-life of me, I couldn't remember what the fuck he said to me. But now, I remember. He told me not to trust you. He told me you'd feed me a bunch of bullshit and promises. He told me you'd tempt me with money, power, and women. Now here we are."

Across the room, the other man smiled. Chris had to work this kid day after day to get a point through. He knew he only needed once to instill the proper knowledge. Here he was watching it surface now, just at the right time. He was disappointed that it took this long for Simon to start doubting that smirking asshole. Chris fancied himself a Player, but all he did was play with people. He had not real control over the world around him, no more than the rest of the Dim populace. His parlor tricks had fooled Simon long. This charade was about to come crashing to a halt.

"Hayes," said Chris, "that son of a bitch."

"What's the matter Chris?" inquired Simon angrily. "Do you really think I couldn't see the evil in your eyes the moment you removed those glasses?"

"Good and evil are open to interpretation," said Chris, "especially beyond the veil. Your concepts of good and evil are based on the moral façade of the living society of your time period. Even in such closed-minded context, I hardly concede to being called evil. I am beyond evil, beyond good, and well beyond the context you are trying to place those words in."

"Well you are manipulative," accused Simon.

"Yes, but to what effect?" said Chris. "I manipulated you into believing yourself no longer disfigured and therefore free from Tatter Town. Manipulated you into understanding that you do not have to be confined to a monotonous eternity?"

"I don't know if that's true," said Simon, glaring at Christopher.

"Look at me long and hard, Simon," said Chris, "and you'll see the truth. Once you free yourself your insight will be greater than most. Many Power Players have a specialization. I think yours could very well be calling bullshit. Keep those eyes open. Don't let Hayes cloud your vision with his suggestions. He has a special way with things like that."

"How can I know you're even telling the truth about that," asked Simon defiantly.

"That stripper with the burns, Laila, the one you clearly got the hard-on for," said Chris.

"Her name is Laila?" asked Simon.

"Yes," responded Chris, "I see I am correct."

"What about her?" asked Simon.

"You saw her burns," said Chris.

"Well yeah," replied Simon, "they covered all of her back."

"Yet no one notices," said Chris, "unless they have true sight. You stared long and hard enough to see through the veil. She obviously burned to death and never fixed herself, but still people do not see. She knows she is beautiful and the universe abides."

"I never said she wasn't beautiful," said Simon.

"Neither did I," responded Chris, "but if certain entities were aware of her condition they would make a move to put her in Tatter Town."

"How do I know other people can't see the burns?" asked Simon.

"You could go around and ask and look like a lunatic, maybe even draw security's attention for scrutinizing one of their dancers," said Christopher, "or maybe you could take my word for it."

"I don't think words are enough right now," said Simon. "Words are too mundane. Show me something."

"I don't have to show you anything, but you can look," explained Chris. "Look around the room, pick any person and stare at them. Remember all they were and all they will be they are right now. The moment of death lasts an eternity, think about all of those moments piled on top on one another. Use your eyes and hold onto that face."

Simon complied. He picked Chris.

"Now tell me what you really see," Christopher said.

"The depths. A tide of souls swimming endlessly. Deprived of oxygen, unseen armies travel with you. You were submerged in the sleepless ocean, only to strive to become her Poseidon. Unfortunately, you drowned."

This time it was Christopher with the look of shock on his face.

"Am I close?" asked Simon sarcastically.

"You are dead on," he replied. "Now can we get back to being civil?"

"Maybe," replied Simon. "Let me just have a look around real quick."

Simon scanned the room for Hayes, so he could get a real look at him. He had just seen him across the dance floor and could not wait to get hold of him with his new eyes. He scanned the room, determined to find Hayes and talk to him. He started off towards the bathroom, figuring it was the last place he had not looked. By the time Simon turned around to look behind him, Hayes was right upon Christopher at the table. He had slipped behind Simon while he was busy looking and had already accomplished his mission. A purple glowing octopus was latched firmly around Christopher's head, completely covering his face

Energy spiraled around the spectral beast. Christopher's limbs flailed briefly then went limp. All the while Hayes stood with one leg bent at the knee and his foot on a chair, in some kind of dramatic, mock-hero pose. This was the last thing he saw before he was shoulder-rammed into the bathroom by a large goon, and the door pinned shut behind him. The man grabbed his wrists and controlled him like a toddler. He wore a black suit, the same as Hayes. Simon was furious and completely powerless. He cursed his lack of knowledge of the un-physics of this new realm. This seemed exactly like regular physics to him.

"Now settle down boy," said the hulking brute, "we're not gonna hurt you. Just Chris."

"Fuck you," shot back Simon. "We're all fucking dead anyway. It doesn't matter what you do I will bounce back, and you can sure as hell bet Chris will."

The brute laughed. "You really think it's that simple? You're dead now, so since you have a body, you have no way to suffer? I guess he didn't tell you."

"Tell me what?" asked Simon.

"That there are still rules that YOU must abide by," replied the malevolent giant. "Rules WE must enforce."

There was a knock at the door. Hayes entered with a smile on his face that made Christopher's normal menacing smirk look benign.

"Let him go, Harry," ordered Hayes. "I think this one can be reasoned with."

"Yes, because this situation is perfectly reasonable," snapped Simon.

"I can understand your anger Simon," said Hayes, "but Christopher must be stopped before he corrupts another fortunate soul."

"How am I being corrupted?" inquired Simon. "If it weren't for him, I'd still be stuck in a loop."

Simon stared at Hayes gravely. He intended to find something out.

"He broke your cycle only to use you to further his sinister plans," replied Hayes, his accusatory tone took a new fury.

"What plans?" Simon could see the true colors bleeding through.

"He is making a pact with the Shambles," said Hayes dramatically, like some late night cheesy horror show host.

"What kind of pact?" asked Simon, genuinely interested.

"We're not sure about the exact details at this moment, but that's about to change. Captain Cephalopod has a way with getting information," Hayes paused and took a labored breath, "but we do know that he's been harassing the living, tampering with planar balance, and a list of other war crimes. Involving the Shambles only greatens the magnitude of his atrocities."

"War crimes?" Simon asked, the truth coming into view.

"We can pretty much do as we please with him due to his violations of the Z-Code," wheezed Hayes. "Zombie suppression laws are still in effect after the nightmare outbreak we helped quell a while back."

He was in the business of keeping people in the dark, but Simon saw Hayes in his eternal death through a thick glass window. His final breaths were labored and painful from toxic fumes. He wore an orange jumpsuit and full shackles. Hayes had been put to death in the gas chamber for mangling children. The sight of a young Shamble girl had set him on a Post Mortal freak out and ensuing moral crusade. His way of handling reality was deceitful. Simon had sensed this in his first meeting, when Hayes had tried to abduct him from the scene of his demise. He hoped that was the last vital detail he failed to remember until it was too late.

"And you, Simon Young, we are going to arrest you for guilt by association in accordance with Z-Code parameter 113, section…" Hayes was cut off by the concussive force of Luger kicking down the bathroom door.

"Fuck your Z-Law, Mr. Hayes," said Luther. "In this bar, I am the Law."

The enforcer was frothing at the mouth and popping veins everywhere. He saw this as a direct challenge. He and Luger were ready to go. A Simon was about to witness his first super heavyweight bathroom fight. They were both fighting to uphold their personal laws. The power of belief. He was ready to see which brand of Justice would prevail. Hayes was already cornered but tried to further flatten himself out against the wall as cockroaches tended to do.

"Fight with us all you like in here," said Hayes, "but the real battle out there is inside your friend's head."

Simon thought about the last thing he saw before being manhandled into the bathroom. Chris flailed and then hung limp with that mind flayer clinging to his skull. Hayes stood there, triumphant looking if not corny. It made Simon sick to think about Chris struggling with that hellish creature.

"I guess your signal is kind of fuzzy since you are nosing around in my realm," said Luger wryly, "but Captain Cephalopod just met Captain Hook."

He dangled the no longer glowing carcass of the purple octopus from his hook hand. Hayes minced his teeth in apparent agony. He loved that cephalopod. Hayes screamed something incoherent and the enforcer bull rushed Luther. Simon could swear the bastard swelled in size. One of the brute's buttons whizzed past his nose.

The titans smashed into each other with the audible crack of post mortal energies colliding. It sounded like a train wreck. The room shook and bits of plaster fell from the ceiling. The enforcer hit Luger's legs with a football tackle. This did not stop Luger's hook from finding its mark. With an overhand swing, he imbedded it in the giant's shoulder blade. He scrambled beside the enforcer and used his leverage to sling him literally through the brick wall and into the street. The enforcer did not get up.

This all looked like ordinary physics to Simon, albeit exaggerated to epic proportions. He chalked it all up to the power of belief. That was getting easier and easier to do. Hayes tried to run for the door while Luger surveyed his damage. He was met halfway by a ragged looking Chris, who smashed him across the eyes with a nightstick.

Hayes stumbled backwards and fell flat on his ass. Simon looked at Chris, the suction cup marks on his face. Simon delivered a soccer kick to the mouth of the reeling Hayes.

"That's the spirit," said Chris before collapsing beside him. Luger leaned in close to Hayes, who was slipping around on all fours in his own blood.

"This is my land, this is my club," said Luger. "I helped build this place, and I fucking died here. My word is law, and there is nothing anyone can do about it, least of all you. You ignorant cock sucker. You should have known that. You are barred for eternity. Your entire "Keepers of The Darkness," bullshit does not fly here. Go fuck yourself. You lose."

"No, I don't," hissed Hayes. "The info and power I usurped from Chris can still be put to use."

"Not if I do this," said Simon, picking up Captain Cephalopod's remains. "Hey, Chris."

"Yeah," Chris said weakly, pulling himself up to a seated position.

"Eat it." This was not a request, but an order.

"You are desperate," said Hayes, "superstition does not work here, not cross cultural and certainly not trans-dimensional."

Chris knew better than to doubt Simon. He chomped down the rubbery sea monster in as few bites as possible. At least he didn't have to worry about choking. A searing purple light flashed from every orifice. He stood up and brushed himself off, looking as spry as any perfectly healthy dead man."

"How do you feel Chris?" asked Simon boldly.

"Good as new," replied Christopher.

"That can't be," exclaimed Hayes in disbelief. "What did you do?"

"Post Mortal enactment of mortal subconscious superstition," said Simon.

"What?" asked Luther.

"Captain Cephalopod was a nightmare creature, a succupus to be precise," explained Simon. "The plane this creature resides on is a dream state from another reality. Superstition in that reality says if that creature steals part of your soul in your sleep, you must go catch an octopus and devour it to get your memories back."

"Damn Simon," said Luther, "nice one."

"But how did you figure that out so quickly?" begged Hayes.

"I looked, and I saw it for what it was, just like you...spineless and lost in a dream," Simon looked at Chris, then Luther. "Now, Mr. Hayes, I believe the soul keeper of this property has demanded that you fuck off."

Hayes picked himself off the ground. He didn't look heroic now, not even in a misguided comical sense. Simon, Luger, and Chris agreed to have a round of shots to celebrate the banishment of Hayes. Although they were sure to see him again, they knew it wouldn't be in their comfort zone. They sat down at the bar. They toasted to space and time being dead like them. They toasted to the power of belief and the concept of territory, despite the lack of tangible boundaries. They toasted to new friendship.

"So I guess you trust me now," said Chris.

"Just enough to never let my guard down," said Simon.

"Then I have taught you well," said Chris.

"But I want to know one thing," said Simon.

"What's that?" said Christopher.

"What was your deal with the Shambles?" Simon asked. "What did you exchange with that girl?"

"Information," said Chris. "They have links to the physical world. I am trying to figure out why their influence is stronger on that plane than the rest of ours. I give her clues about her past and she gives me coordinates."

"Coordinates to what?" asked Simon.

"To meeting points between realms," said Chris with a hint of wonder to his rough voice, "roads between all branches of consciousness. I do not wish to meddle with the living, merely learn from them. That's how you accessed the information about the octopus. We have a door to that realm in the beer cooler."

"No shit," said Simon, "take me."

"Alright," said Chris, "when we are done partying here, we'll have our after party in the alter dream realm. It's beautiful there. That is, of course, if Luger will give us the keys."

"Of course," said Luger, "anything for the after party. We'll go round up some strippers and Shambles and tear shit up proper. We'll be the life of the after party."

Simon awoke in his car. His ride was wrecked and so was he. Sunshine glared murderously through the spider webbings of his windshield. He felt like his guts were cooking.

"Not again," he said aloud, "no fucking way."

He wondered what the fuck was going on. He didn't know how this kept happening. He saw a bottle of Jim Beam in the passenger seat with a cigarette floating in it. Yuck. At least his car wasn't at an awkward angle in a ditch. He was in the strip club parking lot. Chris stood outside cackling.

"I thought it would be funny to bring your car up here and let you placebo drink yourself into an undead coma," Chris said. "You should have seen your face. You almost bought it."

"You sonofabitch…" said Simon.

"Yeah, but it was fun, no?" replied Chris.

"I don't know," said Simon a smirk. "My Quantum Memory is acting up, think you could walk me through the events?"

"Well," said Chris, "I guess one more time wouldn't kill me."

CONRAD YOUNG

Into the Dark

a screenplay by
Anthony S. Buoni
Brittany Lamoureux

FADE IN:

INT. Mu Epsilon Omega (MEO) BUILDING

MIKE and CINDY (attractive college students in their early twenties) are making out in the stairwell of a dorm-style building underneath a sign advertising the Mu Epsilon Omega fall fling festival. They grope each other's clothes, and Mike (shaggy hair and wearing a buttoned shirt) slides his hand under Cindy's green blouse.

> CINDY
> Wait—not here. Which room is yours?

> MIKE

We can't go in there—my roommate already left with his girlfriend.
He called dibs at the party.

CINDY
Well, you'd better think of something fast. If you can't provide a
private place, I'll go back down and find someone who can.

Mike kisses her deep, running his hands through her hair. When he
finishes, he holds her chin and looks her in the eyes.

MIKE
I got the perfect place.

CINDY
I knew you'd come through…with a little prompting.

They kiss again, and Mike leads her down the hall.

INT. MEO HALLWAY—CONTINUING

They stop in front of a wooden attic door with a sign reading KEEP
OUT at eye level.

Mike reaches into his pocket and pulls out a key ring. After fumbling
with them, he singles out a large brass key and smiles

CINDY
What is this?

MIKE
Some kind of attic or storage room. I have never needed it before
tonight.

CINDY

That's a relief.

Mike smirks.

MIKE

This is why you were better off leaving with an RA.

CINDY

I wasn't after your title, big shot.

MIKE

Oh yeah? What were you after then?

Cindy raises an eyebrow and tugs on Mike's collar, bringing him into another open-mouthed kiss.

Mike unlocks the door and returns the key to his pocket. He kisses her again, reaching to the doorknob. He tries opening the door but fails.

He breaks the kiss with a sheepish look and dedicates his full attention to the door, yet he is unable to open it.

CINDY

Gee, my hero.

MIKE

The damned thing is stuck.

He puts all of his weight into it, but the door will not budge.

CINDY

Come on. Those Mai Tais weren't that strong. Hurry. Mike, I'm losing interest over here.

Mike looks over his shoulder, banging against the door.

MIKE

I'm telling you, Cindy, this fucking door won't open. You give it a try, She-ra.

Cindy effortlessly opens the door and crosses her arms. Mike runs his hands through his hair, looking at his feet.

CINDY

After you.

INT. ATTIC—CONTINUING

Inside, the attic is a dusty mess. It is empty, and other then a few pieces of garbage in the corners and floor, it looks as if there was never any human inhabitance.

MIKE

Hope you don't have any allergies.

CINDY

No, but you sure do know how to treat a lady.

MIKE

You haven't seen anything yet.

CINDY
Oh yeah?

Mike draws closer, unbuttoning his shirt.

MIKE
I am about to take you places you've never been.

They begin kissing again; Cindy pulls off his shirt and begins working on his jeans.

MIKE
(kissing Cindy)
You're never gonna walk the same after tonight.

Cindy unzips his pants.

CINDY
Is that so, cowboy?

He begins to unzip her pants, but unseen fingers grab her hair, yanking her head back. Since both of Mike's hands are on her fly, she jumps, turning around to see her assailant. There is, however, no one except for them in the attic.

CINDY
What the fuck was that?

Mike, still working her pants, laughs.

MIKE
What are you talking about, baby?

CINDY

Someone just grabbed my hair and yanked.

MIKE

Oh, so ya want it rough, huh?

Cindy pushes him away. As she feels the back of her head, a worried look comes over her face. She begins to straighten out her clothes.

CINDY

I'm serious, asshole. Something grabbed the back of my head and pulled.

Mike sighs and refastens his pants.

MIKE

I'm telling you there is nobody in here but us. This room is deserted—it has not used in years.

They look into the darkness. We see the room from their POV— moonlight pours into the room from a window overlooking the outside of the building.

MIKE

Nobody here but us…and little, itty-bitty dust bunnies. Nothing scary about them, now is there?

CINDY

Stop it, Mike. Let's go.

MIKE

Come on. You don't want to fool around anymore?

                    CINDY
            You are such a pig.

                    MIKE
            I am a man.

He starts to laugh, but he stops when he sees something shift in the
blackness. Cindy senses his demeanor change. She pulls close to
him, grabbing his shoulder with his hand.

                    CINDY
        What is it?

There is a BEAT as Mike stares into the darkness.

                    CINDY
        Mike? What do you see?

                    MIKE
Nothing. Maybe my roomie is done with his girl by now. He doesn't
    have what us big boys call endurance anyway. We should probab—

Mike is knocked to the ground, and an angry GROWL rips through
the attic. Cindy SCREAMS. Mike is back on his feet in a flash, and
the two race out of there.

INT. MEO HALLWAY—CONTINUING

They burst into the hallway; Mike slams the attic door behind them
and digs out his keys, struggling to get them in the door.

CINDY
LOCK IT, LOCK IT.

MIKE
Damn it, I'm trying.

DEAN MORGAN (an older black man with balding, graying hair who is dressed in a nice suit) grabs Cindy. She SCREAMS, and Dean Morgan raises a hand to silence.

DEAN MORGAN
What are you two doing up here?

MIKE
W-we were just lo-looking around in there, and—

DEAN MORGAN
Looking around? You are both old enough to read right?

Mine and Cindy look stunned by his question.

DEAN MORGAN
Being that you are both college students, I hope that is not an unfair assumption. Anyways, that sign says "keep out", and I know you couldn't have missed it.

MIKE
No, sir.

Mike and Cindy exchange a glance.

DEAN MORGAN
Mike, you're the RA. You know better. Where is the key?

MIKE

Right here, Dean Morgan, but there is something in there. It just at-
tacked us.

Cindy nods. Mike hands the Dean the key.

DEAN MORGAN

Something in there…attacked you?

CINDY

It's true, sir. It grabbed my hair and knocked Mike to the ground.

The Dean looks at them.

CINDY

You have to believe us.

Dean Morgan glances at his watch.

DEAN MORGAN

Look, you two. It's late, and I know you've both been drinking. I can
smell it.

MIKE

But, sir, I swe—

DEAN MORGAN

Ah, ah, ah—I know it is fall fling, and I am exceptionally tolerant
towards my students about these things. You all need to blow off a
little steam. However, it is after 10 o'clock, and I think it would be
best if you said good night to your girlfriend and called it a night.

MIKE

Sir, we are telling you the truth.

DEAN MORGAN
Now, Mike. We'll discuss this tomorrow.

Mike looks flustered for a BEAT, before his shoulders sag and he gives into the Dean's orders.

MIKE
Goodnight, sir.

He tucks Cindy under his arm and leads her down the hall. Dean Morgan watches the two vanish around a corner.

Dean Morgan turns to the attic door, testing the knob. After establishing it is still unlocked, he tries to open it, but, like Mike, the door will not budge.

After a few tries, he manages to get the door open, and he steps in.

INT. ATTIC—CONTINUING

Dean Morgan examines the room carefully. He steps in the center of the room and looks around, sighing.

A mysterious breeze moves dust, blowing papers from the corners towards him. One piece of aged and torn paper hits his feet.

Dean Morgan leans over and picks it up, GROANING. When he returns upright, he swallows hard. He looks at the paper a long time...

CUT TO:

EXT. FITZGERALD UNIVERSITY SIGN

SUPERIMPOSE: 1990

We see a brief montage of Fitzgerald University's campus: buildings, students wandering between classes and chatting to each other.

EXT. COMMONS—DAYTIME

Sitting on a picnic table are four friends: CALEB (19 years old, dressed in khakis and a Polo shirt), BRIAN (also 19, Rock and roll T-shirt, torn jeans), and GINA (striped shirt and long, black dress) sit in front of open books, soda cans, and half-eaten sandwiches.

JARED (a little older, grey shirt and cargo shorts) joins them, slamming his backpack on the table. He snatches the soda in front of Gina.

GINA
Hey, jerk. That is my lunch.

JARED
Your fat ass is never gonna lose weight drinking this crap.
I'm doing you a favor.

Gina looks agitated.

BRIAN
Back off, Jared. That's my woman you're messing with.

GINA

Who said I was your woman?

Brian leans into Gina and begins brushing her hair with his fingers, tucking it behind her ears. She looks a little annoyed with the gesture, but allows it.

Jared looks over and sees a BEARDED MAN lurking around some trees.

JARED

Ah, gag me.

GINA

What?

JARED

See that guy over there? The one looks like he is trying to smell the women walking around those trees?

Gina points towards the man.

GINA

That creep-a-zoid with the beard?

JARED

Jesus, don't point at him. The last thing we want is for him to come over here.

BRIAN

Why, bro? You owe him money for sex?

JARED

Ha-ha. No, he is bad news. The campus cops will run him off as soon as they realize he is hanging out.

                              BRIAN

          Is he dangerous?

Jared slowly shakes his head.

                              BRIAN

          No, he is just a freak.

                              BRIAN

So, Gina, speaking of getting freaky, that new Christian Slater flick is showing at the second run. I hear it's a little dirty, but I don't mind paying a dollar for some good old-fashioned obscenity. How 'bout you and me double date with Caleb and Jared, take it in. You can put on that little black dress you wore last weekend; you know the one with the easy access.

                              GINA

Jesus, Brian. You're such a horn dog. I do like Christian Slater—so hot.

                              BRIAN

Come on, sweet pea. You know it will be a blast.

                              JARED

I can't make it, guys. I am taking Lisa Pelikan to Bella's—you know, that fancy Italian joint in town. I plan on getting some action, and you guys will do nothing but ruin my chances.

                              GINA

Who's going to go with Caleb then? I mean, you don't want to feel like a fifth wheel, do you, Caleb?

Caleb is distracted, staring off across the commons courtyard at SARA (19, purple blouse, black jeans, and a black scarf), walking alone and listening to headphones.

BRIAN
Yo, Caleb? You zoning out there, buddy?

Gina catches on that he is watching Sara walk by.

GINA
You're looking at that girl, aren't you?

CALEB
I, um, ah—

GINA
YOU ARE. You're looking at Sara.

BRIAN
Who?

GINA
Sara Crest. She is so weird.

JARED
I know who she is. She's in our Western Civ class, Caleb. Totally weird.

BRIAN
Weird how. Like—

He holds up his hand as if he had a knife and pantomimes stabbing while making "PSYCHO" SHOWER SCENE music.

GINA

No, silly. She is really quiet. Doesn't talk to anyone. She is always writing in this composition notebook. I tried to invite her to hang out with me and Jared one day after class, and I swear she looked as if she wanted to run away.

BRIAN

That means she's shy. Nothing weird about that.

Brian turns to Caleb.

BRIAN

Hey, Caleb. Want me to go and fetch her for you? I'll tell her you have a twelve inch cock that screams her name in the middle of the night.

JARED

You would be listening to such a thing, you sick-o perv.

Caleb turns red.

BRIAN

I'm his roommate and his best friend. You just wind up knowing things about each other when you have a bond like we do. Right, buddy?

CALEB

I guess.

GINA

Leave him alone. Caleb, if you want me to ask her to come, I can give it s shot.

CALEB

No, you two just go without me. I have a Religion paper for Dr. Halvorson due Monday I need to research some more. Besides, I prefer horror movies. I like to be scared.

The group is approached by HUGO (30's,large, bearded, and dressed in all black), and he points his finger towards Caleb.

HUGO

I know you are staying in the Mu Epsilon Omega building, young man.

Caleb exchanges worried glances with his friends. Brian shrugs before they all look back at him.

BRIAN

We both do. We're roomies.

HUGO

You both had better find some other dorm to shack up in. This school and especially that building and this school are cursed.

GINA

Guys, he's scaring me.

BRIAN

Yeah, man. Kick rocks.

HUGO

Twenty years ago, that building became terribly cursed. A curse that still lingers in the attic, waiting to spread its evil wings on whatever poor soul wanders through those doors.

                    BRIAN
Dude, we pledged the frat already and were accepted. The hazing is over. Get lost.

Hugo looks hurt.

                    HUGO
You need to be warned. I'm helping you because I know.

                    JARED
Just leave. Thanks, but we didn't ask for your help or advice.

Hugo starts to protest, but two CAMPUS SECURITY GUARDS grab him.

                    GUARD #1
Mister, we've told you that you are not allowed to be on campus.

                    HUGO
They need to know. I can save their lives.

                    GUARD #2
Time to go. If you're not going to leave, then we are going to get campus police. Now, I don't think you want to spend the night in jail, but we can arrange that if you want.

                    HUGO
I'll leave. But you've been warned.

Gina mouths "thank you" to the guards as they escort Hugo away.

BRIAN

You were saying that Sara girl was weird. That, Gina, was weird. He must be some townie loon, drunk on cheap wine and smelling the sorority girls' panties when they are in class.

GINA

What was that all about?

JARED

He used to go here.

CALEB

What?

JARED

He used to go here—he was some kind of genius. He was working on his PhD in criminology when he went mad. Word is he is some kind of witch. Now he lives in town and spends a lot of time in the library. He does odd jobs for some of the locals that have taken pity on him. Hugo is his name...I think.

GINA

How do you know all this?

JARED

I'm a sophomore, little miss freshman. There is even a story about the MEO house.

CALEB

What story?

JARED

Twenty years ago, this hippy chick hooked up with a guy she was in love with. Problem was that she already had a boyfriend, some jock or something. The jock was the jealous type, and a girl that liked him ratted the two lovers out at a party one night. Bitch spills the beans about everything, even tells the jock that he could find them in the attic of the MEO building, doing the nasty.

Brian grabs Gina and dry humps her.

> BRIAN
> YEAH—FINALLY SOME ACTION IN THIS BORE.

> GINA
> Get off me.

She shoves him aside and returns her attention to Jared. The others lean closer to Jared as well.

> JARED
> The jock goes up to the attic and finds them in the heat of passion and fucking loses it. He goes nuts, killing them both. I heard that there were pieces of them all over the place. Fingers and toes and legs and arms just everywhere.

> GINA
> Ew.

> BRIAN
> That's wicked, man.

> CALEB
> What happened to the jock?

JARED

When he returned to his sanity—if such a thing is possible after committing something so brutal—he killed himself. Hung himself in the same attic, or something.

BRIAN
Bullshit.

JARED

It's true. I heard it from a teacher my first day of English 1101. She told us their souls still roam campus, and that we should never go to the scene of the crime 'cause their spirits will get us.

Gina's eyes are wide, and Jared takes the moment to pounce at her.

JARED
RAR!

Gina jumps. Everyone but Caleb laughs.

JARED

You're right. It is just some crap they tell the freshmen to get you to understand story tone. The attic is off limits, so it becomes the per-fect device. All right, I got to get, you guys. See you kiddies later.

Brian and Jared shake hands. Jared hugs Gina and slaps Caleb on the shoulder.

BRIAN
See ya.

JARED
Peace.

Jared EXITS.

GINA
So, do you think it really happened?

BRIAN
Hell no. Don't be so gullible. He just wanted to see you piss yourself when he jumped at you. That's all.

GINA
Still…

BRIAN
Still what? Don't tell me you've never been around a campfire and told tall tales before.

GINA
I have. When I was younger, we used to camp in Tennessee all the time.

BRIAN
Do you believe that some psycho with a hook for a hand is waiting on Lover's Lane for you and me to get busy so he can slice and dice us?

GINA
No.

BRIAN
Same thing here. What about you, Caleb? You believe that shit?

Caleb is staring at the MEO building now.

BRIAN

Caleb? You looking for Sara?

Caleb is still staring. Brian snaps his fingers, bringing him back to reality.

                        BRIAN
Welcome back, spaceman. I said: do you believe that shit?

                        CALEB
                No—no, of course not.

                        BRIAN
    See, Gina. Mumbo-jumbo. Let's get some more sodas, my treat.

Gina smiles and bats her eye lashes at him.

                        GINA
            Sounds good. You coming, Caleb?

                        CALEB
                No, I got a trig class soon.

                        BRIAN
Good, 'cause I wasn't buying you one anyway. Let's go, babe.

Gina and Brian EXIT arm-in-arm, laughing and talking amongst themselves.

Caleb remains transfixed on the MEO building.

CUT TO:

INT. MEO HALLWAY

Caleb walks down the hall; a fluorescent light flickers in front of the attic door. There is an older-looking "KEEP OUT" sign affixed to the door, and Caleb pauses in front of it.

He slowly reaches out, testing the handle. It is unlocked, but the door refuses to open. He uses more force, and after a few increasingly hard efforts, it finally opens.

INT. ATTIC—CONTINUING

Inside, we see the same dusty mess as earlier.

Caleb creeps into the center of the room, breathing hard.

A STRANGE WIND picks up, tugging at Caleb's hair.

> CALEB
>> Hello?

Caleb hears a SCUFFING sound, drawing his attention to a corner. He turns slowly.

In a dark corner of the room, Caleb notices a WOMAN'S SILHOUETTE, crouched in the shadows.

> CALEB
>> I'm sorry, I did not know anyone was in here.

He cannot discern any of the woman's features, be he takes a step towards her, his arm outstretched as if to put a hand on her shoulder.

CALEB
Ma'am…?

He takes another step closer. We see no features as the woman remains huddled in the corner.

CALEB
I really did not mean to disturb you—I did not think anyone was allowed in here.

The woman stands and begins walking towards him.

CALEB
Is everything OK, ma'am?

The woman steps into the scant light pouring in from the circular
window, and Caleb sees that she is mangled and covered in blood.

Caleb screams and bolts out of the attic, slamming the door behind
him.

INT. MEO HALLWAY—CONTINUING

Caleb runs into JULIAN (older, overalls, pushing a mop bucket), and
knocks over the mop bucket. Dirty, soapy water spills all over the
floor.

JULIAN
WHAT THE HELL IS THE HURRY, SON?

Caleb, slipping on the spilled water, falls all over himself helping the janitor pick up his bucket.

> CALEB
>
> I am so sorry, sir. I—

> JULIAN
>
> Boy...

Julian looks at the attic door.

> JULIAN
>
> Was you just in there?

Caleb nods.

> JULIAN
>
> Stay out of there. Mr. Dean Morgan does not abide students in there. I heard he expelled the last couple of kids he caught making out in there. It's trespassing, and if I catch you in there again, I'm tellin'.

Caleb nods again, and continues hurrying down the hallway.

Julian looks towards the attic door and shudders.

INT. CLASSROOM

We see a classroom filled with desks and a large world map hanging on one of the walls.

The students listen to a TEACHER who is explaining the Donner Party, occasionally turning his back to write on the dry erase board.

TEACHER

Because the Donner Party found themselves snowed in, they had to resort to cannibalism in order to survive.

Caleb sits in a desk, doodling rough pencil sketches of the woman's face from the MEO attic. Beside him, another STUDENT is sleeping face down at his desk.

Sara sits just behind the sleeping student, and she watches Caleb draw with great interest.

In the back of the classroom, Gina passes Brian a note. He unfolds it, reads it, and flashes a knowing wink. Gina blows him a long kiss and returns the wink.

TEACHER

Of the eighty-three members of the Donner Party that went into the mountains, only forty-five survived to reach California, making this one of the most unfortunate stories of Manifest Destiny.

The teacher notices Caleb's distraction and approaches his desk.

TEACHER

Mr. Reilly, as a history teacher I can appreciate artist's endeavors throughout the development of human civilization, but during my lecture, I would rather you paid attention. Your last exam was less than spectacular, and I fear you are hading for a repeat performance.

The class chuckles, and Caleb sheepishly closes his notebook.

CALEB

Sorry, sir.

Sara frowns.

Brian passes Gina back the note.

The teacher cocks an eyebrow and turns to the dry erase board again.

                    TEACHER
            Ok, who knows why—

The teacher stops when he notices the wall clock.

                    TEACHER
Well, we're out of time for today. I'll see you all next Tuesday, and
        remember that your five-page is due.

The students begin gathering their books and filing towards the door.

                    TEACHER
Now I want that in MLA, cite your sources, and if you have any
problems, you know how to reach me. Don't wait for the last minute
   because I only have as many hours as there are in a day.

As Caleb closes his book bag, Sara stops at his desk.

                    SARA
                    Hey.

Caleb looks up, but he quickly turns his eyes away her.

                    CALEB
            Hey.

                    SARA
        My name is Sara.

Caleb scratches the back of his head.

                    CALEB
           I—I know. Caleb.

                    SARA
           I know.

Caleb puts his backpack on.

                    SARA
           So, you did not do so well on the last exam?

                    CALEB
           That's what he said.

                    SARA
           I saw the first one you took—you aced it.

                    CALEB
           A hundred. And the bonus question about Paul Revere.

                    SARA
           So what's changed. You look like you haven't been sleeping. Every-
                        thing OK?

                    CALEB
           Yeah.

                    SARA
           All right. Look, if you ever need to talk or you want someone to
           study with, I can give you a hand. I think it is easier to work in pairs
                    than to go at some of these alone.

CALEB
Thanks.

SARA
We have that five-page due—I am real good editor, and I can pound
out a citation page like nobody's business.

CALEB
Thanks.

Caleb makes his way to the door where Gina and Brian are kissing.

BRIAN
You keep it up, I am gonna lose my rep as the class clown, buddy.
Giving me a run for the money.

CALEB
Sure. Sorry.

BRIAN
Man, you have been pretty fucking weird lately. What gives?

CALEB
Nothing, I have to go.

Caleb pushes past, EXITING in the hall.

GINA
What is his malfunction?

BRIAN
Too much sperm. His balls are dragging on the ground. He needs to
lose some of the little swimmers before he pops.

Brian shoots SARA a look. Sara puts on her headphones and walks past them.

INT. LIBRARY—EVENING

Caleb enters the library and walks to the back where five microfiche terminals reside. He begins flipping through the books looking through sheets of film stored in cataloged books.

Sara wanders in, watching him from afar.

Caleb settles in front of one of the machines, flipping through old newspaper images.

Sara keeps on wandering by him, grabbing random books and watching over his shoulder.

After some searching, Caleb finds a twenty-year-old article with the headline: MURDER SUICIDE AT FITZGERALD UNIVERSITY. He stops and leans closer.

Caleb pulls out a notepad and begins making notes.

He scrolls through another few frames, stopping at a picture of three attractive college-age kids. He recognizes one photo as the woman from the attic. Underneath her photo a caption reads: DAISY MCK-ENZIE.

Beside her, another male teen dressed in a tux smiles from the screen. Underneath his visage, a caption reads: NICK SANTANGELO. There is copy explaining that these two were victims.

A quick shuffle of the film and Caleb sees a picture of a man in a varsity athlete jacket with a caption reading: ROBERT BATES.

> CALEB
>
> Bates apparently hung himself after strangulating McKenzie and Santangelo. The young man's body was discovered mutilated and posed in what authorities are calling a "satanic ritual".

Caleb sighs and leans back in his chair, rubbing his eyes.

He returns to photos of the crime scene, stopping at them and looking hard.

> JULIAN
>
> What did I tell you about that attic?

Caleb jumps, the janitor having appeared from nowhere.

> CALEB
>
> I was just wondering what the truth was.

> JULIAN
>
> The truth is only the way someone remembers it. Poking around just stirs up bad memories. That incident sullied the name of our good school. It is better to let the past stay where it belongs…in the past.

> CALEB
>
> How come nobody is talking about this?

> JULIAN
>
> Leave it be, son.

Caleb takes another look at the crime scene photos before shutting off the microfiche reader.

                            CALEB
                  All right.

                            JULIAN
    That's a good boy. Concentrate on your studies, or find a woman to
    occupy your thoughts. No good can come from all the pain those
                        families experienced.

Julian EXITS.

Caleb gathers his books and goes over to the card catalog. He flips
through a few before jotting the Dewey Decimal numbers on a small
piece of paper from a pad on top of the files.

He wanders over to a section and, after scanning the spines for a moment, retrieves his desired book.

He does not notice that Sara is still watching him.

He goes to the checkout desk where a LIBRARIAN (young, pretty,
and wearing a pink sweater) takes his book.

                          LIBRARIAN
    Hunting Spirits: A Paranormal Field Book, huh? You getting ready for
    Halloween? Don't tell me you actually believe in this sort of thing.

                            CALEB
                I am not sure what I believe anymore.

                          LIBRARIAN

There's no such thing. I have lived in three different states, and I have never seen anything that even remotely resembles things that go bump in the night.

Caleb does not respond as he signs the check out card and slides it into the pocket on the book's back cover.

LIBRARIAN
It's due back in two weeks, or you'll have to pay a late charge.

CALEB
Thanks.

LIBRARIAN
Happy hunting.

Caleb EXITS.

INT. DORM ROOM—LATER

Caleb is sitting at his desk, pouring over the library book.

Brian is slapping on cologne in front of a mirror. He fiddles with his hair and his collar.

BRIAN
Did you get that Sara girl's digits?

CALEB
It is not like that.

BRIAN

Sure it is. That is why she talked to you. She wants you to give her the Caleb Carrot, man.

CALEB
Come on.

Brian tears himself from the mirror and slides up next to Caleb's desk.

BRIAN
Dude, this is college. What are you doing?

He grabs the book from Caleb's hands.

CALEB
Hey, give it back.

BRIAN
What the fuck is this? Really, Caleb, this is so junior high. I thought you outgrew this along with comic books and Star Wars toys.

CALEB
I still like both.

BRIAN
You have this attractive, although psychotic, woman hot to jump in the sack with you, and you are reading bullshit. You're gonna die a virgin, ya know.

Caleb grabs the book back from Brian.

BRIAN

Worse is that you are going to die a skinny, blind virgin in a Jedi robe that gets his heart broken every Christmas when Santa fails to make an appearance down his chimney.

CALEB

Leave me alone. Don't you have VD to catch?

Brian laughs, punching Caleb in the shoulder.

BRIAN

See, now that's more like it. Show some damn brass ones. I know your grades have been slipping; not just American History, either.

CALEB

Yeah, well…

BRIAN

You got to keep them up. You'll lose everything, bro. The scholarship, the brotherhood—get it together, man.

CALEB

You taking Gina out again?

BRIAN

You know it. You should watch and learn. We'll have your cherry popped in no time.

CALEB

What's up with you two?

BRIAN

What do you mean?

CALEB

Are you two…together?

BRIAN

I would not go as far as to call her my girlfriend, if that's what you mean.

CALEB

So, you are having an open relationship.

Looking over his shoulder at the mirror, Brian runs his fingers through his hair again.

BRIAN

I am. She better not be.

CALEB

Don't you think that is a little messed up?

BRIAN

No, do you?

They pause for a BEAT, looking in each other's eyes, and Brian starts laughing.

BRIAN

I'll leave you to your little fantasy world. I'm gonna be late for dinner. Gina would kill me. Later, bro.

Brian hops up, EXITING.

CALEB
Later.

EXT. COMMONS—DAYTIME

Caleb is sitting with his back against a tree, looking at print-ups of the microfiche articles. He is stuck on the crime scene ones, unable to figure out why they have struck his fancy. He traces his fingers over a shot of the attic, bodies covered with sheets...

SARA
Say: 'I want a taco'!

Caleb looks up to find Sara holding a camera. She SNAPS A PIC-TURE.

SARA
Caught your soul, Caleb.

CALEB
What was that for?

SARA
Newspaper. I am on the staff, and I could not help myself. You looked so serious. What are you studying?

Caleb becomes self-conscious, gathering his photos and books.

CALEB
N-nothing. Just some independent study.

SARA
It's not porn is it? 'Cause I am cool if it is.

CALEB
It's nothing, really.

SARA

Let me see.

Sara hops down, scooting next to Caleb.

SARA

What are these? Are those bodies.

Caleb looks injured.

CALEB

Yeah, it is for a crime class.

SARA

You don't have any crime classes. Gina already told me you were a lit
major.

They exchange a glance.

SARA

I was curious; I asked. Besides, you act as if you are afraid of me. I
had to find out somehow.

CALEB

Why are you so interested in me?

Sara smiles and crosses her arms.

SARA

You're not like other guys around here. there's something…different
about you. Are you going to tell me what you're looking at or what?

Caleb looks at the papers he is holding for a BEAT before turning his attention back to Sara.

CALEB

You're going to think I am nuts.

SARA

You have no idea what they say about me.

They exchange another glance. Caleb starts laying out all the photos.

CALEB

There was a murder in my building. Twenty years ago. This guy, Robert Bates, killed these two—Nick Santangelo and Daisy McKenzie. Daisy was his girl, and he didn't like finding her with Nick.

SARA

Sounds like he had a screw loose.

CALEB

Worse. For what I can find, he knocked out Nick, strangled Daisy, and then chopped them up with something sharp in the attic.

SARA

Lovely.

CALEB

Then he put Nick in this weird pose, as if he was in prayer or something. The papers called it satanic.

Sara picks up one of the crime scene photos.

SARA

I can't believe this happened on campus.

                            CALEB
                          I know, right.

                            SARA
                  Why are you so interested in it?

Caleb takes the photo from her and adds it to the others, returning
them to his backpack.

                            CALEB
                          I just am.

                            SARA
                        I don't buy it.

                            CALEB
                      What do you mean?

                            SARA
    I mean, I know you have been slipping in your classes. Gina even
    mentioned that you have been acting not like yourself. Then, you
              grabbed that paranormal book the other day.

Caleb shoots her a look.

                            SARA
                        I followed you.

Caleb's jaw drops.

                            SARA

It's no big deal. I believe in the other side. I have a big collection
of grave rubbings too. I used to know this kid that collected dead
things. He was my first boyfriend.

CALEB
I have never had a girlfriend.

SARA
We are totally done, if that's what you were thinking. He and I, I
mean. Look, that's not important. What I want to know is why you
are so interested in the subject?

CALEB
I sort of snuck into the attic and saw…something.

SARA
Something? Like what?

Caleb zips his backpack.

CALEB
It's nothing. Nothing.

SARA
If it's nothing, then I want to go.

CALEB
What?

SARA
I want to go up there. I have a camera. We could take some shots.

CALEB
I don't know if that is a good idea, Sara.

SARA

Oh, come on. If we see something, I can shoot it. Evidence for
posterity.

CALEB

I still don't know. The last time things got a little crazy.

Sara grins.

SARA

That's what I am hoping for.

INT. MEO HALLWAY

Caleb follows Sara to the attic door. She has a determined look on
her face as she grabs the doorknob.

CALEB

We don't have to do this.

SARA

Chill out already.

She gives the doorknob a tug. It turns, but it will not budge.

SARA

It is stuck or something.

CALEB

It did the same thing to me. Like it does not want us in there.

> SARA

I can get it, but it will just take some—

Sara GRUNTS and pushes all of her weight into it. The door opens,
CREAKING as it opens.

Caleb looks at Sara.

> SARA

Here we go.

INT. ATTIC—CONTINUING

The two step in. Sara gets her camera ready as Caleb nervously scans
the corners for any signs of movement.

> SARA

This place is a mess.

> CALEB

I really don't think we should be here.

Sara snaps several pictures. The flash lights up the room, but it appears empty.

> SARA

Not much to see. Seems like a lot of wasted space if you ask me.

The strange wind picks up, mussing Sara's hair.

> SARA

Is there a draft in here?

CALEB
We need to go. Come on.

Caleb begins to EXIT for the door.

SARA
Wait, let me get a few more shots.

She hold up the camera, snapping a few more photos.

When she lowers the camera, DAISY is standing in front of her.
Sara SCREAMS, and Daisy shoves her to the door where Caleb is.

Sara falls to the ground, just before the door. Caleb grabs her hand
and begins to pull her out, but something grabs her and begins pulling her back in.

CALEB
Sara, hold on.

He pulls her hard, and she unleashes a PAINFUL SCREAM.

SARA
Don't let go, Caleb.

The tug of war lasts a few BEATS. Caleb manages to pull her out
into the hall. The attic door SLAMS, and the two run down the hall.

INT. CALEB'S DORM ROOM—CONTINUING

Caleb and Sara burst into his dorm room. Sara sits on his bed while
Caleb paces back and forth in front of his desk.

SARA

What the fuck was that?

CALEB

I think it was them…

SARA

Them, Caleb. What does that mean?

Caleb stops pacing and looks at her for a BEAT.

CALEB

Them—those kids that were murdered.
I think they are still up there.

SARA

Why would they attack us? We had nothing to do with it.

CALEB

I—I don't know. Maybe they are mad about what happened to them.

Caleb pulls out his copy of *Hunting Spirits*, and waves it at Sara.

CALEB

I have read here that sometimes souls that are trapped in the places
where injustices occurred often attack the living because they hold
resentments that they can't shake, even in death.

SARA

Revenge?

CALEB

Entities linger because of unfinished business, unrequited love, some instance of severe violence, or revenge. We have every one of those factors in Jared's story.

They share an uncomfortable silence for a BEAT.

SARA

If I had not been there, I would never have believed it. To be honest, I still don't know what I believe.

CALEB

I am not sure what I believe either. I don't think we should tell anyone about this.

SARA

I think I agree. I also think we should not go back there.

Caleb sits on the bed beside her.

CALEB

Sounds good to me.

SARA

Now I know why your grades have been slipping. Do you need any help in your classes?

Caleb looks at her and smiles.

CALEB

You would help me?

SARA

If you needed it, it would be no problem. I wanted to ask you earlier,
but we got…distracted.

CALEB

That would be cool. You know, I was wondering how to break the
ice with you. I'm a little shy sometimes.

SARA

Why would you be shy around me? What are you hiding from?

Caleb swallows hard.

CALEB

Well, I—

The door OPENS and Gina and Brian ENTER, arm-in-arm. Caleb
and Sara jump.

BRIAN

Dorm is mine for a—whoa, dude. Sorry, I did not know you had
company. I didn't see a sock on the door so…

CALEB

No, it's cool, man. We were just talking.

GINA

Hey, Sara. How are you, sweetie?

SARA

I'm, um, fine. A little tired, I suppose. You know, mid-terms and all.
Actually, I was just leaving.

Caleb and Sara stand. Sara leading, they walk past the other couple.
They stop in front of the door and Caleb OPENS it for her.

SARA

Well, it was interesting, to say the least.

CALEB

Yeah. No doubt.

SARA

I am going to develop this film tomorrow. I'll let you know how
the...pictures...turned out.

CALEB

Sounds rad. I'll see you in class.

SARA

Bye, for now.

CALEB

Bye.

He shuts the door, and turns to face Brian and Gina, both smiling at
him.

CALEB
What?

BRIAN
You sly fox. Look at you. Did you bang her?

GINA
Brian, come on. Leave him alone.

BRIAN
Hey, this is guy talk. Well?

CALEB

It is not like that.

BRIAN

Bullshit. You like her and you know it.

CALEB

She is going to help me with my homework. I've been struggling in a few classes and she offered to help.

GINA

That is so sweet.

BRIAN

Oh, no—don't tell me that it's already happened to you.

CALEB

What?

BRAIN

The pussy trance, man. You are already whipped.

GINA

That's wrong, Brian.

BRIAN

But it is true. I can see it in his eyes. You need to give her the meat, dude. Hell, you can use my bed—hell, I've banged Gina in yours.

GINA

BRIAN.

Gina his him arm playfully. Caleb looks at his bed and frowns.

                              BRIAN
                         What? It's true.

                              CALEB
                   That is kind of gross, Brian.

                              BRIAN
           You have to live adventurous, take chances.
                   Lets you know you're alive.

Caleb starts to protest but stops.

                              CALEB
                   You need the room, right?

                              BRIAN
                   For about an hour.

Gina shoots him a look.

                              BRIAN
                       Make it two.

                              CALEB
           Cool. I need to go to study anyway. You guys have fun.

                               GINA
                       Thanks, Caleb.

Caleb nods and EXITS.

INT. DARKROOM—THE NEXT DAY

Sara is developing her photos under the darkroom's ominous red lights. She pulls some of her prints of the stop bath and immerses it in the pans containing the photographic fixers. Next she pulls some of her other prints from the wash and begins hanging them up on a line to dry.

As she works, we see the dangling prints begin to flutter in a gentle breeze.

She moves the final prints from the wash and begins to hang them, stopping when she sees the other prints waving.

From behind, there is a SCUFFLING sound, and she jumps.

SARA
Hey, I'm developing in here. Stay out.

She takes a deep breath and hangs the last prints. She goes to a small sink and begins cleaning up her mess when she hears the SCUF-FLING again.

SARA
Not funny. Come on, I'm working. It is my lab time. It is my only Saturday.

Sara tenses. She moves slowly to the curtains blocking the door, breathing hard. She reaches up to turn off the red light, but something grabs her hair and pulls her down, dragging her back into the center of the room.

She manages to wrestle herself free, getting back on her feet and bolting towards the door.

INT. CALEB'S DORM

Caleb is hunched over his desk, studying. He rubs his eyes and tosses a pen on his desk. He leans back in his chair when a loud KNOCK-ING startles him.

He crosses the room and opens as the frantic KNOCKING continues.

He answers, and Sara pushes her way into the room.

> CALEB
> Um…hey?

> SARA
> It was horrible.

> CALEB
> What happened?

> SARA
> I was in the lab developing photos—the ones we took. Something grabbed me, Caleb.

> CALEB
> What do you mean something grabbed you?

> SARA
> There was no one in the room, but something attacked me. I was so scared, I left without the pictures I was developing.

Caleb crosses his arms.

SARA

That look can't be good.

CALEB

We got to get the pictures.

SARA

I am not going back there.

CALEB

I got to see the shots.

Sara bites her lower lip.

SARA

It was awful, Caleb. What if what grabbed me is still there?

CALEB

I'll go in alone. If something weird happens, I'll get out.

SARA

You promise?

Caleb makes an X over his chest.

CALEB

Cross my heart.

SARA

OK, but the first sign of trouble we split.

CALEB

Deal.

Sara hugs him. He is surprised at first, but returns the embrace.

INT. OUTSIDE DARKROOM

Caleb gives Sara a long look before he grabs the doorknob. Sara reaches out, stopping his hand and mouthing the words: be careful. Caleb nods and ENTERS.

INT. DARKROOM—CONTINUING

Caleb creeps into the red-lit room. He sees the photos, now dry, dangling from the line and begins pulling them off one by one.

Sweating by the time he removes the last one, he turns to see the silhouette of someone in the far corner. The shape approaches, knocking down the developing pans as it nears.

Caleb rushes out of the darkroom.

EXT. DARKROOM—CONTINUING

Caleb, photos in hand, slams the door.

> CALEB
> We need to go.

> SARA
> There is something still in there, isn't there?

Caleb takes her hand and they rush down the hall.

> SARA
> What did you see?

> CALEB
> I don't know, but I don't think it was friendly.

INT. CALEB'S DORM—A FEW MINUTES LATER

Sara and Caleb ENTER, and pause for a BEAT. Caleb holds up the photos and offers a weak smile.

> CALEB
> I got all the pictures I saw. They were on the line.

> SARA
> That was all of them. I have not had a chance to look yet.

> CALEB
> There's better light at my desk.

The two go over to the desk. Caleb flicks on a small lamp and they begin to go through the shots.

The first few photos are of students on campus, studying and socializing. Sara giggles a little when she comes to the shot of Caleb.

> SARA
> You're so cute.

Caleb looks up at her.

Sara flips to the next photo: the first attic shot.

> ### CALEB
> Looks like the attic.

They have three attic photos, and they lay them out side by side.

> ### CALEB
> I don't see anything...

They pour over them a few BEATS when Sara jumps.

> ### SARA
> Oh, my God. LOOK.

Caleb looks down a BEAT.

> ### CALEB
> I don't see...

Sara points to one of the shots.

> ### SARA
> There, in the shadows. There are people there.

Caleb squints his eyes.

> ### CALEB
> I see two shapes—they look just like the thing in the lab, but what
> are—

Caleb stops, jaw dropped.

CALEB

Wait a second.

He opens the drawer to his desk and pulls out a brown folder.

CALEB

These are the papers I printed up from the original murders, twenty years ago. Look there is one of the crime scene. I thought something was weird…look. There.

He points.

SARA

Three of them. There are three in this one.

CALEB

Well, that's how many bodies they found. I think it is them, still lingering there.

SARA

But why would they attack us?

CALEB

I don't know.

Caleb looks over the newspaper printout again.

CALEB

Oh no.

SARA

What?

CALEB

Look at the photo credit.

SARA

Hugo Viejo…who is that?

CALEB

He is this crazy guy they keep tossing from campus. A few days ago he was warning us that this building, this school is cursed. Campus cops ran him off.

SARA

We need to find him. I bet he can help us.

CALEB

There's no telling where he is at.

SARA

I got a car. It is not much, but it will get us into town so we can ask. I bet he's in the phonebook.

CALEB

Are you positive you want to continue this? Seems like it has been nothing but trouble since we went in that attic.

SARA

I'm sure. Whatever this is, it is coming after us. Maybe this Hugo character has an answer.

CALEB

I…I think your cute too.

SARA

Well, that was sudden.

They look at each other a BEAT before falling into a passionate kiss. They embrace each other tightly, but the door opens and Brian EN-TERS, causing them to jump.

> BRIAN
>
> Whoa, dudes. Sock on the door, remember?

Caleb and Sara readjust themselves as Brian hops on his bed.

> BRIAN
>
> Sorry, but I came here to ask you something.

> CALEB
>
> Shoot.

> BRAIN
>
> Tonight is fall fling, and I am gonna need the room until, let's say, midnight-thirty or one. Do you mind?

> CALEB
>
> No, I am going to town anyway. It's cool.

> BRIAN
>
> Going to town? You are going to miss the biggest party this month.

> CALEB
>
> We have a few things we gotta take care of.

> BRIAN
>
> Ah, I see. Well, you have fun with whatever it is you crazy kids are doing, and I will be here, getting drunk and laid.

Caleb and Sara exchange a glance.

CALEB

I guess we'd better get started.

SARA

Good plan.

Caleb gathers the photos and begins to EXIT.

CALEB

See you later, man.

BRIAN

Don't do anything I wouldn't do.

Brian laughs as Sara and Caleb EXIT.

INT. SARA'S CAR—A LITTLE WHILE LATER

Caleb flips through a phonebook as Sara drives.

CALEB

I'll be damned, he's in here.

SARA

So, where are we heading.

CALEB

Get this: 1313 Mockingbird Lane.

They exchange a smile.

CALEB

Know where it's at?

                        SARA
Yeah. Not too far from here. If all goes well, we'll be back in time
                    for Twin Peaks.

                        CALEB
                I am hooked on that show.

Sara nods.

                        SARA
            It drives me nuts, but I am too.

Caleb reaches over and brushes her cheek with his fingers. She
makes doe eyes at him.

EXT. HUGO'S HOUSE—A FEW MOMENTS LATER

There is nothing extraordinary about the 1313 Mockingbird Lane
residence save for a stone gargoyle beside the front door.

Caleb knocks in the center of the large brown door, taking a step
back.

Hugo answers the door, wearing a nice suit and smiling.

                        CALEB
        I am sorry to bother you sir, but I—

                        HUGO

You have come because you went up in the attic, and now something
is following you.

Caleb and Sara look astonished.

Hugo waves them in.

> HUGO
> Come on in, we have a lot to talk about.

INT. HUGO'S HOME—CONTINUING

Despite the plain exterior, inside of Hugo's home resembles a muse-
um. Bookshelves loaded with tomes line the walls. Skulls and hour-
glasses decorate the end tables, and Hugo lights an incense stick.

> HUGO
> This is dragon's blood I have blended with clove—good for protec-
> tion and power. Please have a seat. Tea will be ready in a minute.

Sara and Caleb sit beside each other on a loveseat. Caleb offers his
hand, and Sara accepts it, clutching it tightly.

> HUGO
> The cards told me you would be coming. I knew you were going to
> go to that cursed place that day on campus. It was in your stars.

> CALEB
> I never believed in things like this.

> HUGO
> They never do.

CALEB
I just…got curious.

HUGO
One cannot escape their destiny, my young friend. Sure, the path
may vary, but the end is always the same. I drew your cards today,
and I saw nothing but sorrow.

SARA
Cards?

HUGO
Tarot. I like the traditional Rider-Waite deck myself—a marriage
between modern and old, it is scary accurate.

SARA
Can you read mine?

HUGO
I am afraid that we do not have time, love. We have to go tonight
and try to end this cycle of despair.

CALEB
Tonight?

HUGO
Let me get the tea. I have a story for you both.

Hugo EXITS, and we hear him PREPARING TEA in another room.

Caleb rubs Sara's arm, and she leans into him. Hugo RETURNS with
a tray containing a teapot and two teacups. He tells his story as he
pours them tea.

HUGO

I was well into my education that horrible night. I was working part time as a crime scene photographer to better my skills at an art I have always held a deep passion for. Nothing like that had ever been seen in this sleepy town.

He hands Sara and Caleb their glasses.

HUGO

I was appalled at what that Bates kid did to them. Like an animal, he'd torn them apart, and then, like a coward, he hung himself.

Hugo offers sugar to the couple. They nod and he gives them both two lumps as he continues.

HUGO

Little did I know, the worse was on the horizon. I have always had a…knack for seeing things just beyond normal perception. We are surrounded by things most people simply choose to ignore as they grow hardened to this world. I knew they were there the moment I stepped in. What I did not count on was that they would follow me.

Hugo watches them take a long pull from his tea.

HUGO

The Fitzgerald University Three are still on campus, but they have different agendas. McKenzie and Santangelo are benign—they mean only to protect the school from that monster Bates. Have you noticed how hard it can be to get in the attic door?

Caleb nods.

HUGO

I believe it is McKenzie and Santangelo trying to keep people out so nothing bad happens. Because of their sudden deaths, those two remain trapped in the attic, but Bates' hunger for revenge allows him a little more play. Things had fallen silent because the attic was left alone. All that's changed now.

SARA

How did you get them to leave you alone?

HUGO

I never said I have. They are confined to campus, but I have taken precautions. I don't think you missed my sentinel at the front door.

The couple nods.

HUGO

There was a reason they used to be on all those old buildings. They serve their function well.

CALEB

How did you know we were going to be here? Why were you expect-ing us?

HUGO

What is going on at Fitzgerald University as we speak?

SARA

It's fall fling.

CALEB

The anniversary.

HUGO

Twenty years ago tonight. Bates' energy will feed of the party, making his extremely dangerous. I can't tell you how many students never come back to class or die from alcohol poisoning during this festival. It is a shame, really...

SARA

So, how do we stop them on campus?

HUGO

Good question. I have dedicated my life to studying paranormal activity, and I have a few things I have wanted to try. Problem is, I get run off the campus. My last stunt earned me a trespass. I'll go to jail if they catch me there again.

CALEB

Then what are we going to do?

HUGO

I've prepared a kit. It includes ancient superstitions passed down from village elder to village elder. It also includes this:

He reaches under the coffee table and pulls out a wooden Ouija board with a planchette to point out the letters.

HUGO

I made this based on instructions from an old voodoo psychic down in swamps outside New Orleans. I was saving it for this chance.

Hugo traces the alphabet with his fingers. He looks back up at Caleb and Sara.

HUGO

Are you ready?

EXT. OUTSIDE OF THE MEO BUILDING—DUSK—FALL
FLING PARTY

Students gather outside the MEO, socializing and drinking.

Brian wanders through the crowd, stopping in front of a small circle
of people.

> BRIAN
> Have any of you guys seen Gina?

An ATTRACTIVE WOMAN in a sundress shakes her head before
returning to the conversation.

> BRIAN
> Thanks.

He looks into the crowd some more.

INT. OUTSIDE THE MEO ATTIC—AT THE SAME TIME

The Julian, dressed in his normal janitor attire, is carrying a black
garbage bag past the attic door when he hears a low MOAN coming
from the attic. He looks over to the door and frowns.

> JULIAN
> God damned kids, fooling around in there.

He tosses the garbage bag beside the door and pulls on it. Unable to move it, he SWEARS under his breath. He pulls hard, and the door finally gives.

> JULIAN
> All right, you little bastards, party time's over.

He ENTERS.

INT. ATTIC—CONTINUING

Julian storms into the attic.

> JULIAN
> I told you kids it is time to go.

The door SLAMS, and Julian spins around. There is no one there.

> JULIAN
> All right, no funny business. Come out where I can see you.

The room is silent a BEAT. Julian looks around, yet he can discern no trace of anything.

Julian begins to head for the door. Before making it, he is stopped by semi-transparent FIGURE with indefinable features and wearing a red letterman jacket.

Julian takes a step back, but the figure lunges forwards as Julian SCREAMS, his howl is muffled by the party outside.

EXT. FALL FLING PARTY—NIGHT

Brian, still wandering through the noticeably larger crowd, runs into Jared who is finishing a cigarette.

> JARED
>
> Dude, what's up? Can you believe this? It's gonna be a hell of a night.

They slap hands.

> BRIAN
>
> Hey, have you seen Gina around?

> JARED
>
> Gina? Don't tell me you're still messing with her.

Brian crosses his arms.

> BRIAN
>
> What's it to you?

> JARED
>
> She's a tramp, man. You know it, and you know you can do better than that.

> BRIAN
>
> All right, I'll pretend I did not hear that. Have you seen her or not.

Jared lights another cigarette.

> JARED
>
> I have, but you aren't gonna like it.

BRIAN

What are you talking about, Jared.

JARED

She is by the door to the dorms…making out with some swim team
member, or something.

BRAIN

What?

JARED

Man, she is a tramp. You aren't planning on having any thing real
with her, are you?

Brian does not answer, but his expression conveys his anger.

JARED

Besides, man, I thought that you both had some kind of arrangement—an open relationship or something.

BRAIN

You have no idea what we have.

JARED

Knowing you both, it's probably herpes.

Brian shoves Jared. Stunned at first, Jared returns the shove.

A circle of students begins to gather, but before Brain can hit him,
several JOCKS (wearing their red lettermen jackets) separate the two.

JOCK #1

Easy there, killer. This is a party, not a massacre.

JOCK #2
Yeah, you guys kiss and make up.

Brian shoves the jocks off him and points at Jared.

BRIAN
This isn't over, Jared.

JARED
Bring it on anytime, asshole. I ain't scared of you.

They glare at each other a moment before Brian strikes off into the crowd.

INT. SARA'S CAR—NIGHT

Hugo, in the back seat, is leaning forward and talking to Sara and Caleb.

HUGO
The white candle's flame will turn blue when an evil presence is near. That's the point of no return. Now, the sea salt needs to be as close to a perfect spiral as possible. If Robert Bates makes a move near it, he will be drawn into the spiral, and the salt will capture him. His evil energy will weaken and get lost in the spiral. If that works, take all the salt, and wrap it in that cloth I gave you. It has a binding spell on it, and Bates won't be able to slip out. We'll bury that bastard on holy ground.

CALEB
What if that does not work?

HUGO

Tell him goodbye on the Ouija board. Tell him goodbye and do not return. It is not a permanent solution, but it will buy you enough time to get out of there.

SARA

How about Daisy and Nick? How do we set them free?

Hugo is quiet a BEAT.

HUGO

I have two theories on this. One, that once Robert Bates becomes neutralized, they will be avenged, and their souls may rest. Two, in the event that they are not at peace, we will come back and do a separate ceremony to cleanse both their souls and that horrible attic.

SARA

What if none of this works?

Hugo leans back.

HUGO

I don't know, Sara. I don't know.

EXT. FALL FLING

Brian walks to the door of the MEO building where Gina is leaned against VINCE, also dressed in a red letterman jacket.

BRIAN

HEY, GINA, WHAT ARE YOU DOING?

Gina has a worried look on her face as Brian approaches. Vincent grabs her arm and pushes her behind him.

VINCE

Look, I don't want any trouble.

BRIAN

I'm not talking to you. I have no beef with you. Just let me talk to my girlfriend and let us work this out.

GINA

Girlfriend?

VINCE

You're talking out your ass, bro. I suggest you back off before this turns into something you don't want.

BRIAN

Get your damned hands off my girl. This is your last chance.

GINA

Your girl?

Vince begins to lunge for Brian, but Gina grabs his arm.

GINA

Vince, wait.

Vince looks stunned.

VINCE

For what?

GINA

Brian, you have never called me your girlfriend before.

BRIAN

I know.

GINA

Why not?

Brian scratches the back of his head.

BRIAN

I—I don't know. Guess I'm afraid of getting hurt.

Vince, a look of disgust on his face, spits on the concrete steps.

VINCE

You know what? You can have this little slut.

Brian draws back and punches Vince, knocking him out. The gathered crowd cheers.

Gina rushes to him, kissing him.

GINA

I am so sorry, Brian. I didn't know you really cared.

BRIAN

I do. I do. Let's get out of here.

She kisses him again, and they enter the MEO building, arm in arm.

INT. DORM ROOM—A FEW MINUTES LATER

Brian and Gina ENTER the room, kissing passionately. Brian grabs
a sock from a nearby dresser and affixes it to the doorknob.

They claw and tear at each other's clothes, stumbling towards Caleb's
bed. Brian pulls his shirt off, but stops before they proceed.

> BRIAN
> Wait, I think we should use my bed.

> GINA
> Our bed?

Brian smiles.

> BRIAN
> Yes, our bed.

Kissing as they fall onto the other bed, Gina straddles Brian and pulls
off her top, exposing her pink bra.

> BRIAN
> Damn, you are beautiful.

Gina leans in close to Brian's left ear, WHISPERING.

> GINA
> You like this?

Brian nods as Gina wiggles.

> GINA
> My panties match.

Brian leans up to unhitch her bra, but Gina pulls back, shaking her head and playfully shoving him back on the bed.

Brian GASPS as she drags her nails across his bare chest, leaving faint pink lines in her fingers' wake.

She slowly moves her arms to her back. While unhinging her bra, she is pulled off him by Bates' silhouetted form and slung to the back wall. As her body falls to the floor, it tears off a rock band poster.

Gina SCREAMS as she watches Bates lift Brian in the air, hold him against the wall, and then snap his neck. Brian's lifeless body slumps to the bed.

Gina, shaking of the fall, begins to get up, but Bates grabs her leg and drags her under the bed. She claws at the wooden floor, but her fingernails break after leaving deep claw marks across the wood.

EXT. FITZGERALD UNIVERSITY ENTRANCE—NIGHT

Sara's car pulls up to the FU entrance. Caleb and Sara EXIT the vehicle, leaving Hugo in the car.

Caleb is carrying a black backpack filled with the magical supplies over his shoulder.

HUGO
If it gets to be too much, leave that place. Don't let yourselves get hurt. We can try again another night, when I have had more time to prepare the two of you.

Sara and Caleb exchange a glance, and then clasp hands.

HUGO
Do you remember everything?

SARA
Yeah. We got it.

HUGO
Now, they should all be in the attic, but if Bates is roaming the campus, the invocation spell is on that piece of parchment.

Hugo looks at them both a BEAT.

HUGO
Good luck, kids. May the God or Goddess of your choice protect and bless you both.

Caleb and Sara turn and head onto campus.

EXT. FALL FLING—CONTINUING

Sara and Caleb wave through the crowd. They pass a campus cop chatting with a student. After a BEAT, they run into Jared, who is holding a red cup.

JARED
Hey, stop a sec.

Caleb and Sara freeze. Jared notices they are holding hands.

JARED

Well, look at you two.

He slaps Caleb on the ribs.

> JARED
> 'Bout time you grew a pair. Speaking of brass balls, where is your little-dick roommate?

Caleb and Sara exchange a glance.

> JARED
> I mean you, Caleb. No wonder you been foundering in your classes.

> CALEB
> Oh, Brian. Um, I haven't seen him. He said something about needing the room tonight. He's probably in there with Gina or some other woman.

> JARED
> Well, you need to let me in the room. I know that he won't answer to a knock if he is banging some dame.

> CALEB
> Jared, man, I am kind of busy right now.

Jared grabs Caleb by his shirt collar and pulls him near.

> JARED
> Look, I ain't got no problem with you, Caleb, but I'm gonna rearrange Brian's face unless we settle a little shit tonight.

> SARA
> YOU'RE DRUNK. LET HIM GO.

JARED

Back off, weird-o. This is between me and your boyfriend.

CALEB

All right, all right. I'll take you to the room.

Caleb and Sara exchange a look.

Jared lets him loose. Sara rushes to Caleb's side, fixing his collar.

JARED

Now that's better. Now I don't have cream that little jerk.

CALEB

I got to know, what happened?

JARED

Come on, I'll tell you on the way.

INT. MEO BUILDING—CONTINUED

The trio are walking down the hall leading towards Caleb's dorm room.

CALEB

He finally admitted it.

JARED

He was ready to punch me in the jaw over her.

Caleb whistles in disbelief.

SARA

I think it's sweet.

JARED

Not all of us believe in love, sister.

SARA

Do you?

Jared does not answer.

They stop in front of the dorm, there is a dirty white sock hanging from the doorknob.

CALEB

That means they're in there.

He pulls out his keys.

JARED

That's a pretty crusty sock there, Caleb. Ex-girlfriend of yours?

CALEB

Ha-ha-ha.

He KNOCKS TWICE and unlocks the door. They all exchange a glance before Caleb opens the door slowly.

CALEB

SORRY. COMING IN. Make sure you are under the covers. There is someone here to see you.

INT. DORM ROOM—CONTINUING

Caleb steps in and flips the light switch. Sara SCREAMS.

Brian's body, now mangled, is on the bed. He looks mangled, and
blood splatters coat the walls.

Gina's head and outstretched arms poke out from under Brian's bed.

> JARED
> What the fuck is this?

Sara turns her eyes away, sinking her head into Caleb's shoulder.

Jared turns to the couple.

> JARED
> What did you sick bastards do? Now I know why you didn't want me
> to come up here—so you could clean up your fucking mess.

> CALEB
> We didn't do this, Jared.

> JARED
> Yeah, then who did? I'm getting campus police.

Jared starts to EXIT, but Caleb grabs his arm.

> CALEB
> Wait, I swear we didn't do this. I can explain everything.

> JARED
> Well, you'd better start talking fast.

Caleb takes a deep breath.

CALEB

Do you remember the story you told us when that crazy guy approached us?

JARED

The murdered kids. So what?

CALEB

They are still here, on campus.

JARED

Don't tell me you believe in that stupid gypsy's bullshit.

SARA

It's true, Jared. That murdering bastard did this, and those two poor teenagers are also trapped in the attic.

JARED

Pfft.

Jared starts to leave, but Caleb stops him again.

CALEB

We were in a hurry because we were going to stop them. If you don't believe us, coma along and see for yourself.

JARED

And get blamed for this shit. No fucking way, man. No fucking way.

CALEB

I'll take the fall for all of this.

SARA

NO.

CALEB

It does not matter as long as we stop this monster and set Nick and
Daisy free.

JARED

Nick and Daisy—so you're on a first name basis with dead teenagers.
Nice.

CALEB

Jared, come to the attic with us. I'll prove it.

Jared crosses his arms.

JARED

You'll just kill me too.

CALEB

You know I would never do such a thing.

Jared looks him up and down.

CALEB

Fine, call the cops. Tell them I'll be in the attic.

Caleb looks at Sara. Her eyes well up with tears.

CALEB

Are you ready?

SARA

Yes. I'm ready.

They look back at Jared and begin to EXIT.

> JARED
> All right. I'm coming.

Caleb starts to say something, but Jared cuts him off.

> JARED
> I'm coming to prove how crazy you both are. Then, when nothing happens, I'm calling the cops.

> CALEB
> Fair. Come on.

They EXIT.

INT. OUTSIDE ATTIC DOOR—A FEW MOMENTS LATER

Jared, arms crossed, stands behind Caleb and Sara.

Caleb takes a deep breath and grasps the doorknob. He tries to open it, but, as always, it will not give. Jared CHUCKLES.

> JARED
> Having trouble there?

Caleb shoots him a look.

> CALEB
> You try it.

Jared pushes in the front and tries to open the door. Once again, it will not open. He looks back at Caleb, giving him the same look.

> JARED
> Easy, now. I got this bitch.

He tugs hard, and the door opens. He extends his arm.

> JARED
> After you, kind sir.

Caleb ENTERS.

INT. ATTIC—CONTINUING

The three ENTER slowly. Caleb takes his backpack off his shoulder and unzips it as he approaches the center of the room.

After handing Sara the white candle, he removes the Ouija board and sets it in the center of the room.

> JARED
> Ouija board? That's cute, guys.

Caleb shoots him a look. He removes a white, silken cloth that looks like a little bag. He unties the top and carefully creates a salt spiral next to the board.

Sara strikes a match and lights the white candle, setting it in the attic's windowsill. The flame offers a normal glow.

> JARED

Setting the mood, eh? You two are some silly bitches.

CALEB

Please, show some respect. We are about to get into some weird
stuff. The candle says there is nothing evil here. Let's take this
chance to free Nick and Daisy.

Sara joins them and sits cross-legged on the floor beside the board.
Caleb sits in front of the board and looks up at Jared.

CALEB

Please join us. You are now a part of this. Sit on the other end of
the Ouija board and mind the salt.

Jared rolls his eyes but respectfully walks around the salt and takes his
place across the board from Caleb.

CALEB

OK, we should touch the eye and get started.

They all touch the wooden pointer and look at the board.

CALEB

I invoke Nick Santangelo and Daisy McKenzie. Are you there?

Jared CHUCKLES.

JARED

I really can't believe you two.

Sara SHUSHES him.

CALEB

I'll try again. Nick Santangelo and Daisy McKenzie, if
you are present give us an answer.

The planchette's eye begins to move.

JARED

Come on, guys.

The eye moves towards yes on the upper right hand side of the
board. Jared SIGHS.

CALEB

Will you please make your presence known?

Jared starts to laugh, but NICK and DAISY materialize, translucent
and featureless like Robert.

JARED

Oh, shit. What the fuck, you guys?

Sara SHUSHES him again.

CALEB

We are here to help. Please, lead him into the salt spiral when we
summon Robert Bates. Your souls will finally have peace.

Nick and Daisy say nothing, hovering in the corner of the room.

CALEB

Are you ready?

Sara nods, but Jared trembles, speechless.

CALEB

I now invoke Robert Ba—

Before he can finish the sentence, the candle's flame turns neon blue and a breeze comes, scattering the salt spiral.

Jared is flung from the circle, and Robert Bates looms over the Ouija board.

CALEB

GOOD—

Before he can finish, the Ouija board soars to the other corner of the room. Sara rushes to retrieve it.

Caleb is knocked over towards the attic door.

Jared gets up and tries to punch Robert in the back, but his hand goes right through the apparition. Robert turns around and attacks Jared. Nick grabs him, slowing him down but Robert effortlessly shakes him off.

Caleb is trying get in the center of the room with the Ouija board to set it back up, but he cannot find the planchette.

CALEB

The eye, the eye—where is the eye?

Sara looks around and sees it at her feet. She grabs the eye and rushes to meet Caleb in the center of the room.

Robert's fist punches into Jared's chest, pulling out his still-beating heart. Jared looks stunned as he falls to the floor. A pool of blood expands around him.

Caleb sets up the board and Sara sets the eye on top of the board. They both put their fingers to the board

> CALEB AND SARA
> GOODBYE, ROBERT BATES,
> DO NOT RETURN.

Robert HOWLS before vanishing into the darkness of the attic. The white candle's flame returns to its normal glow.

All is SILENT.

Caleb and Sara exchange a glance and see Nick and Daisy, holding hands.

A white light appears in the roof of the attic. A spiral of this comes down like a tornado, sucking Nick and Daisy into its vortex. They spin and spin, until they become consumed in the whirl. The tornado ascends back to the ceiling, vanishing.

Sara and Caleb look at each other before falling into a tight embrace.

> SARA
> What now?

> CALEB
> We do the right thing.

Sara lowers her head.

EXT. MEO STEPS—A FEW MINUTES LATER.

Flashing lights bounce off the MEO building. Cop cars and ambulances are everywhere.

Caleb and Sara stand arm in arm, talking to two POLICE OFFICERS. Dean Morgan stands in the circle with his arms crossed.

                    POLICE OFFICER #1
      So, are you going to tell us what happened up there?

                         CALEB
      I don't know. I went in my room and found them in there.

                    POLICE OFFICER #2
      We have eyewitnesses that saw you two leaving the party with one of
                  the victims. How do you explain that?

                         CALEB
          Like I said, sir. I told you everything I know.

                    DEAN MORGAN
        Please, son. If you know anything, tell them.

Caleb shakes his head. Dean Morgan looks towards Sara, but she looks towards the ground.

The cops exchange a glance.

                    POLICE OFFICER #1
      I'm sorry, but you both have to downtown for questioning.

Caleb nods.

                    POLICE OFFICER #2
        Put them in different cars. Let's get them out of here.

SARA

WAIT. Can't we ride together?

POLICE OFFICER #1

Sorry. Come on, let's go.

Police Officer #1 goes for Sara's arm, but she rushes to Caleb and kisses him passionately.

The cops grab her, pulling her away.

They look longingly at each other as they are separated.

They are shoved into different cop cars and driven off campus.

EXT. FITZGERALD UNIVERSITY ENTRANCE—CONTINU-ING

The cop cars pass the entrance sign where Hugo stands, his head lowered.

HUGO

One cannot escape their destinies, my young friends.

As the cop cars pass, Hugo dematerializes into the night.

CUT TO:

INT. DEAN MORGAN'S OFFICE

SUPERIMPOSE: 2010

Dean Morgan returns to his office, setting the RA's attic key on his desk. In his other hand, he carries the photo he found on the attic's floor.

He opens a drawer in his desk and pulls out a bottle of scotch and a tumbler, pouring himself a tall drink. He takes the entire glass with one gulp.

He stands and crosses his office to a bookshelf. He pulls out a file, returns to his desk, and pours another tall scotch.

He opens the file and we see a yellowed newspaper with the headline: TWO STUDENTS CHARGED WITH THE MURDER OF FIVE AT LOCAL UNIVERSITY.

Underneath the headline, we see pictures of Sara and Caleb.

He flips the clipping over and we see another headline reading: STUDENTS CLAIM CAMPUS IS HAUNTED.

Dean Morgan rubs his eyes as he flips the paper over. We see the original story clipping with the picture Hugo took. He compares them and gasps. He runs his fingers over the figures in each picture.

He jumps up, and EXITS.

INT. MEO ATTIC—A FEW MINUTES LATER

Dean Morgan ENTERS the attic after a brief struggle with the door.

He looks around but it appears still.

DEAN MORGAN
Are you still here?

A small breeze kicks up. He looks over his shoulder and sees a transparent figure in a red letterman jacket in the corner.

He takes a step back.

Robert lunges and Dean Morgan SCREAMS.

FADE OUT

ANTHONY S. BUONI
BRITTANY M. W. LAMOUREUX

WHITEBLOOD

Thomas Whiteblood was in love with a woman. He was one of those rare and fortunate souls who loved and was loved in return. One autumn day he stood beside her on the shores of the gulf just as the sun was crawling down the western horizon. There they stood quietly together, while Thomas held her close in his arms to shield her from the cold wind blowing in over the foaming waves. The beach was an image of desolation, empty of people and beautiful in its naked silence.

Thomas kissed her face, the face of the woman he loved. Her eyes were closed and her lips were red and dry from the salt in the air.

Her face was cold, so cold that he spoke her name aloud.

"Eleanor," he whispered. He felt the burden of her weight press against his arms more than was normal. He spoke her name again but she did not answer. He feared to let go of her lest she fall into the cold white sand. Her head sank into his chest beneath the enclosure of his arms, pressing against his heart and forcing him to feel the beat. He dropped down to his knees and she fell with him, her dark hair flowing in rushes like the waves breaking against the nearby shore.

"Eleanor," he said again. His voice was drowned beneath the crash of a wave. She lay in his arms like a sleeping doll. She never spoke. He stared down at her, watched as the sunlight crept across her pale face as though it were leaning in to kiss her goodnight. She had sand in her hair. She hated having sand in her hair.

Thomas watched the sun set on her face and when night had fallen he still held her there on the cold shore. He rested her in the sand, then lay down beside her and stared up at the stars. They had often lain awake through the night and watched the stars together.

* * *

She is dead. Thomas wrote the words on a blank page in a journal he kept. *She is dead, I am alive, and that is that.* The words were cold, mechanical, as though they'd been written by someone who had never known love nor ever cared to know it. *She died in my arms on a Thursday in November. She died because her heart failed.*

She died in your arms on a Thursday, and you lay with her on the cold, barren shore, and though the night drew on you like a needle in your vein draws blood, you did not move, you did not go for help, you did not weep over her corpse, you just lay there like some twisted…like some perversity of human nature. What you have always been. Why she loved you at all.

What I have always been. She loved me because I am what I have always been.

Outside the night was coming over the trees skirting the eastern field. The barn was glowing at him from the window—a red outpost that seemed farther off than it really was, the sun dipping beneath it. He knew the small hill would be yellow behind the barn because it was the hill that he and Eleanor used to visit almost every other night before sunset. They would walk down the hill and follow the hidden path into the trees where the stream ran dark and cold into deepening woods, where sunlight broke into flurries through a filter of leaves and pine needles.

Does it help you to remember those times?

He ignored the question and got up from the desk. Pulled the coat she had given him from the kitchen chair and putting it on, stepped outside onto the back porch.

The air was dry in the breeze and colder now than it had been before sunrise that morning. He thought about the air being dry in Florida and about how he waited for this time of year to come because it was a rare and precious thing. But now he couldn't think about it because she was gone and he used to always tell her how much he loved it and she would say but it's so cold and I miss the summer and he would laugh and shake his head because one day of cold was more than she wanted and it was all he ever waited for.

He caught himself laughing and put a stop to it. She was gone and he could not laugh about things they had shared.

But she would want you to laugh, to remember those times. Wouldn't she?

What difference does make what she would want if she isn't here to want it? The assumptions we make about the dead. The stupid goddamned assumptions. She wanted nothing but to be with me forever and now she can't and somehow I'm to believe that she doesn't want that anymore just because she's...

Tightening his coat, he stepped down from the porch and walked out into the field. Walked up to the side of the barn where the wood was stacked and grabbed a load to build a fire with. The wood felt rough and cold against his naked hands. Dry, willing to burn through the night.

It isn't hard doing things like chopping wood, building fires. Makes things better in some sort of way. Work always makes things better for some reason god only knows.

After the funeral, the house had been rife with the solemn presence of well-meaning people. Family, he called some of them. They would not let him work because everyone knew that you didn't work when you were grieving. He let them stay for a while because he knew it made them feel better, as though by being near they offered

him a kind of consolation. He let them believe it so that they would
leave sooner. So he could get back to work.

Go back to being the man you have always been and stay that way
and don't change but go on being that man and die that man.

Why is it that people think they can offer solace to a man? A
man finds no solace in people that he doesn't find within himself.
If they'd just left me to my land, to my quiet labors, they would've
shown then that they knew something of what it means to be human...

But that's the problem with the world. It's full of humans who
don't have the damnedest notion of what it is to be human. And
damned if you haven't stacked too many logs.

He was going to set the bundle down in the grass before the top
two could roll off. He was leaning forward to lay them down gently
on the soft earth. A black spider scurried across the topmost log and
he dropped the whole stack. The spider vanished into the dark grass.
He checked himself by rubbing his arms, his hair. Fear at sight of a
lonely black spider.

You are more human than you thought you were. It's a good
thing, too.

After a moment, he bent down and arranged the logs into a neat
pile, then stood up to face the eastern woodland where now darkness
draped over the trees like the veil of a woman in mourning. Above
the trees, the moon hung like the great bulb of some distant lamp-
post, a voiceless and solemn guardian who would keep watch through
the night.

But even the moonlight is a kind of shadow, another form of
darkness in its own right. There is no light but only levels of shadow
I realize now.

"Wouldn't it be fun to go somewhere where the moon was big-
ger?" she said to him while staring up at it. To him it seemed she
stood like she might have when she was a child, her head tilted slightly and her hands restlessly searching until they found one another.
He wanted to put his arms around her but instead he just stood next

to her and kept the space between his body and hers constant, as though he were trying to hold two magnets half an inch apart without letting them touch.

Breathe.

He felt someone inhale for him. He could sense the earth turning and for a moment he stood upon the axis of perpetuity, in the shadow of a red barn and in the shadow of the trees beneath the moon.

The wheelbarrow is inside the barn. Should go get the wheelbarrow and use it to carry the wood back to the house.

* * *

Within the barn, it was colder, darker. When he opened the big door, he felt the inward flow of air as the breeze brushed passed him and swept into the stagnant hollow covered by a tin roof. He felt the inner chamber exhale the brisk, stale and odorless air of a vault that's been sealed for time on end. For a moment, he stood amid that flux as if caught between past and future with no present to be found. Then he entered the barn, hushed.

The light switch was on the left wall beside the old refrigerator. He went to turn it on so he could see to get the wheelbarrow.

Daddy!

The voice slipped in through the open door behind him. He turned and faced the door. The moonlight came in from the field and inside the barn it began to glow but he stood outside of it. The door creaked as it shifted in the wind and beyond it, the long grass swayed, rising and then falling again. He forgot about the wheelbarrow.

Daddy! The voice came from somewhere out in the field. It was a child's voice. Thomas thought it must have been a lost child crying for its father—but there were no other houses near his land, not for miles at least. The idea that a child could be out this far, alone, helpless...

He rushed to the door and ran out into the field. He ran along the side of the barn through the waves of dancing grass, the earth in a boisterous stir about him. The wind was against him as he ran, throwing his hair behind his ears. The wind blew cold but he did not feel it.

He looked toward the eastern woods but there was no one there, and so he ran behind the barn. When he came to the crest of the small hill, the northern trees loomed greater than those in the east, blanketing the field before him and spreading their darkness. The way to the hidden path was difficult to see even in the moonlight, but he knew where it was, and so he made for it as though the child's voice had come from there, from beneath the canopy of trees where he and Eleanor once walked.

Daddy! The voice came to him again, this time clearly from the direction of the hidden path. He was going the right way at least. The child did not sound as though it were in peril. The cry was that of someone lost and afraid of being alone.

"Where are you?" Thomas cried out. His voice broke from the cold and the running, sounded brittle in the wind. He came to the path and followed it into the woods. There the gloom enveloped him like a snare laid up for his coming.

Daddy! Daddy! The voice was close now, coming from a bend in the path ahead. He looked for the child but there was no one. He slowed his pace a little and followed the bend as it wound toward the stream. He could hear the trickling of the water even amid the violent rustling of leaves overhead.

Daddy, I can't find you!

"I'm here! I'm coming!" he cried.

He came to the stream and standing beneath the oak where he and Eleanor had once made love was a small boy clothed in shadow, no more than a silhouette. Thomas could tell he was a boy by the way he stood, like a man in search of something and yet terrified of what he might find. The boy stared up at Thomas with eyes that were like faint grey stars. He was not a tall child, could not have been older than seven.

Daddy! The boy ran to him and Thomas knelt to catch him. He felt the boy's arms close about his neck and latch on as though they would never come loose. They were like ice against his skin—the boy was so cold all over, thin and frail. He could smell the boy's hair so close to him now, and it reminded him of the way Eleanor used to smell and he felt the tears streaming down his face as the child breathed against him.

Daddy, I was... afraid... because I couldn't... find you. Where did you... go? Why did... you leave... me? The boy sobbed between his words.

"I didn't know you were here," Thomas said. "Never again. You'll never lose me again."

Promise? He felt the boy's tears running down his neck, soaking into his shirt, freezing in the chilled night air.

"Yes, I promise. I promise."

Okay.

He held the boy beside the stream in the dark and they cried together beneath the rustling branches in the cold.

* * *

You don't even know his name.

He is my son.

What is his name then?

Maybe I'll ask him. What difference does it make? He is mine. I know it.

She never gave you a child. You and she had often talked about having children, had even planned on it. But the time for that never came and now all hope has passed.

He called me Daddy. I heard him call me Daddy. He ran into my arms and his hair smelt like hers and his eyes, they're like mine and—

Daddy... The voice sounded muffled as it came from behind his shoulder. He was carrying the child across the field toward the house. The moon had risen into the night and what few stars there were shone down upon the field, upon the father carrying his son.

"Yes?"

Are we going home?

"Yes," he said. "It's only a little ways further. It'll be warmer there."

He walked past the pile of logs he had gathered for firewood, past the barn with its big door left open to the outside, past the shadows and the frail memories of things that meant nothing to him now.

What if the child's family is looking for him? What if the real father is out there now, running around in a panic because his little boy is lost in the dark?

No one is looking for him because he is mine. He is my son.

You never had a son. You never had—

He is my son I know he is He called for *me* Called me *Daddy* Ran into my arms His hair smells like hers used to I know he is mine.

You know that this isn't real. None of it is.

I don't care if it isn't. I don't care. It's real to me right now in this moment. Please just let me have this moment if nothing else.

Very well.

He took the boy into the house and went to lay him down on the couch beside the fireplace.

No! The boy held to him tighter. He didn't think the boy could have held on any tighter.

"I'm just going to lay you down and get you some blankets."

No. You are going to leave me again.

"No, I promise I won't leave you. I'll stay right here."

I'm cold. My feet are cold.

Thomas noticed for the first time that the boy had no shoes. He reached down and touched one of the dangling feet. It was so cold that it stung his fingers. He began rubbing the foot with his free hand.

"I can build you a fire. There's already some wood by the fire-place, see? I can build it right here in front of you and I won't have to go outside."

The boy held to him and was not lax in his hold. He felt the boy's warm breath on his neck, the perfect motion of his chest heaving upward and then receding as he drew life into him.

We are alive together. You are alive and I am alive. We are alive together.

Okay.

"Okay." The boy's weightless arms slipped down from his shoulders, and Thomas laid him down on the couch.

Look at him. Look at his eyes and his lips and his hair.

I am looking.

He is my son. I told you he was. He looks like her too. There's more of her there than me I think.

Yes.

He got some blankets and covered the boy from neck to feet, then tucked the blankets underneath him. He made sure to wrap the feet tightly. Thomas caressed his hair and the boy looked up at him but did not say anything.

"I'm going to build you a fire now. Is that all right?"

The boy nodded.

Thomas knelt on the hearth and stacked the wood inside the fireplace. He looked back at intervals to check on the boy, saw that he was falling asleep. After the wood began to catch, Thomas went to the couch and gently lifted him, then sat down so that he could hold him while he slept. He woke briefly and so Thomas quietly hushed him.

"Go back to sleep, son," he said.

Stay here.

"I'm not going anywhere."

Promise?

"I promise. Go back to sleep now."

Okay. I love you, Daddy. The boy grew quiet and seemed to have fallen back to sleep. Thomas did not say the words he wanted to speak. He held the sleeping child and watched the fire swirl into a blaze.

You couldn't tell him that you love him because you don't know if you do.

I couldn't tell him because I'm afraid if I tell him then he will go away and never come back. I love him more than I have ever loved anything.

Then why not say it?

The last person I said I love you to died in my arms. So I will not tell him that I love him. I will not make that mistake again. The devils and the angels alike will never hear me speak those words. I know that they will not strive to take from me that which I do not love.

Do you really think that you can hide something just by refusing to say it?

I can try. It's all I know to do. They will not hear me say that I love him because I will not say it.

So be it then. But I do not think that you can protect him that way.

I have to try.

He held the boy for a long time and watched the fire devour the last of the wood. When the ashes had long set, he still kept awake until before long he looked through the window and saw the sun climbing up over the trees skirting the eastern field. The boy did not once stir through the night, but slept as one who does not dream.

* * *

Sometimes before sunrise, he saw it through the window walking alone in the field. It walked from the eastern woods and moved toward the house, swaying like a shadow at the bottom of a clear stream. It came to the window and looked in. There were no eyes but it looked in and it looked at the boy for a long time.

Thomas held the boy, pretended not to see it, waited for it to leave. It turned away and moved with forceful, plodding steps back into the eastern trees well before the sun's first light touched the field.

* * *

The sun has come up over the field and he is still asleep on the couch. I was careful not to wake him. I closed the shades so the light would not disturb his sleep. He is so thin, so pale. He will need to wake soon and eat something, but that can wait a little while longer. I find myself repeatedly looking back at him to see if he is still there... I am afraid that he will vanish, just as he appeared. I thought that with the coming of day he would dissolve like some ghostly apparition that can only dwell under cover of night... but morning has come and still he remains. I am not dreaming.

I can't help but think that somehow this is Eleanor's doing. I don't pretend to understand any of it, but somehow I've been given the chance to have what I could never have... somehow the parallel tracks of fate have merged and two separate destinies have come together to become one. The fate I should have had and the fate I am living now, they have intersected in a sense. In another life, perhaps a life that only exists within the essence of dreams, the boy sleeping on my couch is my son... but in this life he could never be, and yet he is here for reasons and by such causes the likes of which I may never understand.

But I am happy that he is here, though his very presence frightens me for all that it implies and more. I have considered the possibility that he may be a hallucination, and as such I plan to test that possibility today sometime after he wakes. Still, everything about the manner in which he came to me points to the supernatural rather than the psychological. He is a ghost and yet he breathes.

I have heard of ghosts in the sense of those whose time has passed... but ghosts of those whose time never came to be... that is something I cannot even begin to fathom and so I dare not try. This is some sort of curse or miracle or a mingling of the two.

He is waking up now I think...

* * *

When the boy awoke he sat up on the couch and stared at the fireplace in a daze, his hair matted and sticking out in places. Thomas watched him from where he sat at his writing desk. The boy held his gaze on the fireplace with eyes that seemed to see nothing, then his head tilted slightly and his eyes wandered until they found Thomas sitting in front of the shaded window.

Daddy? The voice came from half-parted lips, frail and a little breathless but louder than a whisper.

"Yeah, buddy, I'm right here."

Thomas got up, walked over to the couch and knelt down beside it. He reached up and combed the boy's hair with his fingers. It was soft and buoyant, like a mixture of air and water, the way Eleanor's had been. The boy just stared back at him with eyes that were cold yet hopeful, as though he were trying to discern a familiar face.

"Are you hungry?"

The boy nodded. Thomas smiled and then lifted him from the couch. Carried him to the kitchen and set him on one of the tall chairs in front of the bar.

"What would you like? Eggs, bacon, cereal?" Thomas opened the refrigerator door and looked over at the boy.

A waffle and bacon.

Thomas smiled. "I didn't think about waffles," he said. "A waffle sounds good."

He pulled a pan from one of the lower cabinets and set it on the stove. After he put the bacon in the pan and it had begun to fry, he got out the eggs and the butter and the waffle mix. The boy watched him without saying anything. Soon he had the mix in the iron and he stood turning the strips over in the pan while looking back at the boy as often as possible.

"What do you want to do today?" Thomas asked him.

What can we do?

"Anything you want," he said, and then he remembered something. "But before we do anything we have to buy you some shoes."

The boy seemed to consider that statement for a few moments, as though he were trying to remember an event or solve some mystery. Thomas watched him, noting the way his eyes searched within themselves. Again he was reminded of Eleanor and he felt his heart sink into itself.

I don't remember what happened to my shoes.

"It's all right. We'll buy you some new ones."

When the bacon and the waffle were ready Thomas put them on a plate, then placed the plate in front of the boy and watched him douse the waffle in syrup. He poured the boy a glass of orange juice and slid it across the bar to him.

Are you going to eat, Daddy? The boy had already eaten half of the waffle and some of the bacon. He ate like any boy would.

"Maybe in a little while," Thomas said. He turned and went to the sink to throw some water on his face, then wiped the water off with a dry dishtowel. He turned back to the boy and smiled.

Are you okay, Daddy?

"Yeah, I'm fine." He wiped underneath both eyes with one of his knuckles. "You go ahead and finish your breakfast." The boy went back to eating. Thomas watched him for a moment and then, "Have you decided what you want to do today?"

We can do anything?

"Anything that is capable of being done and that is within reason."

Within reason?

"Yeah that just means we can't do anything that's against the law or that bothers other people. We can do all the good stuff we want though."

Okay. The boy finished the last piece of bacon. *I wouldn't want to do any of the bad stuff anyway.*

Thomas laughed. "Good. It wouldn't be nearly as fun as the good stuff."

Can we go to the beach?

Thomas stared at him for a little while, thinking of things that he had not thought about during the course of morning. Things that had momentarily abandoned him for the first time since that day she died in his arms.

"Yes," he said. "After we buy you some shoes and some new clothes."

The boy smiled. He didn't say anything but ate the last few bits of his waffle until he had cleaned the plate. After he had eaten everything, he took the glass of orange juice and drank it down without pause. Color began to show on his face. The life in him was gaining strength.

* * *

They rode into town in the black truck. The boy was quiet for most of the way. Thomas looked over occasionally to check on him, sometimes to make sure that he was still there, sometimes just to glance and wonder what he might be thinking about. The boy stared out the window and watched the things that passed, the other cars and the signs and the one-story buildings.

He doesn't mind the quiet. Eleanor could not often stand quiet and so she always talked and you would listen and you loved all the things she would say.

He likes to think about things more than he likes to talk about them.

Like you.

Yes, like me.

They drove on in silence. Autumn clouds gathered as the morning aged, until the sky was a grey woolen blanket that locked in the cold and held the sun's warmth at bay. It was colder even than the day before and the wind, ever as boisterous, could be heard humming outside their windows. He could tell that the boy liked listening to the wind.

Soon the truck pulled into the parking lot of the shopping mall. Seagulls circled over them and perched on the tall streetlamps. When he had parked he looked over at the boy, who was staring back at him the way Thomas sometimes stared at himself in the mirror. He looked at the boy's feet, at the socks he had given him to wear. The socks were folded down because the boy did not like them covering his legs up to his knees.

"How are the socks?"

Itchy.

"We'll get you some better ones. You sit there and I'll come around and get you. I don't want you walking without shoes." He grabbed the handle to open the door.

Daddy...

He turned back to the boy. "Yes?"

The boy stared down at the floorboard.

Did Mommy love me?

Keep it together. He is watching you now, closely.

Thomas just looked at the boy for a while and thought. He stared into his grey eyes and for a moment felt he might be staring into that narrow part of himself where there was a fragile glimpse of something that resembled perfection.

"Your mother loved you more than she loved anything in this world or any other. And she loves you still."

You think so?

"I just said it, didn't I?"

The boy got quiet and looked back down at his socks. He took long, quiet breaths.

Eleanor always did the same thing whenever you said something like that. She would get quiet and breathe long and deep.

I only meant that I believed in what I said. Because I know it's true. I didn't mean to come off harsh.

You never do.

"Hey," Thomas said. The boy looked up at him. "I wouldn't have said it if I didn't know it to be the truth. She always loved you and she always will. You believe me?"

The boy nodded slowly.

"Okay. I'll come around and get you."

Daddy?

Thomas stopped and turned again. "Yes?"

Do you love me?

Thomas looked into his son's eyes but said nothing. His left hand was fastened on the door handle. He felt as though he were hanging over a great depth and the handle, his only salvation.

You have to answer the question.

No I don't. I don't have to answer this one. I'm not going to answer this one.

You will break his heart if you don't. A broken heart could be worse than any dark and terrible thing your mind can conjure for him.

I will not say it.

He is waiting for your answer. He is beginning to doubt. You could lose him that way. Have you considered that?

Damn you.

You are losing him. For christ's sake, say something.

"What do you think?" Thomas said, almost forcing the words. The boy's eyes wandered across the dashboard as he thought it over.

Eleanor always hated it when I avoided a question by asking another. She hated it more than anything and she wouldn't speak to me for the rest of the day or night.

But he is different in many ways. Like you, he is not intimidated by a question, only challenged by it.

He welcomes the challenge as an opportunity.

Just as you often do.

I don't know. The boy sat with his back against the seat and with his head tilted slightly downward.

"Son…" The boy just stared down at his socks.

"Hey." Thomas reached over and flicked the strand of hair that was hanging in front of the boy's eye. The boy looked over at him again. "I think you know," he said. The boy kept silent. Thomas smiled and said, "Now let's go buy you some shoes and some clothes so we can go to the beach. You still want to go, don't you?"

The boy nodded.

"All right." Thomas got out of the car, walked to the other side and lifted the boy out. The gulls were still circling overhead and the boy watched them while Thomas carried him across the parking lot. As they came to the entrance, some people walked out of the mall. They looked at Thomas and then they looked at the boy.

They can see him. My god, they can see him.

Yes. I knew that they would.

Thomas carried him to the section where the shoes were and set him down in one of the chairs. A woman came and asked if they needed any help. Thomas pointed to the boy and said that he needed some shoes. The woman asked what size and Thomas looked at the boy and the boy just shrugged. The woman smiled down at him, then brought out a Brannock and measured his foot.

"What happened to your other shoes?" she asked him. He just looked at her without answering.

"He lost them out in the woods and he's outgrown his other ones," Thomas said. "We'll be buying more than one pair."

"Well all right then," she said and then smiled again. She showed them several different kinds of shoes and the boy looked at them and picked out the ones he liked best. Thomas bought three pairs of shoes and let the boy carry the empty boxes as they walked to the section where the children's clothes were.

You saw it. She looked at him and talked to him and smiled at him.

Yes, she did... she did.

* * *

He helped the boy take off his new shoes and his socks, then set them together in the sand. The boy looked out in awe over the waves rushing one after another upon the smooth shoreline. To Thomas he acted as though he had never seen the gulf, and then Thomas thought that perhaps he never had.

Is it cold? The boy looked up at him.

"Roll up your jeans and go stand where the water can wash over your feet," he said.

The sand is really cold. The boy drove his foot into the sand and made a print.

"Go and try the water."

You have to come with me.

"All right."

Thomas took off his shoes and socks, stuffed the socks inside the shoes and then set them next to the other pair. He rolled up the legs of his jeans and then the boy's. They walked up to where the waves were stretching and then dying upon the glossy sand. Grey light from an overcast sky descended on the water, which seemed almost colorless nearer the shallows but farther out it became like basalt, a mingling of dull blacks and porous whites.

It's cold! It's really cold! The boy jumped and splashed as the water swelled over his feet and ankles. He looked up at Thomas and smiled.

"Well you're only going to get colder if you keep splashing like that."

It's fun. The boy waited for the next wave.

"Well then keep doing it."

Thomas watched him run back and forth across the wet sand, dancing and splashing as the cold saltwater foamed up over his ankles. He was laughing and whenever he looked up he would see Thomas smiling back at him. The boy turned and ran away from another surge of water as it chased him up the shore. When he came to the dry sand he stopped, his thin arms dangling at his sides. Another rush came in behind him but he did not notice it.

"What is it?" Thomas walked up and stood beside him.

The boy was silent as he held his gaze on the nearly deserted beach. Thomas noted shapes of people off in the distance in both directions but the boy was not looking at them. The boy started to walk and Thomas began to move alongside him, watching him.

"Where are we going?"

The boy did not answer but kept walking, leaving wet tracks in the sand. Thomas could feel the sand caking around his ankles and between his toes as he followed the boy farther along the beach. Gulls hovered over the dunes, their cries borne by the wind out into nothing.

They followed the curve of the beach a ways until from a distance they could see the jetty reaching out across the water like the arm of some earthen giant who may have fallen there long ago. Thomas recognized the place now. The boy stopped there and stood looking down at the sand.

Is this it?

"Yes." Thomas heard the words but wasn't sure if he had spoken them. The boy's eyes were fixed on the spot, his lips drawn together in the form of a kiss that wasn't there to be given.

Why did you bring me here?

"I had forgotten... I didn't realize how close we were. We can go back—"

Did you try to save her?

"No," he said. "I didn't."

You could have tried, couldn't you've?

"I don't know... maybe."

How come you didn't try?

"I... I didn't try because..."

The boy looked up at him. Tears were flowing along the curves of his cheeks now reddened from the cold. Thomas never looked at the boy but stared at the place where he had lain with her through the night under those forgotten stars.

"I didn't try because I loved her," he said. "I loved her and so I let her do what she wanted. I always let her do whatever she wanted... because I loved her."

I think you're lying. I think you were afraid to try. I think you were so afraid.

Thomas knelt down in front of the boy and put his hands on his shoulders. "My whole life I waited for her," he said. "And you know what happened? I got her and I promised to love her for as long as I lived, but she left before the end could come and now I'm here holding on to my empty promise, gazing through the keyhole of door that can never be opened to catch a glimpse of everything I will never be. I didn't try to save her because she didn't want to be saved."

You don't know that. The boy was crying harder.

"You weren't there. I was. What do you think you know about it?"

I could have saved her. I wouldn't have been afraid to try.

"You couldn't have done a thing. Just like I couldn't. But you won't see that so you just go on believing that you could have done something." Thomas made no effort to suppress his tears but let them run down over his lips and below his chin.

I wish it had been you and not her.

"That makes two of us then."

I want to go home now, but I don't want to talk to you anymore. The boy started off in the direction of the parking lot and never looked back to see if Thomas followed.

* * *

No light but lines of shadow.

I can hear the waves, thunderous. They roar so loudly and I am frightened they will rush over me and take me into them, into the very depths of heaven. Wind so cold, so strong it blows sand up into my eyes as I watch him go. These waning tears make mud of the sand.

No light... but shadow.

And I watch him walk away from me under the awning of grey clouds that do not thunder. No voice but the wind and the waves.

You could have told him. You can still—

It isn't within me to speak those words. I cannot give him what he wants and so he needs to go somewhere else.

How do you know he isn't going to wait for you in the truck? You think he's going to disappear, don't you? You'll get to the truck and he'll be there.

Either way he is as dead now as she is. He is dead because I cannot tell him. He was dead the night I found him there under the oak.

He is your creation. Remember that. What happens to him is in your hands.

He is a life of his own now, free from my control. He will choose to leave and never return. No, he's already made the choice.

Only because you leave him no other. You are the one who is dead. You are the one letting life drift out into that sunless nothing of an earth.

Will he wait in the truck?

I don't know. I don't care.

Then all is as it was and ought to have remained.

You don't mean that. I know you don't.

All is as it ought to have remained.

Stop saying that. You don't mean it.

All is as—

Stop it. Stop saying it.

What should I do then?

Go after your boy.

He isn't my boy. He's a ghost spawned from the depths of my darkest—

Bullshit. Go after him.

What is he doing?

He's stopping to pick up the shoes you bought him. He won't put them on because he doesn't want to get wet sand in them. Now he's walking toward the parking lot with a shoe in each hand. Good thing you didn't give him the keys or he'd leave you here.

I'm certain he would try.

I'm confident he would succeed.

He can do anything he wants.

Yes. Yes, he can.

Will he stay?

Go and catch him while there's still time.

A man strolling along the shore with his hands in his pockets and his eyes cast downward. He looked up at Thomas, who was still watching the boy. Thomas didn't notice the man but held his eyes on the distant thing, now almost out of sight. The man turned his head and looked where Thomas was looking.

"They tell you to let 'em have their space," the man said. "Room to grow."

Thomas took his eyes away from the boy and looked over at the man standing some six feet from him, nearer the water. He was a thin and older-looking man.

"What?" Thomas was looking at him, his face and hair and clothing. He wore a green jacket and his jeans were rolled up. He wore tennis shoes without socks.

"I think differently myself," the man said. "You have to watch 'em. All the time."

"What are you talking about?"

The man took a step toward Thomas, looking him hard and cold in the eye. The man's hair was wild and touched with grey, his eyes almost colorless or a shade of something that Thomas could not name. Behind him, the gulf was billowing under clouds that foretold winter but Thomas didn't see them billowing.

"You let 'em out of your sight for one minute and one minute is long enough to pay the price. Wolf's always there waiting to snatch 'em up. After that you never see 'em again but you know they're out there somewhere buried in pieces in the dirt or stuffed in a sack that

got thrown into a lake or maybe they were incinerated and their ashes
are blowing in the air you breathe."

Thomas stared at the man but didn't say anything. His body was
tense, suspended from the ground up and hanging like a weighted
line over the sky. He could feel the blood rushing to his head.

"But people don't listen to me so what bit of a goddamn difference does it make?" The man sniffed in the dry breeze and then
looked back down at the sand. He went on down the shore without
saying a thing more, his hands in his pockets. Thomas watched him
for a little while until he was a dark and frail outline against the jetties.

What time you had is now gone.

Thomas turned and ran barefoot through the sand toward the
walkways that led to the parking lot. Ran past the spot where his
shoes were and sprinted across the walkway, the planks throbbing
beneath him. He could see the truck from a distance but the boy was
nowhere in sight.

* * *

She stood in the doorway in front of the sun. Light bursting
around her and she, the darkness within. In her, the two were joined
inseparably, light and shadow. Chaos set to rest in her.

She stood looking at him from the open door and he could see
the pale glow of her eyes despite the fiery sunset behind her. He sat
on the couch and waited for her to speak.

"Aren't you coming?" she asked. Her voice reminded him of the
quiet running water of a stream flowing forever into the night.

"I don't know," he said. He didn't move from the couch.

"You won't come because you think he needs you," she said.

"I need him," he said.

"You don't know what you need anymore, Thomas."

"You want me to abandon him? You want me to abandon our
son?"

"I don't know him. He isn't of me."

"How can you say that? He wants you to love him. I told him that you—"

"Who told you to tell him anything? How can I love what is not of me? I love you, Thomas. That is enough. Come with me."

"I can't," he said.

"The sun won't be up for much longer," she said, looking back over her shoulder. "We used to walk the hill at sunset, you remember?"

"Yes," he said. "I remember."

She looked down at the floor, rubbed her hands together slowly, caressing.

"The devils inhabit these fields," she said. "You've brought one of them into our home."

"Don't say that. It isn't true and you know it. He's only a boy for christ's sake."

"There is no Christ in him or in you."

"Go to hell." He stood up and glared into the dying sun, the gleam of tears in his eyes.

"I have, Thomas. It is where I abide now. And you abide there with me as long as you keep yourself apart from me."

"I'm not going with you," he said. "I risked everything for you... and I'll risk more for him. Soon you will see him as I do and then you will know."

"You really believe... you really love him?"

"More than you can imagine," he said.

She stood for a moment in thought. Her dark hair, flowing in buoyant waves down to her shoulders, shone red against the light of sunset.

"Then love him, Thomas," she said finally. "And whatever you do, don't lose him."

"You said he was a devil. I heard you say it."

"I still believe he is a devil," she said. "All the same, hold on to him and don't let go of him as you did me."

"Do you still love me?" he asked her. He looked into the shadowed veil that guarded her face and saw her smile. She smiled as she had on the day that he'd asked her and she'd said yes.

"Always," she said.

After a moment, he asked, "Are you certain that you know nothing? Nothing of him?"

"You are asking if it was I who brought him here, but I've already told you. He is not of me."

"I thought that he was your gift to me," he said, casting his eyes to the floor.

"I can give you nothing now," she said. "You will not come."

"No," he said. "I will not come. Not yet. Not until I've finished here."

"You'll never be finished here, Thomas. I love you but I will not wait for you."

"I waited for you. Too many ages to count I waited."

"I'm sorry I could not be like you, Thomas. I tried so very hard to be like you."

"You could have had whatever you wanted with me."

"I had everything I wanted and more," she said. "But the ages of this world were not meant to keep me as they have kept you."

"Now that he has come it may be different," he said.

"How do you explain his coming, Thomas? How do you explain any of it?"

"How do you explain me?" he said. "What I am? Like you, I do not remember the day that I was born. No one ever does, do they? He does not remember losing his shoes. He does not remember a thing but that he awoke in the night, alone in the cold under the oak."

"And what do you remember?" she asked. "About yourself, I mean."

"You used to always ask me that. The answer is the same now as it was then: 'I am here.'"

Sun nigh submerged beneath the hill. Her shadow fading into the night. Her beauty encompassed in her darkness.

"Thomas," she said, whispering now. "If I had stayed, you would have been exposed. People would have seen, and in seeing they would have come to know. My wish for you has always been that you would find peace."

"Peace is not reserved for the likes of me."

"But for the first time you know what is most important to you," she said. "And you must fight to keep it. You must fight like the men who live and die fight. You too are a man with destiny in your heart. In that you may yet find peace."

"My destiny has been withheld from me," he said.

"Yes," she said. "Until now."

He saw her fade into the shadows cast beneath the sunless sky. He saw the red barn in the doorway only it wasn't red anymore, the trees hovering behind it like a host of robed cardinals all standing in rows. Then the room grew dark and no light shone on the horizon. Shadows laughed and danced about him until he too laughed and danced with them.

And at last sinking into their tepid embraces he found not the light of morning.

* * *

From the window, I can see her walking alone in the field. It is midday. A bright sun shines down and she shines with it even in her sadness. She does not want me with her now and so I write in my journal. She is so sensitive and I in all my ageless wisdom am incapable of knowing when to say something and when to keep quiet, even after these many years.

But what am I supposed to say to it? This terminus of her and everything with her? How can I accept for her what I have never been able to accept for myself?

She reads my journal sometimes and I don't mind it. She puts smiley faces by the passages that make her happy and sad faces by the ones she doesn't like and sometimes she draws confused faces by the passages that I write when my thoughts run free. That's all the critical analysis I've ever gotten from anyone and think I prefer it that way. She will read this sometime tonight probably and when she does, I hope it does not hurt her and I hope she does not cry. I hope she knows that what she has already given me is more than I have ever prayed for.

She is walking back toward the house now and I think she knows I'm watching her. She walks as if she knows she is being watched—there are times when I watch her and she doesn't know and her walk is different.

I hope you don't cry when you read this.

* * *

The boy was not in the truck. The parking lot was empty but for a few cars.

Hold it together.

Pavement was gritty against the rough souls of his feet. Wind blew swirls of dust and sand up into his eyes. He could taste the grit and the coldness but he could not breathe them in. The sand stopped in his throat and the air never made it past the seal of his lips.

Can't. Can't breathe.

Never really could to begin with.

He wanted to call out for the boy… wanted to call him and see him running over the hill to his right or out from under the walking deck maybe, dark hair swaying like a fiery liquid and eyes burning as the nearest of stars on a clear night.

Call out to him.

I never gave him a name. I don't know what to call him.

Give him one now then. Give him a name and call that name as though you've called it a hundred times before.

It had begun to rain lightly and the pines were shivering in the cold. He leaned against the truck and let it hold him. His feet felt warm and rough against the dry asphalt black as the hole that was somewhere deep inside of him. He wanted to lie down on the hard ground and sleep. Until the earth swallowed itself into nothing and him with it.

For god's sake, call out to him.

He called out a name, frail beneath the hum.

Again.

He called the name again, louder.

I remember the night I found him...

It was only last night.

I remember he was so afraid to be alone. He was beautiful in that mirthless dark beneath the trees. His eyes shone even in the deep forested night and his voice was like an angel's voice. I was so afraid of being alone.

You've always been alone.

And I've always been afraid.

You think it has taken him? The one you sometimes see walking alone in the field before sunrise? The one with black eyes that see without looking.

God, stop.

The time it was at the window and it just stared at her through the glass while she slept but you lay there and pretended to sleep but you watched and you knew that it knew you watched. Just like with the boy last night...

Please... no more of this.

Daddy?

He turned sharply and saw the boy standing in the rain, wearing his shoes untied. He'd come from the restrooms; Thomas could see the stalls some small distance behind the boy. He knew the boy had come from there.

I had to go the bathroom, the boy said. *I tried to tie my shoes in there but I couldn't do it.*

Thomas ran to him and drew him up into his arms and held him close.

"It can't take you," he said, and he started to laugh while crying.

The boy pushed away from his shoulder and looked him in the face. *What can't take me, Daddy?*

"I don't know," he said and laughed again. "It could never take me. It won't be able to take you either." The rain started to come down harder. People were running from the beach to their cars in the parking lot.

How come?

"Because we're the same," he said.

We are?

"Yeah."

I'm sorry I said I didn't want to talk to you anymore. Are you mad?

"No... no, I'm not mad. You have nothing to be sorry for. Nothing at all. I was angry, but I wasn't angry at you. I could never be angry at you. I love you, son. I always have and I always will. You hear me?"

The boy nodded.

You said it.

Yes I said it, and let them all be damned.

He put the boy in the truck out of the rain and got in on the other side. The engine hummed to life and he turned on the heat to warm them both. The boy put his hands up to the vents and scrunched his fingers in toward his palms.

Where are your shoes? The boy glanced at his bare foot pressing lightly against the gas as the truck started to back up.

"I left them on the beach," he said.

Don't you need them?

"There are more important things," he said. "I have other shoes at home."

Can you show me how to tie mine when we get home?

Thomas smiled. "Sure," he said. "It's really easy."

Did your daddy teach you how when you were little?

Thomas didn't look at the boy. He focused on the raindrops falling harder, breaking against the windshield and dispersing into hundreds of tiny droplets. The distorted glare of lights from other cars as they passed... the back and forth throbbing of the windshield wipers...

"If there had been a daddy," he said, "then I suppose he would have taught me how. But there wasn't one, so I taught myself... like with everything else."

You didn't have a daddy?

"No."

How come?

"I'm not sure," he said. "That's just how it was when I woke up for the first time."

What about a mommy?

"Nope," he said. "No mommy either. Don't suppose I ever really needed one though. I was always good at taking care of myself."

Daddy?

"Yeah?" He felt the boy hesitate to go on. He glanced over at him and could see the deliberation within his little mind, the struggle and the fear. He waited, focusing on the road. The rain was falling hard now and obscuring their way. It did not often rain this hard in November. Or did it and had he only forgotten?

Were you a little boy like me once?

And what do you say to that?

I shouldn't be afraid to answer his questions.

You rarely answer this one for yourself.

That's because there is no answer to this question.

There is if you go deeper. He expects an answer.

"If I ever was..." he began. He was quiet for a moment. "As far as I know I've always been like this," he said.

Shallow, but serves its purpose, I suppose.

The boy thought on this for a few moments. *For how long?*

Thomas shrugged. "A long time," he said.

A few moments went by and the boy didn't say anything. Thomas was thinking about how she had always asked him all the same questions and how frustrated she would become at the way he answered her or didn't answer her.

Well, he heard the boy say after the silence.

"Well what?"

At least I have a daddy, he said.

Thomas held his gaze on the road, felt the boy staring at him as if awaiting a response. He could've almost believed it was her sitting in the passenger seat... but he did not want it to be her and for the first time was happy that it was not her.

"Yeah," was all that he said, and then he looked over at the boy and smiled.

* * *

Thomas was standing on the back porch when the boy drove up in the blue truck. He had bought the truck for the boy as a wedding present over a year past. The boy's wife was sitting in the front seat, smiling at something he was saying. She held her arm outside the open window and waved to Thomas as the truck pulled up and slowed. Thomas smiled and waved back, then walked down the steps from the porch as they were getting out of the truck.

The sun shone brightly over the field and the grass was green even for mid-summer. It was a hot day; the boy wore shorts and she wore a skirt. They both had sunglasses and sandals on. The woman came to him first and put her arms around him, kissed him on the cheek and told him he looked good. He smiled and thanked her.

"You look beautiful as ever," he said.

"I'm fatter," she said.

"Never met a pregnant woman who wasn't," he said and she laughed softly.

The boy walked up to him then and hugged him. "You look different and you look the same," he said. "Have you been working?"

Thomas smiled. "Mostly writing and rereading old books I read years ago. I do what outdoor work I can at night or early in the morning before the real heat comes. But today I rested because I knew you were coming. Are you hungry?"

"Yes," the woman said before the boy could answer. They all laughed and walked up to the porch together. Thomas led them to the door and ushered them in. He looked one last time at the truck, then at the sunlit field. Then he went in after them and closed the door.

* * *

"Do you remember when I carried you across that field one cold night when you were about seven?" Thomas asked him. They sat at the bar while the woman cleaned and put away dishes that Thomas had told her not to touch.

"No," the boy said. "I don't. What was I doing?"

"You had wandered off into the woods alone while I was in the barn and you got lost. Scared you pretty bad. I got to you as quick as I could and carried you back to the house and built a fire for you. You don't remember?"

"No," the boy said. "I guess I made myself forget. Where did you find me?"

Thomas thought for a moment, not because he had to think to remember but because the memory was so strong in him that he had to dilute it. For him it was an event still too close to his heart to be labeled as past.

"By the old oak," he said. "You were standing under it when I got to you. I held you and promised that I would never let you get lost again."

"That's sad and sweet," the woman said. "Odd that you wouldn't remember it."

The boy nodded but did not say anything. It seemed to Thomas as if he were trying to remember and fighting within himself to lay hold of the memory should he find it.

He won't remember.

No. All these years and I never once spoke of it. I knew that he wouldn't remember.

You didn't want him to remember.

No, I didn't want him to remember.

"I have no memory of that night," the boy said finally.

"Well," Thomas said, smiling. "You were uncommonly tired that night and you slept for a long time after. I didn't want to wake you. I felt you needed to sleep the trials of that night away into a dream. And I think that's exactly what you did."

"Yeah," the boy said. He sat for a moment in thought, and Thomas watched him in his silence. Very little had changed about him over the years except that he had grown taller and stronger. Thomas could remember him putting on muscle after his fourteenth birthday. He could remember many things as if they had only just passed.

"I wish Mom could have been here for this," the boy said, pointing with his eyes to his wife and the baby she carried inside of her. "I wish I'd had the chance to know her... to remember her."

"So do I," Thomas said. "I've written a lot about her in my journal. Which reminds me..." Thomas got up and went to the writing desk by the window. He took the journal from the top drawer, walked back to the bar with it and handed it to the boy.

"What's this for?"

"It's yours now," Thomas said. "I'm giving it to you to read and finish if you want. There are some pages left. Your mother got it for me a long time ago and I want you to have it."

"What are you going to write in from now on?" the boy asked. He held the journal with delicate hands, staring down at it as though it were something ageless and mythical.

"I'll go buy a new one maybe," Thomas said and smiled.

You lie to him with so much love and with so little effort.

It is better this way.

So you've convinced yourself. But what happens when he reads what you wrote the night—

I've always meant for him to read it. He will wonder what it means, but it will not hurt him to read it. I know it won't.

You are as strong as ever, and you can be here to love them both and to help them. Why must you leave?

I know that it's time... I've known for many years now, but I've waited because I love him so. I will see my grandchild, and then I will be finished.

"Thomas," she said. He looked up at the woman.

You thought it was Eleanor.

So I did... for a moment.

"Yeah?"

"We've narrowed the list down and we're torn between three names," she said.

"Let's hear them," he said. He listened to her as she talked about the different names. The boy said he liked the second one best so far but that he liked the other ones too—he said this because the woman gave him a look. They both laughed together as they playfully argued over which name was best.

Thomas sat quietly, listened and thought about the names.

* * *

We brought the baby over today and when we got there, we were both surprised he wasn't on the back porch. I knew something was wrong but I didn't say anything. I think she knew too. The door was unlocked and so I went in ahead. I looked in every room but he wasn't there. I went out to the barn, thinking he would be there and that he hadn't heard us drive up. He wasn't there either. Nor was he by the old oak. I don't know where he is... all I know is that he is gone and that he will not be coming back from wherever he has gone to.

On that day over a year ago that he asked me if I remembered the night, he carried me across the field, I lied. I did remember it. I think about it every day and have never been able to reason it out. I never asked him about that night because I was afraid of the truth—I'm still afraid. I often go back and read about that night in his journal and I think about what it could mean. I remember the day at the beach when I went to the spot where she died and I knew it for what it was though I never knew her... I think about it but I have no answers.

My father never spoke of it but in his writings, he mentions the nightwalker that would sometimes appear in the field and at the window. I'm glad he never spoke of it. The only account he ever recorded is dated the same day as the beach. In that account, he wrote about the different times he saw it in the field and the times it came to the window... but he never wrote what happened that night while he thought I was asleep.

So I write it now as I saw it.

He must have seen it walking toward the house and so he put down his pen, got up from the desk and went out to meet it. I snuck up to the window and watched. He walked up to it and it walked up to him and they both stopped in front of each other. They stood there for a long time. I'll never know what passed between them.

I saw the nightwalker turn away from my father and vanish into the trees. My father stood with his back to the house and watched it go. He stood facing the shadowed wall of trees long after it had left. I never saw it again after that night and my father never again wrote of it.

I can't be sure, but I think his disappearance has something to do with that night. Something he had to finish.

She asked me where he could have gone, and I told her that deep down I knew this day was coming. That was no kind of answer, I know. Of course, she didn't understand. How could she? But that was all the answer I could give her and it's all the answer I can give myself now.

One thing I'm sure of though... wherever he is, Thomas Whiteblood is doing what he does best.

And I am proud of him. I am proud of my father.

* * *

On the last night, Thomas dreamed that there was a little boy, and that he was the little boy. Paddling in a small boat along a black river in the night, surrounded by a dense forest where the branches reached out across the river toward each other from both banks, forming a canopy over the water. No starlight and no moonlight but he could see a little ways into the dark on all sides, as though he had just enough light within himself to spare. There was music playing from somewhere behind the trees, somewhere close by maybe.

The music frightened him but stirred something in him as well. Like a breath he needed to catch but couldn't. The music got louder as he paddled farther down the river and he thought about turning the boat around and paddling upstream. He knew he wouldn't do it but he still thought about it, as if the thought itself were a kind of comfort.

The water, black as tar, sloshed against his paddle. He came to a bend and veered away from the current and entered a small alcove where dead tree limbs jutted from the water's surface; gaunt hands reaching out from a stagnant pool toward their living brethren. He brushed against one of them and he felt it trying to grab the inside of the boat. Pushed away from it with his paddle and let the boat drift into the center of the pool.

Something said that this was a place of certain importance. Perhaps it was he who said it. He would not have stopped otherwise. He could still hear the music playing from someplace deep within the shadowed woodland before him. Tones in the minor fitting for such a night.

He paddled to the shore and climbed out slowly. His shoes got wet and made a light splash as he pulled the boat up onto the bank. He let the boat rest on the gnarled web of roots that infested the bank from one end to the other all away around the cove, then looked into the deepening stretch of woodland, searching for a path amid shadows. He took one step forward and a veil of branches opened their way to him. From there he followed the music.

Following a hidden path, he drove himself deeper into the forest. Pushed through a net of prickly bushes and came upon a glade where the tree branches could not reach across and an opening to the night-clouded sky mirrored a bald hilltop at the center of the glade. This was where the music was coming from he was sure, but there was no one that he could see. He could feel eyes watching from the cover of the surrounding woodland as he approached the crest of the hill.

Upon the hill, he stood and looked up toward the sky. The clouds parted, and the light of stars dripped down silver and cold, beading upon his face like sweat droplets. He ignored the eyes that watched him from the forested dark—they would not come out because they were afraid. The music played louder than he thought it could and it frightened him more. It is good to be frightened, he thought. He stood the ground because it was now his ground.

It is my music. The forest and the river and the hill are also mine.

He looked up once more to the stars and welcomed their questioning glances.

And these stars... I wonder if they do not also belong to me.

He sat down upon his hillcrest under heaven and listened to the music as the night drew on into deeper night, until those who watched from the surrounding woodland had retreated back to their own lands, until the stars themselves blinked out and slept, until the music trailed off into an oscillating ring and eternity at last measured itself immeasurable.

W. ADAM BURDESHAW

PROMISE

she comes to me. always after midnight, always clad in the same flowing white gown, the silken dress she wore at our wedding. her hair hangs below her shoulders in wisps as hungry and wild as barren tree limbs reaching for the constellations above the cemetery; twice as ticklish too. her chin crowned by a parted pink smile and round nose, and those exploring lips begin at my ear and work their way to my wanting mouth, leaving warm kisses to cool against the darkened bedroom air filling with the sweet scent of opium incense.

even in the dark, i can sense her half-closed eyes devouring me as if i was a meal in some expensive and glamorous restaurant only upper-crust types can afford or pronounce.

she slides an exposed leg over mine, sending chills down my arms and chest—her slender fingers brush against my hardening nipple. i gasp when our bodies shift, altering my supine position so that i'm facing her on my side. my hands brush over her tattoos as our tongues roll over each other. my eyes clench as she explores my back with her black painted fingernails, running the length of my spine as if she were plotting an exotic indian ocean voyage on some archaic,

yellowed map. maybe my occasional scattered freckles are first magnitude stars of indecent constellations helping her find the way...

   i press my hips into hers. she moans in my ear, tugging my sweat-
soaked hair with her alcohol-soaked breath. entwining, our bodies
become strawberry licorice, flexible and sweet, and any observer
would not know where i ended and she began. she pulls back, slipping the gown's straps with a shake of her shoulders before pressing her white calendulas against my bare chest, our hearts beat, beat,
beating in unison, as one. my lower lip trembles when she hooks
the straps of my black pajamas with her thumbs and tugs. we hold
our breaths as we remove the rest of our concealing garments in one
deliberate motion.

   there is nothing more between us, only flesh pressed against flesh,
but it's not time just yet. i taste the salt of her pallid skin, becoming inebriated from her luscious musky pheromones. i nibble little
pinches of her while working my way to her thighs. her hands get
lost in the tangled forest of my hair, pulling tufts above and behind
my pointed ears.

   when i get to her pale soles, i wash them with a tan sponge and a
silver pan filled with lukewarm water scented with bruised green tea
leaves and fresh pomegranate rinds, polishing each tiny toe no renais-
sance sculptor could duplicate with even the finest italian marble. i
massage her legs, coating them with frangipani oil from a new orleans
voodoo shop, and then rub her back with only my bare, guitar-rough-
ened hands. wrapping my arms around her neck, i smell her hair,
letting tresses mesh with my beard before flicking my tongue on the
bottom of her right earlobe.

   she turns around, facing me, sliding her hands to my hips. throbbing, i find my way to the warm wet, letting her swallow me with her
eager lotus. i lean her back—on top of our discarded clothes snarled
in the purple velvet sheets we begin moving our bodies like a squee-
zebox at a full moon gypsy bonfire. we don't gulp each other down.
instead, we take time to feel every inch and each fold, gyrating in
opposite pelvic directions. we take turns pressing ourselves together,

discovering new ways to pleasure each other capable of baffling antiquities' chinese masters. no need for their forbidden herbal aph- rodisiacs or hand-drawn pillow books, our prolonged duration arises from each other's desire of one another.

as the sun breaks the wine colored east sky, we collapse like waterfalls, coming to rest like a welder's iron statue. our bodies fused together until the alarm goes off, and i sit up alone on my cramped apartment's beat up couch. i slap the rectangular snooze button and lay back down, haunted by a woman i haven't touched in longer than i cared to remember.

i turn to my side, facing dick dastardly chasing after a fleeing mes- senger pigeon on the muted TV, promising to remain faithful until i join her icy side under the salt. on a coffee table we bought from wal-mart, a puppy dog calendar in need of another black X over the next empty box.

TOBY UNION

CAFÉ ELYSIUM

~PINKY~

Wiping stubborn grape jelly splotches off tabletops is not my favorite part of the job but it comes with the biz. Some of our more desperate clients make an uncivilized mess all over those uncomfortable vinyl seats that chirp when you shift, and the restrooms have seen their overwhelming share of depravity, but what cuts me to the bone about this post is wishy-washy customers. You know the ones that can't make up their minds even with color photographs crowning boldface, detailed descriptions of our menu selections—it's not like we have a million items—just steak, eggs, fish, or burgers. If vegetables happen to be your thing, we have a lovely garden salad with chickpeas, tomatoes, and cucumbers served up with a tofu shake... it's the easiest thing. Those morons drive me rabid when they scratch their heads and crinkle their brow while I tap my pen on my vacant order pad, waiting for a lone, starving thought to flicker in their dumb eyes. What can I do? It's what I do.

I was eradicating one of those jelly Mona Lisa's when the dangling cowbell announced (with a *ping-a-tonk*) Mr. Dirge had brought another paltry woman through the front door.

My boss was wearing his usual: black Armani slacks with matching long-sleeved button up, white tie, and snappy Italian leather shoes. A jet-black widow's peak points over piercing eyes and you never know what might come out of his thin lips. His stern presence causes me to stiffen up and work harder, but he is a fair employer. Doesn't ask much, just that I do what I'm suppose to. I don't pry into his affairs and he leaves me be…it works for both of us. He has a dignity and class about him that, despite his austerity, makes me look up to him.

On the other hand, the trash with him appeared to be a capital example of human wreckage. She was wearing a gray hoodie a size or two larger for her and the rotten thing was soiled what might have been dried coffee or grape juice. Her tattered blue jeans were held together by various patches of every color, size, and pattern, her knees worn and grass stained. Attached to her ankles were shoes that had once been Converses, and a wafting odious aroma begged me to wonder what sickening gutter Dirge plucked her from. I disliked her instantly, but a patron is a patron.

Dirge escorted her over to table 7, and motioned her to sit. She shot him a dirty look but complied, sliding into the booth. I heard it sing *Amazing Grace* as she settled in and rested the right side of her gaunt face on my clean table. I knew my expression gave away my anger, but I pursed my lips together, faking a smile as Mr. Dirge smoothed past me and exited the front door into the darkness.

I pulled my order pad and black ballpoint out of my pocket and strolled over to table 7 where I sat, *squeak, squeak, squeaking* in the seat across from her. I find this level of closeness heightens intimacy between order taker and client—just another special touch I like to offer. I laid the order pad on the table and began tapping my pen over unfilled blue bars.

"Welcome to Café Elysium. Know what you want or would you like to talk?" I asked in the nicest voice I could counterfeit.

"Stop making that noise, it's hurting my noggin." The heap before me groaned before wrapping her arms around her head. This one was going to be tough.

I looked at the untouched menu nestled betwixt the glass sugar igloo and the napkin holder that looked like an unattractive lunchbox. Normally I pull the laminated page out, setting it in front of the consumer but her lack of hygiene and self-respect didn't deserve my usual A-one service. To tell the truth, I found her repulsive and I didn't give a hot damn *what* she wanted.

"Do you know what you want to drink? I can get that ready for you while you make up your mind." I was trying to push my own never-ending thirst out of my mind.

She remained motionless as I licked my lips, and in the back of my thoughts, a nagging desire to bop the back of her head. I put the pad and the pen back into my pocket and *squeak, squeak, squeaked* my way out of the booth with, "How 'bout water? I'll be right back."

I didn't wait or care for a response. The faster I took her order, the faster she would leave.

I pushed open the red swinging double doors with the diamond Plexiglas windows, rushed to the drink station, and started scooping ice into one of our plastic sixteen-ounce cups. We use nonbreakable drinking tumblers so angry customers can't destroy them—I know it sounds odd, but it happens. Once a guy missing his legs tried to stab me with a dinner fork, but my reflexes allowed me to dodge his brutal, uncalled for attack. It's funny because I usually choose to wait before the meal to break the ill news to them so they can chew on more than their comestibles. I had the water up to the line just shy of the rim when Flyswat emerged from the depths of the kitchen.

Flyswat is not the biggest piece of jerky in the bag, but he has heart. Don't know what his real name is but I call him Flyswat because I believe that, in a past life, he was an annoying insect that met an abrupt end after pestering the wrong human, thus explaining his natural banality. He stumbled over to my drink station clad in a white undershirt, grease-stained apron, and checkered chef's pants—whistling Dixie and holding a frying pan.

"Did we get an order? I thought I heard the bell."

"Not yet, Flyswat. This one's a mountain but, don't worry. I'll climb her."

Flyswat's brown eyes widened, "Mr. Dirge brought us a *mountain?*"

I smiled and patted him on the shoulder. Even after working together all this time, he still manages to tickle me. I don't know what he did to find himself in our situation but he's blessed in his ignorance.

"I'll be right back," I said, pushing my way out of the double doors and carrying her unordered baptism in my hands.

I set the cup in front of her but she didn't budge—if I didn't know any better I could have sworn she was dead.

The menu was still in place, but I impatiently asked, "Do you know what you want yet?" playing the notion that, after a few moments, she would shed her shell and become loquacious.

"I don't have any cash," she responded, never looking up.

I smiled...progress at last. "That's of no matter here, darling. Just tell me what you feel like eating, and I'll make sure my cook whips it up."

There was a pause before the woman crawled out of her chrysalis and met my gaze. I took a step back for *she had the most beautiful green eyes* that I had ever seen. It was as if I finally caught a glimpse of the human tucked deep within the slop pile. What's worse is, a long time ago, I would have said they made her...*cute.*

"I don't need to pay for the food?" she asked. I noticed what might have been a sly smile pull at the corners of her chapped mouth. I noticed her teeth were yellow-green, and her gums... The whole affair was in serious need of a dentist's loving care.

"My boss has seen that it's covered."

She leaned over, grabbed the menu, and began scanning items. I could tell by her hungry jade glare that she hadn't eaten in a while, and my guess was that she was steak people.

"While you look, would you like a soda or tea?"

"Water's fine," as she flips the menu over to the plain back. I love it when they're easy. Moments like this make my atonement almost pleasurable. "I'll have a steak, medium rare."

I seldom miss a beat—by the time she spoke, I had it halfway scrawled down.

"No problem. I'll be right back, OK?"

I returned through the diamond doors to the kitchen where Flyswat, mumbling something about Abe Lincoln's sordid name, was kicking a large, silver oven. I tore her order off the pad, handing it to my coworker.

"I told you," I said and then, singing, I backtracked to the dining room to tend to our guest.

As I approached her table, I noticed that she had sipped some of the water through one of those candy cane straws that come one hundred to a pack and was toying with a Splenda packet...funny how people worry about such simple things as sugar or calories. I sat across from her, squeak, squeak, and slipped into my best poker smile.

"What's your name?" I asked, piling on the honey.

"Pinky."

"Well, Pinky, it's a pleasure to make your acquaintance. Tell me, what's the last thing you remember before you came in with my boss? He was the nice man in the expensive suit."

Her stare went a billion miles away. I noticed her thumb scrape at her cuticles—a disgusting habit but better than smoking...I guess.

"I was outside Aunt Tiki's with No-no, shooting some horse we copped from Angel."

"Ah, that must have been it. The smack."

"What do you mean 'the smack'?"

"Pinky, I hate to be Bad News Mercury, but I'm afraid the smack wasn't good or you took too much or some*thing*. You see, before reaching whatever destination your fate has in plan, you have come here," I looked around, "to Café Elysium. It's sort of an in-between place where you can enjoy some final carnal pleasures."

Disbelief deluged her face and she says, "You mean I di—"

I cut her off with, "I don't know what *you* call it, but you're here."

"Why are you here? How come you didn't reach your destination?"

"Let's just say I did something fate didn't like." I smirk, not wanting to divulge my thousand reasons for drowning that bastard Gordon in the Grand Lagoon oh so long ago. Besides, it's my problem and I'm dealing with it…am I not?

We stare at each other a moment and then she unrolls the napkin that carefully envelops our fancy silverware. After placing the fork tines down on the white blanket she's made, she crosses it with a butter knife, making a neat X. Everyone takes the news differently—some cry, some yell, some cuss, some laugh. Occasionally, you get the soul who wants to demolish everything in sight; however, most folks are Zen with it. More than you'd believe. Pinky seemed to be handling it swell.

We were in this moment of peace when the dining room filled with the din of pots and pans crashing followed by Flyswat shouting something vile and unrepeatable. Pinky and I exchanged an awkward glance.

"Was that the guy making my food?"

"Umm, I'll be right back," as I squeaked out of the booth and ran to the kitchen. As soon as I caught Flyswat in the dish room, I punched his arm, hard.

"*Ow*. That hurt," he said, rubbing his arm.

"I know it hurt, that's why I did it. We have a pleasant, albeit dirty, customer waiting on our quality food, and you are tearing up my restaurant. You're making us look like goons, ya moron."

Flyswat's eyes turn to the white sneakers he keeps clean despite his nasty job, and I feel bad for yelling when I see he's near tears.

"I'm sorry, Flyswat. I just want to keep an air of...professionalism here."

He looks up and I feel that his tears are passing, but the moment is smashed with the ping-a-tonk of the front door's cowbell. We both glance towards the diamond doors and Flyswat mumbles, "Mr. Dirge has another one."

"Always," I respond as push back out to the dining room where I see Mr. Dirge, seating a couple who are dressed to the nines and splattered in blood. I suspect a car wreck. Pinky stares off into space and I'm glad she's one of the ones who can't see the others coming in. I guess it's a precaution so people don't get freaked out before they hit where or whenever they're going. Perhaps it's because most folks face it alone...

"Your food will be right out," I assure Pinky and before I can greet my new guests, she reaches out and stops me.

"What happens after I eat?" Her eyes widen. "I mean, what next?"

"Some people have a cup of java, some have tea, some offer advice or make a final observation, some smoke—although I hate the smell—and others waste time clinging on to what they had. I hate to force people out but it happens. Anyway, once you are finished and ready, you go out the door with the red exit sign overhead." I point to the left-hand side of the building where—beside the pink, ladies' restroom door—there is a glass outlet. Pinky nods, and I am happy to be of assistance...after all, I am here for her needs.

I brush pass Mr. Dirge on my way to table 13, giving him a quick nod, and I pull out my order pad.

The blood-soaked couple are in good spirits (they're newlyweds), and I could be happier for them, facing eternity together. She wants Coke and, while he's ordering root beer, I hear a bell's ding signifying Flyswat has finished Pinky's steak. I excused myself from the happy couple's table and strolled over to the window where Pinky's steak was waiting under the heat lamps. I picked it up and began walking towards table 7, but I discovered Pinky wasn't there.

I looked up and caught a gleam of light flash across the exit door as it silently shuts—the only remnant of Pinky a hint of unpleasant breeze.

Everyone takes the news differently and still, after all these years, I just can't figure...

I replaced the steak under the heat lamps and slapped the adjacent silver bell—bing. Flyswat appeared at the window clad in a worried look.

"Did she send it back? Did I cook it too much?"

"No, that one was in a hurry. Looks pretty good. Why don't you eat this one, Flyswat?"

His face lit up.

"I love steak, it's my favorite," he beamed, pulling the festive-colored plate that reminds me of Cinco de Mayo from the window. I went through the swinging diamond doors to the drink station and filled the newlyweds' plastic glasses with ice. I was pouring the root beer when, once again, the cowbell sang ping-a-tonk.

~NATALIE~

Rushes come and go, but I do get to enjoy the lulls that sometimes seem to last, well, an eternity. I often like to fill those listless voids by touching up my makeup in the bathroom mirror. I think earth tones accent my features best; some base for color, a little dab of brown above the eyes, and, finally, a lipstick I fancy called Fall Forrest. When I'm low and I serve someone wearing my color, I hit them up. Most have no problem kicking me their make-up, being they're already deceased, but some folks are greedy until the end—I guess sometimes you can take it with you.

I was putting on my face when I heard the *ping-a-tonk* from out front, and I stuffed the kit into this cute, black kitty-cat purse a charming ballet dancer kicked to me after she tipped-toed into the passenger seat of a drunk driver's red Porsche. You wouldn't believe all the folks I meet who've gone out from that cataclysmic blend of adult beverages and automobiles—you'd think there would be laws against that troublesome combination.

I stashed my black purse in one of the lockers located in the vestibule between the kitchen and the employee bathroom, rushing my way past the swinging door with the Plexiglas diamond, to witness Dirge handing this young woman an order pad and a pen. The familiar scene reminds me of my first few moments here.

I can't tell you how long ago it was. Outside there's no sunrise or sunset, just stars against eternal black. Inside there are no clocks anywhere to indicate when we are. When I first came to Café Elysium there was an amiable waiter named Juan tending to Dirge's endless customers, and he taught me the unpredictable ins and outs of the afterlife service industry. He said very little, never alluding to how long he thought he'd been here or why, but he was always patient and kind. There was no telling how long we worked together, and one day, when the reality of my punishment had sunk in and I was crying in the employee bathroom, he vanished. I don't know where he went to, but I heard the cowbell and hurried out, finding I was alone to take the next order.

Been just me and Flyswat ever since.

So, after Mr. Dirge hands this girl I figure is around 19 or so the order pad and pen, he shot me a look telling me I better take this seriously. I felt my ears burn with anger, but he's the boss, and I have to follow orders. Dirge is the type of man I don't want to fool with, save I wind up in a worse place. Effortlessly, Dirge turned and exited through the entrance, leaving this scared-looking girl staring at the blank order pad's blue bars.

She's a strawberry blonde, blue-eyed thing with a little peach fuzz on her upper lip. I've always found women with mustaches unattractive, but I have a razor I got from a hiker mauled by a badger in my purse, and I'll train her to have better respect for herself. She's wearing this blue blouse and black slacks, and I guess she's pretty, but there's no way in Hades she's better looking than me.

"Welcome, darling," I said. "Are you all right?" I laid as much drawl in my voice as this Southern Belle can muster, letting her believe I might actually be her friend.

"W-where am I?" she stammered, and I instantly discerned she's a Yankee.

"Why," I replied, "you're in a diner." I really drew out the last word, sugar coating a terrible situation. "Let me get you something to eat before we start your training."

"Training?" she asked.

"Well, Mr. Dirge gave you a pad and a pen, meaning you're my new help. Good thing, too. I could use some help around here."

"I'm not a waitress," she said, lower lip trembling. "I'm a student at Drexel."

"You were a student at Drexel, honey," I corrected, feeling a little bad for her. So young, so naïve. "But let's get some food in you before we get the next rush."

I grabbed her by her left hand (maybe a little harder than the poor lamb deserves, but I got to get it straight right away who the boss here is) and took her to table 9. She squeaked into place as I slid the menu before her and set silverware rolled in a napkin on her right.

"What 'cha like to drink?" I ask, pulling out my order pad.

"Um, Sprite," she replied.

"We got that here," I told her. "One Sprite, coming up." I went to the drink station and filled up one of our cups with the ice scoop, topping the glass with soda. I'm thinking she's a salad girl, possibly grilled chicken, but, as I set the glass in front of her, I bite my tongue, waiting for her to speak. "Figure out what you're having yet?"

"I'll take a hamburger plate, well done, and no pickle," she ordered, taking me by surprise. I thought for sure she was salad people, the type always worried about their figure and what other people think.

I jotted her order down. "I'll be right back and we're gonna have a little chat, OK?" She nodded and I walked to the window where I place most of the orders. Peeking in, I noticed Flyswat wasn't cleaning the grill or prepping onions, and I sighed, not wanting to go back there.

"FLYSWAT," I hollered, hating to lose face in front of our green waitress. After a moment passed and he didn't appear, I pushed my way back through the swinging doors and looked around the empty kitchen. Thinking he might have slipped into the employee restroom, I went through the vestibule and banged on the door. "FLYSWAT," I called again, unable to mask the annoyance in my words. With still no sign of my cook, I went to the cold box where we keep our refrigerated stock.

There's this stainless handle and, when I yanked, the door came open with a sucking sound. A wall of cold air tingled my flesh, and aside from the normal boxes of produce and thawing meats, there was nothing inside. I groaned and turned, shutting the door and starting for the icebox, where we store frozen goods, when I heard Flyswat's voice behind me.

"You need something Miss Brite?" he asked, little smile on his lips.

"Flyswat," I said, startled. "Where were you? I was looking all over."

He blushed. "Oh, I was just, uh, in the stockroom, checking up on straws."

I watched him carefully. "We got one. I think she's gonna stay."

"Stay?" He looks puzzled. "She won't go through the door?"

"It's not that," I laughed. "She's a new waitress. Mr. Dirge brought her in and handed her an order pad."

"Just like you," he grinned.

"Yup. Here's her order." I handed him the ticket.

"Hamburger girl...neat," he said as we headed to the kitchen. "Have you told her yet?"

"I'm about to," I replied, pushing my way through the double swinging door as Flyswat opened a reach-in and pulled out one of our huge, ½-pound burgers. Flyswat claims we have the best because they're never frozen. He fixes the ground beef up with a bunch of his secret spices and quiet magic. The burgers are our best sellers, and I would certainly recommend them to an unsure patron.

She was sipping on her Sprite when I *squeaked* across from her at the table.

"How's your soda pop?" I asked, sitting back.

"It's nice, thank you," she said, looking around at the table and the restaurant, everywhere but my eyes.

"Since you'll be working here, let me introduce myself," I said, offering an honest smile. "My name is Valerie Brite. What do they call you?"

"Natalie Reynolds, and I don't remember ever wanting to work here."

I smile, unable to contain myself. "Natalie, it's a pleasure to meet you." I extended my hand. Natalie accepted it, and I can't help but notice her black nail polish and how cold her fingers feel. "I'm afraid I have some unfortunate news for you."

Her brow tightened up. "Unfortunate?"

"Yes." I rested one hand on my hip, shifting my weight to my left foot. "It is." I sighed. "Now, I don't want you to freak out—are you the type that flips?" She slowly shook her head. "OK. Sweetie, you're dead, and I guess it's my job to train you how to work in this place, Café Elysium."

"Dead?" A frightened look crossed her face.

"I'm sorry, Natalie," I said as I reached out for her cold, cold wrists, noticing the wounds, her reason for being here. "I'm not trying to frighten you, and I'm not attempting to do you any harm. I just want you to understand that everything you knew before is gone."

BING sang Flyswat's bell. Her meal was ready.

"Excuse me," I said, winking before I squeaked out of the seat and went to the pick-up window where Flyswat peered out, smiling like a cockroach in a trash heap.

"You tell her I made it real special," he said. "I made a smiley face out of the onions, just for her."

"Flyswat, I don't think that's gonna help. This girl has just had her fate handed to her—smiley faces and games have no place here."

His grin dropped, and he sulked back into the kitchen. I spun around and walked the burger to her, smelling the warm steam wafting form the meat. When I got to table 9, I saw Natalie pulling out a hard pack of Camel Lights.

"Hey, now," I said, *thumping* the plate in front of her—I saw the lettuce shake as the onion visage became lopsided. "There'll be none of that while you're here."

"What?" said Natalie, the cigarette dangling from her lips. "I can't smoke."

"Only the best of men and the worst of women smoke. Café Elysium ain't no brothel. This is a classy place, and we're gonna show these folks some respect."

Natalie pulled the cigarette from her lips and reinserted it into her pack, which disappeared under the table. She looked at her food a moment, as if unsure where to start, and then looked back up at me.

"Enjoy, darling. After this it's time to go to work."

"Do we get a break, Valerie?"

"Only when Mr. Dirge doesn't have any customers. Sometimes we get long breaks."

"What about sleeping?" she asked. "Don't we get to sleep?"

"We don't sleep." I wished she would shut up and eat so we could get on with it. "After a while you won't feel hunger. Eating becomes a choice. You never get tired, and you can drink whatever you want. You will be thirsty. Our job is to help make our patron's transition between their world and the next as easy as pecan pie."

"What if I don't want to do this? What if I go back through that door, and forget all about this?"

"I'm afraid that's not possible, Natalie," I was unable to hide the somberness in my voice. "You made a mistake, and, now, you must pay for it…just like me. Just like Flyswat."

Squeak, squeak, she slid out of the booth and began yelling. "THIS ISN'T FAIR. I DON'T HAVE TO DEAL WITH THIS IF I DON'T WANT TO. YOU CAN TAKE THIS JOB AND SHOVE IT." She stormed over to the entrance and pulled the handle open, a blast of ultra-violet light and a horrible cacophony of screams, static, and moans blew in. Before Natalie knew what was happening, Mr. Dirge was standing in the doorway, shaking is head. Natalie fell to her knees and began weeping, covering her teary eyes with her hands. Dirge calmly shut the door, silencing the violent disturbance.

I couldn't blame her—I've done the same thing. Now, she knew exactly how serious her—our—situation was. We're damned, and there's nothing that can be done about it.

I walked over to her, helped her up, and lead her back to table 9, where we squeaked across from each other. She looked so sad… I understood. All those little things you never finished, all those petty hopes and dreams unfulfilled. We sat in silence, her food remained uneaten. Flyswat came out of the kitchen and checked on his meal; I noticed he was hurt by her not trying it.

Ping-a-tonk and I jumped up, seeing a guy who looked as if his bones had been broken. After Dirge left and I got him settled, the guy told me he fell off a cliff while bird watching. I asked him how it felt to fly. He laughed, said it was nice, and then ordered scrambled eggs and bacon, side of hash browns. He was a nice fellow, Nick I think was his name, and he walked out the EXIT door, smiling and whistling, totally bringing up my gloomy mood.

I checked back on Natalie, who still hadn't touched a single morsel.

"Do you want me to clear this off?" I asked. She shook her head, and I sighed. It was time to get this lazy horse riding. "Well, are you ready to start taking orders? There's bound to be one any moment now."

She looked up at me, scrunched up her eyes, and asked, "When did you die?"

"1968, darling," I said. "How about you? When did you bite it?"

"You don't know what year it is?"

"Afraid not. See any clocks around here?" She looked, then shook her head. "So, when was it?"

"2011."

"2011—I'll be. I guess I have been here a while. It really hasn't felt like that long," I offered, trying to cheer her up. "Come on, let's get to work. I'll show you around our little restaurant, let you pick a locker."

She slid out of the seat (*squeak, squeak*) and stood, stretching. I picked up her untouched food and placed it by the pick-up window, under the heat lamps.

"We call this the window. Here's where we drop off orders and pick up food. All you have to do is holler, and Flyswat will tend to your needs. He's a good cook, a little slow, but a fine, fine man. He won't try anything funny, you understand?" She nodded. "These double doors lead into the kitchen, but, first, there's the drink and salad stations." I pushed open the doors and we entered.

The drink station was how I left it, tidy and almost full of ice.

"Here is where you get folks their drinks. I want everything kept clean, I can not abide a mess. After you fill up the cups with ice, put it under the spout. Press this button here and hold it until you reach the lower line on the inside of the glass. If we run out of ice, tell Flyswat. He'll refill the bin."

She seemed to understand my instructions. At least Dirge brought me someone who listens.

"Beside the drink station is the area where we prepare salads," I told her. "It's basically a bin with the mix that opens up so you can assemble quick side salads. Piled up here are these empty plastic bowls, but when they want a special salad with grilled chicken, use these large ceramic ones." I pointed to a stack of bowls.

"I guess all these other smaller bins are veggies?" she asked, pointing to a row of covered ½ pans.

"Aren't we a quick one," I said, delighted. "Yes, around the bowl it goes: tomato on top, two cucumbers at one o'clock, carrot slices at three o'clock, broccoli at five, three onion rings at six, cauliflower at seven, and a small dab of chic peas at nine, and three black olives at eleven. In the center, place a little alfalfa sprouts—it's pleasing to the eye." I opened up the reach-in underneath the salad station's countertop and pulled out three sliding trays containing soufflé cups filled with dressing. "We have to prep these up once in a while. We have ranch, creamy Italian, bleu cheese, thousand island, and French. If someone wants the classic oil and vinegar, that's here too in this container." I held up the special bottle to be certain she understood.

"I was a waitress once," she said. I looked into her eyes, trying to draw out a tangible emotion.

"Really? Then this should be a walk in the park," I replied.

"I didn't like it."

"Then I guess this is a fitting punishment for you, Natalie." I was unable to hide the sarcasm in my voice. Natalie shot me a look, and I wondered how smoothly things were going to run after all.

~DOUGLAS~

Sometimes you can't win.

Things had been going a little bumpy with Natalie. She caught on quickly but refused to take initiative. She'd hang back, make me take all the orders. I forced her to wait on this elderly lady, and Natalie wound up spilling her sweet tea all over the table and her lap. She went through the EXIT cussing, barely eating her fried chicken sandwich. I know Dirge allows a training period, but I don't want her inattentive behavior reflecting on my teaching ability.

Dirge is a force I don't want to tinker with.

I was thinking I smelled cigarette smoke when Dirge walked in this guy whose suit matched the boss's in style and cost. Where Dirge usually wears black, this guy was in brown. About sixty, he came in with a sour look on his puss. When Dirge seated him at table 4, I *squeaked* in across from him and set the menu in front of him.

"Hi, how are you?" I threw on another fake smile to accent my Southern drawl.

"I'm dead," he said flatly. "What's it to ya?"

"Well," I started, "do you want to talk about it, or are you ready to order?"

"What if I just want to sit here a while?"

"You may take your time, but when we hit a rush and someone else needs that table, you're gonna have to go."

He leaned back in his booth, letting loose a smug smile. "You can't make me go through that door."

I felt every muscle in my body tense up. You get the type that pulls this sort of aggravating stunt, and I still haven't figured out the proper formula, the right way to handle it. They have to go through, it's just the universe's order—I'm here only to let them enjoy one last bit of who they were. It's so simple—I can't, for the life of me, understand why letting go is so difficult.

"Sir, it's not my place to make you go through that door."

"See," he laughed. "I knew we'd come to a consensus."

I held up my pointer finger. "*However*, my employer—Mr. Dirge—is the big man around here. And I'm sure he would be delighted to escort you through that exit, when the time comes." I leaned in a little closer, whispering, "*And I'm certain you won't appreciate the way* **he** *does it.*"

His eyes widened, and he tightened his lips, disgusted by his obvious defeat. It was my turn to lean back in my booth and smile. We didn't speak a few moments. He reached over and snatched out the menu from behind the lunchbox-shaped napkin dispenser and slapped it down on the table, grumbling. I noticed there was a splotch of chili on the top left-hand corner and I knew I was going to have to get onto Natalie about it—we're not running a pigsty.

"I bet you're a steak guy," I said, pulling out my order pad from my blue apron stuffed with straws and ballpoint pens. "Well done—right?" He glanced up over the menu, shooting me a frigid look from his hard, brown eyes.

"Right. And I'll have new potatoes for the side. Does it come with a salad?" he asked, never flinching.

"I can serve a side salad if you'd like," I smiled.

"I would, but I want it after the meal."

"That's a little unusual. Why after?"

"A salad is so delicious." He set the menu down and clasped his fingers. "It's as good as any tart."

"What to drink with that, honey?"

"Scotch...on the rocks. Chivas Regal. Eighteen year if you have it." He waved his hand in a swift circular motion.
I frowned. "I'm sorry, but we don't have any alcohol."

"No scotch?"

"No scotch."

"Well, I'd say we have a problem then. If this is my last meal, it better be exactly what I want. If it's not, I'm not going to have a good time of this, and where would that put you?"

"I don't suppose it matters where I stand. You still have to go through that exit."

"You, as a servant of the public, shouldn't treat people like this."

"I'd say that could go both ways, sir," I replied, all humor gone from my voice. You can't let them get to you; the afterlife is way too long.

"Do you even know who I am?"

"Afraid not." I yawned.

"I'm Douglas McSweenly, and I make more money in a half day's work than most men make in their entire lifetimes."

"I guess that really doesn't matter now, does it?" I said, wanting to get this guy through the door more than ever. I've often noticed—

whether the person is rich or poor—greedy patrons are the hardest
to deal with. After all is said and done, after all those trivial things are
reduced to rubbish, the avaricious are the most difficult to deal with.

Douglas McSweenly shot me a murderous look as I *squeaked* out
of the seat and stood next to the table, a broad smile pulling my lips.
I glanced over at Natalie, and saw her watching me, frowning. I could
tell she was appalled by the way I was handling my customer, and I
wondered what she would've done had she been in my shoes.

"Someone ought to report you to your supervisor," he snapped,
and I burst out laughing.

"Sir, would you like something to drink while your steak cooks?"

"Just water," he said softly. I could tell by the look on his face the
gravity of what was unfolding had finally struck him. A few moments before, he was someone important and powerful. Now, he was
just another face in the haze—one more name in that long docket of
souls who had simply lived at one time or another. Everything he'd
taken for granted was gone, and the time to move on had come; his
brown eyes watered, softened, and I knew, somewhere in the back of
his selfish mind he thought he was going to live forever.

"Would you like a lemon for your water," I asked, trying to soften
realization's unkind blow.

"Lemon," he answered softy. "Yes. Please."

I smiled. "All right. I'll put your order in and be right back with
your drink. When I get back, we can have a little talk if you'd like."
He looked up at me, unsure of what to say. I wasn't trying to bring
him down, but what we're doing here is serious, and I need everyone
who goes through that EXIT door to understand exactly what they
are leaving behind. I didn't realize what I was losing until the moment I was left alone with Flyswat, and I bet Natalie is going to need
time to adjust, too. He nodded, and I went to the pick up window.

"Flyswat," I called. He appeared right away, smiling.

"We got one?" he asked, unable to hide his eagerness. His
simplicity never fails to warm me—I guarantee you he doesn't even
know he's deceased. He still eats like he's alive, often complaining

about being tired. I haven't slept or even so much as hiccupped since I've got here, the only remaining earthly desire remaining is an unquenchable thirst. I've learned to ignore it most of the time, but here and there I give in to the constant burning in my throat.

"Steak, well, side-new," I recited, dangling the ticket on the spinning order holder affixed to the window and pushing it so Flyswat could read it. After walking through the double swinging doors, I stopped in front of the drink station and grabbed one of the cups. Natalie followed me, looking as mad as a blind cat in a bathtub.

"What's wrong with you, honey?" I asked as I dispensed water from the spigot.

"You are horrible," she said. "That man just passed away, and look at the way you're treating him. It's not right, Valerie. You shouldn't do people like that."

I thought, *who do you think you are, little girl*, as I pulled out the lemon wedges from a reach-in under the station. I wanted to slap her sassy mouth, but I swallowed my anger like a proper lady and put two wedges on the lip of Douglas McSweenly's cup.

"Explain to me why you're acting this way, Valerie," she pleaded.

"I don't have to explain one tiny detail, Natalie. This is my shift, and I am your boss. These aren't the pearly gates, darling. We don't have to be anything but what we are. Dirge brings them in and we feed then send them out—it's the simplest thing. It's paramount you understand that. If you can't get with it, I'm going to have tell Mr. Dirge you aren't going to cut it here."

"You're a monster, Valerie Brite."

I slapped her across her left cheek. Her jaw dropped and her hands went to her already reddening face. We stared at each other a moment, feeling the hatred between us grow. She opened her mouth to say something but, before she could speak, we heard the ping-a-tonk from out front.

"You best take that order," I warned her, "or there'll be hell to pay."

She studied my eyes, gazed into my soul, and knew I meant business. I wasn't playing around any more; the time had come for her to step up. She sighed and pulled out her order pad, about-facing through the swinging doors. I picked up Douglas McSweenly's cup and calmly followed her, walking it to his table.

I watched her talk to a black gentleman in a blue and white basketball jersey and blue sweat pants as Dirge returned through the front door. She was even smiling as he ordered a Vanilla Coke, and I felt the tension dissolve from my shoulders. I set the ice water in front of McSweenly and offered one of my truest smiles.

"Only two?" He motioned to the lemons.

"Don't push it," I answered. "There has to be enough for everybody."

He shot me a glare and pulled one of the wedges off the rim, squeezing it. I watched an extra squirt roll down the outside of the glass, mix with the condensation, and pool on the tabletop.

"Did you want to talk?" I asked, one hand on my hips. "Get anything off your chest before you get your meal?"

"Sit down, girl. I've got some advice for you."

I *squeaked* across from him, made eye contact, and folded my arms across the cold table. "Advice...for me? I'm not sure how your no doubt infinite wisdom is going to be able to help me."

"First of all, you're a very pretty girl."

"Thanks," I blushed. At least he had good taste.

"The problem is that you aren't a very nice one. I came in here—a customer—and you didn't show me the least bit of respect. That's the sort of attitude that is going to prevent you from advancing in life—or whatever your situation may be."

"Is that so?" I asked, annoyed.

"Indeed. In fact, if you would just smile and not be so much of a smarty pants, people might actually like you."

"Like me? I hate to break it to you, Douglas McSweenly, but people are the least of my worry. I've done this a long, long time, and I could care less what people think about me."

" Really? Then why do you put on all that make-up and strut around here like the cock on the walk?"

He had me speechless for a second. "You pompous cuss. You tell me I'm rude, and all the while you don't have a single concern for your fellow man, or woman in this case." He looked surprised. Since I had him pinned, I continued, "As if it's any of your business, I wear make-up for me, not anyone else." A sly smile crossed his lips, and he sat back in the booth.

"You have spunk, girl."

"My name is Valerie."

"Valerie," he repeated, tasting my name on his lips. "Why are you here?"

"You don't want to know."

"Sure I do. I'm interested. Knowing people is how I made my fortune."

I thought hard about how I should answer him. It happened so long ago, and I try not to think about it much. Honestly, I hadn't told anyone other than my trainer how it all went down. I wish I could forget that humid Florida night, that bloody mess I'll never be able to wash off my hands.

"I made a mistake."

"What kind of mistake?"

"The kind that disrupts the harmony of the universe, Douglas. A mistake that not even Death could forgive."

"Do you think this is the only Halfway Café out there or could there be more?" he asked, and, out of the corner of my eye, I saw Natalie by the pick-up window, hanging onto every word.

"I couldn't tell you, Douglas. All I know is that my customers speak or at least understand English. I've never had a patron I'm unable to communicate with, so I suspect there are more places like this—where people can feel…safe."

"That's exactly my point, Valerie," he said. "I didn't feel safe or even welcomed here. If it's your job to help souls crossover, than do your damned job."

And that was it. My 'damned job' was exactly that. I felt every-
hing inside twist, tightness tore at my chest, and my spirits utterly
lropped. As much as I hated it, he was right. I figured I'd better
vork on my customer service.

BING sang Flyswat's bell, and I scurried out of my noisy seat,
ushing to the pick-up window where Flyswat beamed. Douglas'
teak was perfectly marked with the crisscrossed patterns from his pit
grill, and the three sliced new potatoes sprinkled with fresh parsley
at neatly to the right of the meat. An attractive piece of kale was at
he top of the plate, bordering a soufflé cup filled with Flyswat's secret sauce—a concoction one part Worcestershire, one part culinary
genius—also sprinkled with green herbs to make the liquid esthetic.

"Looking good, sweetie," I said as I lifted the plate from under
he heat lamps. Flyswat stopped a second, looking like a nine-year-
old getting an ice cream on Sunday.

"T-thanks, Miss Brite. I love to cook."

"I know you do, and you do it well, Flyswat." I swore I saw him
blushing. He nodded and I turned, glancing over to Natalie, huddled
by the swinging doors, and offered a weak smile and a nod.

I walked over to Douglas McSweenly's table and set his order
down. He leaned forward and inhaled the steam rising off the meal
and smiled.

"Smells good. I don't know what I think of death yet, but, so
far the food's nice." I smiled and began to turn and let him eat, but
he reached out and gently brushed my arm. "Please. Sit with me. I
would love to eat my last meal as Douglas McSweenly with you."

"Really?" I asked.

"Really. Although I had many lovers, I never married anyone,
never settled down. One of my favorite things about life was eating
a good meal with an attractive woman. It's so simple, but I guess it's
the simple things that life worth living, right?" I nodded as I *squeaked*
into the booth across from him. He gestured towards me. "Would
you like some of my steak?"

"No, thanks."

"Suit yourself." He picked up his rolled silverware. He unrolled the napkin and daintily set the fork and knife on top of it, then he picked up the soufflé cup and sniffed Flyswat's secret sauce. "This smells wonderful. What is it?"

"House recipe. Totally hush-hush."

He poured the sauce over his steak and potatoes, setting the empty soufflé on the side of his plate. He picked up his fork and knife and cut into the steak—I saw the inside was as white as a dove, a perfect steak—done but juicy. I knock Flyswat for being a simpleton, but I must confess, he's a hell of a cook.

He took a bite and smiled. "Mmm." I watched him slowly chew up the bite, savoring it. Douglas McSweenly, a man devouring every last drop of what he was.

"So, Douglas, how did you become a rich man?" Smiling as he skewered on of the potato slices, I knew this one was going to be good.

"My father made the family wealthy. He spent his entire life selling things he found in thrift shops to rich people who wanted to feel closer to the class gap. He had a little shop near some of the more upscale section of Panama City Beach, and those nice folks in the big houses didn't seem to mind overpaying for used clothes, trinkets, and art. I guess it was in vogue during his time. Mother and I helped around the shop, and I took it over after I finished a four-year at FSU, in Tallahassee. Life was good to me—I met many interesting characters and had many good times. My father set up some successful stocks, and, when I inherited his fortune, I invested in rental properties. Panama City Beached boomed, and I began to live the good life."

"I know the area well," I said.

"Do you?"

"I lived there…a long time ago."

"When was that, exactly?"

"Too long to matter. How come you never married, never found anyone to share it all with?" I asked as he gobbled the potato slice.

"Truthfully?" he asked. I was glad he did not push about my past.

"Truthfully."

"There was this one woman I would have given a ring to, but I couldn't get over myself."

"I don't follow. What do you mean?"

He sighed. "I'm afraid I couldn't bring myself to share." There was some far-off look in his eyes—I've seen the same flat glare on several of my more regretful customers. Crazy how a person can fall back into a single memory, and that simple retrospection can swallow someone up. Every smell, every sound, every tiny detail of one incredible moment comes rushing back all at once, forever burned in a soul. Happens to me too.

"What?" I asked. "You just offered me part of your meal."

"I know," he said, cutting into the meat again. "Perhaps that was me atoning for my wrongs. Maybe I was trying to make one last connection before cashing in all the chips and going home...wherever that is."

"You already knew you were dead when I seated you, Douglas. How did it happen?"

He looked up at me with this sort-of half smirk, and I gathered the subject made him uncomfortable. He set the silverware on the left-hand side of the plate, next to the steak, and leaned back in the booth. He cracked his knuckles and then opened his blazer, revealing a slit in his white dress shirt surrounded with dried blood.

"I was stabbed by a robber," he said. A strange serene befell his face. "I was leaving an ATM when these two masked men jumped me. I wouldn't come off my money, and one of them stabbed me. His buddy got scared and they both ran away, empty-handed." He reached inside his blazer and pulled out a wad of cash, saying, "I died with a grand in my wallet. No money in world could bring that ambulance to me any quicker, and I passed watching the stars peacefully burn thousands of miles away."

I quickly glanced out the diner's window at the constellations flickering beyond the abyss. It's true how far away they feel. Totally hopeless.

He picked his silverware back up, and I watched in silence as he ate, occasionally sipping the lemon ice water. His manners were impeccable—after every other bite of his meal he dabbed the napkin against his lips, and the careful manner in which he drank the water allowed not one rogue drop to escape. When he finished, he rested the silverware on the plate and again dabbed his lips with another clean napkin, covering the plate when he was done.

"Enjoy your meal?" I honestly cared.

"Yes, Valerie, I did. Thanks to you and your chef, it was the best I've ever had."

"I'm glad."

"Valerie?"

"What, Douglas?"

"How did you die?" he inquired.

"In a lot of pain and joy at the same time," I told him.

"You come off as an educated woman. Not the type I'd expect to find in your shoes. Did you have a good time on Earth? Did your life take you far?" His words sounded somewhere between curiosity and worry.

"Far enough to land me here," I said, never breaking eye contact.

He looked down at his napkin-covered plate and sighed. "I'm sorry. I won't pry any further." I knew he understood.

"It happened a long time ago. So long, it doesn't even matter any more." He nodded and reestablished eye contact, and I saw what I originally took as coldness had melted into sadness, like a wounded animal begging for mercy. Although knowing Douglas McSweenly for only a shot time, there was no doubt he would not whimper as he walked through the EXIT. An admirable man.

"It's time," he said. I nodded. "How much do I owe for the food?"

"It's covered."

"I guess I got to tip you then." He reached into his blazer.

"No, no, no. I have no use for it."

He waved his hand. "I insist. The service was superb." He pulled out his wad of bills and tossed it on the center of the table, behind his cleaned plate. The cash slid, and I saw Benjamin Franklin's forehead ten different times. He squeaked out of the booth and adjusted his tie. "I guess it's time for me to get out of here."

I squeaked my way to his side and gave him a hug. "Are you nervous?"

"Nah. Whatever awaits beyond that door doesn't phase me. Know why?" I shook my head. "Because I'm walking through a rich man." He winked, turned, and strolled through the door, never looking back.

I watched him go, wondering what was in store for him. To tell the truth, I was envious of the fearlessness he exhibited. I picked up his glass and plate, leaving the cash on the table—as I said, I have no use for it. Besides, even if I did need it, you never want to look needy. It's not becoming. I walked the dishes through the swinging door and into the dish room where I placed them by the sink for Flyswat to attend to.

"FLYSWAT," I called out, but, again, I couldn't see or hear him anywhere. I shrugged it off, assuming he was tending to work in the stockroom, a part of the diner I tried to stay away from.

When I pushed my way back through the doors, I saw Natalie's customer heading towards the EXIT, looking over his shoulder twice before he pushed the door open and stepped into the starry vortex outside. The restaurant was empty again, and I was left with my two co-workers, a table to wipe clean, and my thoughts.

I went to the table to straighten it up and noticed the ten hundred-dollar bills were gone. I looked around, but I was the only one left in the dining room. Someone had robbed me, and I had a strong inkling who the culprit was.

~THE CRASH~

Whenever there's an unthinkable accident—like tonight's horrible bus crash—It floods the restaurant with a bunch of scared and
confused diners. I've handled several such occasions with ease, sac-
rificing my usual relaxed state of mind for a job well done, but when
tensions mount and things go terribly haywire, the most experienced
waitress is liable to lose her cool.

The rush began with Mr. Dirge opening the door. Normally, he
escorts the clients to their tables, but in this instance, he just held the
door open and let them pile in. It seemed as if they wouldn't ever
stop coming—one after the other after the next—before I could get
my order pad in my hands, almost every booth in the joint was full.
I later gathered that a passenger bus blew a tire on I-95, crashing
into three or four civilian motor vehicles and killing almost everyone
involved.

It was pure pandemonium.

I don't know what order they arrived, but there was folks looking
for loved ones, some looking for luggage, some cussing at Dirge as
they entered, and others just plain lost in the whole messy ordeal. I
couldn't find Natalie—I assumed she was in the employee bathroom,
smoking cigarettes—and, when I called for Flyswat, I couldn't find
him either. The most unsettling moment of the rush's beginning
was when I saw a mother take her screaming toddler out through the
EXIT because she could find her screaming child's stuffed platypus.
That one hurt…bad. Finally, they stopped coming, and I got everyone seated.

"I'LL TAKE YOUR DRINK ORDERS IN JUST A MO-
MENT," I called out. "Y'ALL BEAR WITH ME, AND WE'LL
GET RIGHT TO THIS."

I needed Natalie by my side, helping, but I wasn't afraid to handle
this by myself. I slipped into the employee bathroom where I found
Natalie as I expected her. Sitting on the sink, arrogantly puffing away
on a smoke.

"WHAT ARE YOU DOING, GIRL?" I hollered. "WE'VE GOT WORK TO DO—WE'RE SLAMMED."

"I'm busy." She took another long pull from the cigarette and blew the smoke in my face. "I'm sure you can handle it on your own."

"YOU BETTER GET YOUR FANNY OUT THERE AND START TAKING ORDERS, MISSY. WHERE'S FLYSWAT?"

"I don't know." She threw the cigarette to the ground. The cherry exploded into an orange supernova on the black and white checkered patterns. The cigarette, still smoking, rolled to the drain in the middle of the floor. "He's been missing a lot lately. Guess he's just tired of your crap."

I almost lost it. I wanted to grab that sassy little trollop by her hair and shake her until some sense found its way into her thick skull.

"Look, we've got a job to do here. The way I see it, it's not that hard, and you meet some interesting people, folks no other job would ever let you come in contact with."

"I don't care much for people. Never did."

"I don't care much for you, Natalie." I started for the lobby to take drink orders. Looking back, I shouldn't have turned my back on her. I should have realized the look in her eyes meant she'd reached her breaking point.

Natalie grabbed my hair and pulled herself off the sink—despite my situation, I can still feel. I saw red and went to my knees with an ear-piercing yelp. She got a cheap shot in my rib cage, but I retaliated by standing back up and shoving her into the sink. I guess I knocked the wind out of her because she loosened up her hold, giving me the opportunity to spin myself around and slap her across her face. He blue eyes blazed, and she charged—we both hit the green door of the bathroom stall, and I heard the snap of the sliding lock buckle on the other side.

"I'M GONNA KILL YOU," she screamed.

"I'M ALREADY DEAD." I pounded my fists against her shoulders and arms. I wanted to dig my fingernails into the side of her face, take a chunk out of her almost-pretty looks, but I couldn't quite reach around. She screamed when I kneed her right thigh, attacking harder than before. Flyswat pushed open the door, and through the fury I saw a startled look cross his face.

"**Ladies**," he shrieked. "Miss Brite—stop—stop." He rushed behind Natalie, pulling her off. "You two better stop. Mr. Dirge is g-gonna be mad...real mad. I d-don't wanna get in t-trouble." I've known Flyswat a long time, and he only stutters when I yell or when Dirge asks questions. I gasped when he finally extracted Natalie off me.

"I hate you, Valerie." Tears rolled down Natalie's face. Flyswat tightened his restraint, holding her arms behind her back. She squirmed and tugged but he wouldn't let her go.

The back of my head throbbed, and my ribs ached. A glance in the mirror revealed my disheveled appearance. My hair was a disaster, knotted and sticking up, and my make-up was smeared. I looked like a freak, and I still had tables to wait on.

"This isn't over, Natalie," I warned. "We'll finish this later—you and me."

"Bring it on, Val. I'm not scared."

"You should be, little girl. You should be."

"Come on, guys," pleaded Flyswat. "We can't fight like this. There're a lot of hungry souls out there, and we need to tend to their needs—that's why we're here. That's what we do...remember?"

I looked at his eyes. He was about to weep, and I knew he was right. I looked dreadful, but I couldn't stop. Something told me more souls would be in behind this lot, and there would be no rest for us. I knew by his clean apron Flyswat sensed it too.

He relaxed his hold on Natalie, and she shrugged her shoulders when she slid free. Glancing over, I decided she looked just as disarrayed. It was almost...funny. I didn't let humor overwhelm the moment, though. It was time to get to work.

"Tidy yourself up, Natalie. I'll be out there getting all of the drink orders. When you've made yourself up, start filling up cups with ice so we can knock them out." She nodded, and I turned to Flyswat. "You have enough prep to handle this?"

"You know it, Miss Brite."

"Good. Let's turn and burn."

I looked over to Natalie again. She was fixing her hair with a brush she got from her third or fourth table, and her compact was out on the counter attached to the sink. I've noticed she fancies blues and reds like the common streetwalker, but the colors she has out are closer to my predilections—a beige foundation with a hint of blush and chestnut lipstick—really quite tasteful.

I flattened my hair down with my palms while exiting the employee bathroom, Flyswat in close pursuit. We split up at the dish room, and I passed the drink and salad stations, pushing my way through the swinging doors to the cacophony of the dining room. The wall of sound was appalling—some were crying, some were laughing, and most were just engaged in bewildered conversation.

I began to make my rounds, table to table, writing as fast as I ever had in my life. I used my own system of shorthand for the drinks, placing tally marks behind abbreviated codes for each beverage. By the time I had gathered the orders, I had six Cokes, four Sprites, a root beer, ten iced teas, two waters (one with lemon), and three coffees. One gentleman desired hot tea, but switched to water when he learned we don't serve Pennyroyal.

I completed the rounds quickly—faster than I would normally care to. As I mentioned before, I like to make folks comfortable with what's going on...most of the time. There are always exceptions to the rules. Douglas McSweenly, for example, rubbed me the wrong way, and he started out with my less than concerned service. What can I say, I'm only human. Sort of.

I pushed my way back through the swinging doors and saw Flyswat filling fry baskets with frozen French fries.

"Where's Natalie?" I asked. He looked over at me and shrugged. "Has she come out of the bathroom yet?"

"I think so...is she out there?"

"I didn't see her." Unable to hide the despair in my voice, I moaned, "Darn it, I told her to fill up the glasses with ice."

Flyswat set the fry basket down. "Don't you worry, Miss Brite. Just leave the ticket, and I'll fill the drink orders. They'll be ready by the time you get back with the first six orders." Sometimes, enough pressure turns otherwise inert minerals into a gem, such as a diamond. This was one of those moments. I guess there can be genius in simplicity. I nodded, accepting Flyswat's plan.

Back through the swinging doors and into the frenzy, I started at table 8, working my way counter clockwise around the dining room in groups of six or seven. Flyswat was right, by clumping up the tables we were able to get the kitchen in a flow. After the first six, I picked up the drinks he'd prepared in exchange for the batch of orders. By the time I had taken the next set of tables, the original orders were steaming in the window, and we worked the diner into that sort of motion until every table had been waited on.

After I gave the last table their final meals, I strolled back over to the pick-up window and looked out over the dining room, filled with life, or what used to be life. I sighed. They had worked me to the bone, but I felt as if I handled everything smooth. I peered through the window to the kitchen and saw Flyswat using a grill brush to clean the burnt carbon off his pit grill.

"Hey, Flyswat," I called in. It took him by surprise because he jumped, dropping the brush on the kitchen floor with a *clatter-clink*.

"Oh, wow, Miss Brite." He took a beep breath and shot me a sheepish grin. "You scared me to death."

"Good job tonight." He blushed and looked at his toes.

"T-thanks."

"Have you seen Natalie around anywhere?"

"Not since I pulled her off of you, Miss Brite." He picked up the brush and returned to scrubbing.

"I wonder where that wench ran off to." I still had the hardest part of the evening ahead of me. The clean up would be no problem, but telling my customers they needed to go through the EXIT when they were finished was a completely different matter. As usual, some of the diners knew their numbers were up, but others had no idea how they wound up in the small diner with the infinite galaxy beyond the glass windows.

I handled delivering the news as I always did—kind to those deserving and stern to the unworthy.

One unsuspecting table thought they were the mark of a ruse on some hidden camera TV show when I broke the news to them. I assured them it was no trickery, and they were not going to be on television. Funny, over the duration I've been here, I've heard many people talk about a myriad of subjects, but it seems a lot of my folks love TV. I've always enjoyed novels—but I hear all types of stories about their favorite programs and how upset they are for not ever being able to find out what happened to so-and-so. Sure, I liked TV when I was alive. It was fun, something to do. I liked other things— swimming and guys and music. When I imagine how important people have made a little box with flickering pictures, I laugh. Maybe I'm just out of touch.

I've kept up with expressions for the most part, but fashion is mysterious to me. I've seen people with silver in their faces and ink in their skin like godless savages, and I wonder what kind of shape the world is in. My father would have killed me if I ever drew in my flesh—he raised me up proper. Maybe I'll never understand, and that's where the trouble between Natalie and me stems from—we're from two different times, worlds even.

At another table—a family of three—the mother began crying and blubbering, which in turn frightened their nine-year-old daughter. The father, bless his heart, hugged his bawling daughter and massaged his wife's shoulders, assuring her everything would be hunky-dory. I couldn't watch them go out, so I preoccupied myself with another table.

About this time, the tables that knew they were no longer among the living were finding their way out the EXIT, and some called to me, others grumbled, and one or two laughed as they pushed their way into endlessness.

A funny thing about this place and the people that come through here—some of them have no idea that they are dining amongst other people. They go through the entire meal ignorant to a soul or two sitting in nearby booths. They don't seem to ever bump into others, and my only explanation for this is that they are running off some grander plan to keep the end of their paths as simple as possible. They also can't hear the other patrons; again my feelings about why this happens are nothing more than casual hunches.

Then, there are the ones that see every poor passer-through in the restaurant. They comment on things the other patrons are saying and even have the ability to take things from them—trust me, when it happens, it really messes with those who can't see anyone else—not that I think it's funny, or anything.

One of last tables (grilled chicken sandwich and fries, side of mayo) took me by surprise. When I told the guy with a satanic looking rock and roll T-shirt and torn blue jeans his meal was paid for and he was on his way to destiny, he laughed. I thought he was some kind of devil worshipper by the looks of him, but he explained his devotion to the church and how he hoped to be reunited with his scripture-loving grandmother. I told him I thought he looked evil, but he insisted it was just his style and that he would be holding hands with Christ once he ventured through the EXIT. Talk about mixed signals.

The rush passed, and I was left with just one gentleman dressed in swimming trunks who entered the restaurant towards the end of the rush. He'd made the tragic mistake of jumping into the deep end of the YMCA pool after eating three double cheeseburgers and a medium fry at a Wendy's in Philly—needless to include, he sank like a lead egg.

I stood by hall leading to the customer bathrooms, surveying the havoc the catastrophic pile up on I-95 had wrought. Every table was dirty, and the checkered floor looked as if a three-year-old had uneashed his wrath, tossing whatever wherever. To think folks would have the self-respect to not litter for just a few short minutes before crossing to the beyond…people. The mess was vile, and I had no desire to clean it up. Handling the incident took a lot out of me, and it was time for Natalie to pull some of her weight.

I pushed my way through the swinging doors and headed straight for the employee washroom, thinking she was still ogling herself in the cracked mirror. When I stormed in, I was ready to pounce; however, to my dismay she wasn't there. Other then the unappealing lingering aroma of burnt tobacco, there was no trace of my lazy coworker. I grumbled and went to the kitchen where Flyswat was filtering his fryers.

"Where is she, Flyswat?"

He flinched. "Uh, I haven't seen her, Miss Brite, and I just came from the coolers. Umm, Did you check the bathroom?"

"First place I looked, Flyswat. She's just disappeared."

"Well, what about the stockroom? Did you go back there?"

"No. Haven't looked in there yet." Really, I hate going back there. Two reasons: first, there's always dry goods to unpack, organize, and store (I despise the extra work) and, second, for lack of a better word, it's simply scary back there. When you go back into the stockroom, it's quieter than a tomb, and there is something in the stillness that gnaws at my nerves. It's not a place for a lady.

"Just go on back," Flyswat urged. "I've put up all the stock for the week, so nothing's should be in your way."

"Thanks," I groaned, not wanting go back there. The things you do for your job, right?

I sighed and went through the kitchen, into the cramped hall, where the flickering fluorescent lights pain the eyes. My footfalls echoed clump, clump, clump. The hallway opened into the L-shaped stock room, and I marveled at Flyswat's organization.

All of the dry stock was stacked in one corner—the napkins above the toilet paper and the hand towels beside the salt and pepper packets. On the right, a shelf filled with the table condiments.

Ketchup, hot sauce, pickled jalapeños, and mustard packets rest above
rows of our canned salad veggies, like chic peas and black olives. No
food touches the floor, for sanitary reasons.

The back of the rectangular room turns left, and, in addition to
other stock odds and ends, it is where the water heater, soda lines,
and main ice machine are located.

I turned and went to the back, where I found Natalie curled up in
a ball on the right-hand side of the ice machine, crying.

"Oh, no," I said, kneeling before her. She looked up at me, the
mascara she applied in the restroom at the beginning of the rush running down her cheeks.

"I don't want to be here," she sobbed, greenish-brown mucus
running from her right nostril. Part of me still wanted to slap her,
but I couldn't deny another urge to hold her.

"Well, it's our lot." Unsure of the proper words, I hated being in
the spooky stock room with this woman I barely knew and liked even
less. "Whether we want it or not."

She pushed hair stuck to her brow out of the way, and I saw the
scars along her wrists again. I wondered what pushed her to the
point of taking her own life, but I knew this was not the time to be
nosey. I was sure there was a logical reason why she ran down an
already inescapable fate, but at this point in our relationship, I needed
not pry.

"Are they all gone?" She rubbed her eyes and smeared her mascara even more.

"They're gone, but they've left an awful mess." She looked into
my eyes, blinking twice. "It needs to be cleaned up. If we work together, it'll be spotless in a jiffy." I extended my hand.

She hesitated. "Is Mr. Dirge going to punish me?"

"I don't know," I sighed. "Help me clean this up."

She took my hand and I pulled her to her feet—she steadied herself on the ice machine before she regained her balance. She wiped
her tear-stained eyes again, and sniffed. The girl needed to spend

some time in front of a mirror, but there was no time for that. We had work to do.

As we walked back towards the hall leading to the kitchen, our footsteps *clumped, clumped*, mixing with the sound of our breathing.

"What was that door behind the ice machine?" asked Natalie, regaining control of her voice.

"Door?"

"Yeah, I saw something that looked like a door when I was… when I was crying."

"I don't know. I try not to go back there."

"Why not?"

"I just don't like it, Natalie. I get a weird feeling—like I don't belong."

"I've felt that way since I got here."

I stopped and stared at her. This girl fled from something horrible, and found herself in purgatory. A lousy hand, indeed. I had no words for her—I nodded and continued to the kitchen, Natalie close behind.

~VANION~

All types come through my doors. Some are pleasant…total joys to wait on. They're they type that kick down make-up or clothes, or leave you laughing from a good joke. Others are rude. Some come, making no impression—as if they were ghosts drifting along. Some rock your world, entirely changing you.

It had been going slow. A table here and there or the occasional two-top from an automobile wreck or double homicide, nothing outrageous like the I-95 pile up. Natalie was taking orders regularly, and it was no surprise to discover she was a bit of a whiner.

It seemed as if nothing satisfied her. If it wasn't a complaint about the customers, it was her nails or her hair or the same unquenchable thirst plaguing me. I found it annoying, not because things bothered her, but because she wouldn't cease her irksome nagging. The price you pay for getting to know people.

We were wiping off this one table where this woman in her mid-thirties dropped her cup of coffee after we told her what type of water she was in. Her drink ran off the table and onto the booth, and the lady started yelling and pounding her fists on the table, knocking over the salt and pepper. She went out the EXIT yelling about who was going to take care of her cat, leaving me with the lingering impression that she was the victim of cardiac arrest.

"I didn't like her," Natalie said. "She reminded me of my Aunt Lucia. Ug." I didn't say anything, just kept on wiping the tabletop. "People leave a lot of loose ends behind, don't they?"

I stopped wiping and frowned, not wanting to get into this one. "I guess they do." Worse than loose ends, most folks die with secrets, too. Big ones...

"I bet she henpecked her husband," she said.

"I wouldn't know."

"She was wearing a ring. What kind of desperate fool slaps a ring on a cow like that?"

"Men have many reasons why they do things." I was unable to mask my sly smile. "Whether they make sense or not is another story."

"I never married."

"Nor I."

"All the guys at school thought I was a little strange." I detected a little nervousness in her voice. "Go figure."

"I was the toast of the town when I was alive. My father had money, and I was quite a dish."

"I bet." I hoped she wouldn't poke further. "If you were the hottest thing since sunburn—" The *ping-a-tonk* of the front door cut her short.

"I got this one," I told her. "You finish here." Natalie rolled her eyes but continued scrubbing the sticky mess.

I saw Dirge escorting this handsome guy to table 13. He was
inky and dressed in all black. His long-sleeved dress shirt hung
open, revealing a muscular build and a tattoo of a crescent waxing
moon on his shaved chest above his right nipple. The way he followed Mr. Dirge, you'd think they were best friends—he strolled in as
if he didn't own a care in the world.

He *squeaked* in his seat, Dirge breezed out of the restaurant quiet
as ice, and I stood before his table, order pad in hand.

"Hey, sweetie," I said. "What are you having to drink tonight?"

"Hmm," he said, scratching his chin's stubble—his unkempt
roughness reminded me of Gordon. "I guess since this is it, I'd better make a wise choice." He knew. That always makes it easier, but
he seemed so calm, collected, as if he'd waited all his life for this.

"I guess so," I said, flirting. He smelled of burning cloves with a
dash of cinnamon—irresistible.

"I've always been a fan of red wine mixed with Diet soda. Do
you have any Merlot?"

"I'm sorry, hun. We don't have any wine, beer, or liquor here."

"Pity." He cocked an eyebrow. "A last penchant unfulfilled." He
chuckled. "I'll have root beer, my lady." I smiled and wrote his drink
order down on the bottom of the blank ticket.

"I'll be right back with that," I said, and he shot me a wink. I
felt myself blush—he was incredibly charming...hitting on me too.
I glided over to the swinging doors and hopped in, whistling a little
tune.

As soon as I started filling up his glass with ice, Natalie bounced
over to me.

"My stars, Val," she squeaked. "Do you know who that is?"

"No. He's trying to pick me up."

"You're kidding."

"No. I think he likes me. Do you know him?"

"Not exactly," she said. "But I listen to his music."

"Music?"

"He's a rock star. His name's Vanion, and he sings for a band called Bad Apple. They had a couple of hits recently. I saw them in Birmingham last spring at the Verizon Center—they totally rock."

"A rock star, huh?" I play a little piano, but it's been an eternity and I'm nothing special.

"You have to let me serve him." She steepled her fingers.

"WHAT? A little while ago I couldn't pay you to take a table. Now, you want to wait on him?"

"I want to do more than wait on him," she giggled.

"Natalie." I couldn't believe she was acting this way, but I understood where she was coming from—he was easy on the eyes.

"Come on. Let me take him, please."

"No, and quit begging—it's unattractive." She puckered up her face, and I filled Vanion's glass with root beer, letting the fizz settle before topping it off.

Natalie huffed and flew through the swinging doors—they *chirped* as they swung back shut. I grabbed a straw from my apron and balanced it between my pointer and middle finger, picking up the cup with the same hand. This allows me to rest the straw on top of the cup when I set it in front of my thirsty customer, like it's ready to be sipped on. Yet another one of my signature touches.

I went through the swinging doors—they *chirped* again—and I saw Natalie hovering over Vanion, laughing and running her hands through her hair. I knew she was only flirting, but it boiled my blood. He was my table, my responsibility. When I got to table 13, I pushed Natalie out of the way with my hip.

"Hey," she said as I rested the root beer before Vanion.

"Excuse me," I exaggerated my Southern drawl, "but this man was thirsty."

Vanion smirked. "Really, there's no hurry."

"See?" said Natalie. "He's not in a hurry."

"Why don't you make yourself useful for once and go help Fly-swat do whatever it is he does in the kitchen," I suggested, pulling out my order pad and pen. Vanion ripped the paper casing from the straw.

The front door sang *ping-a-tonk*, and I saw Dirge lead this obese woman to table 42.

"You got one," I said to Natalie. "Better see what they need." Her forehead scrunched up, and she whipped out her order pad and stomped over to the new table. I smiled, focusing my attention on Vanion, sipping his drink. "I'm guessing you're a steak man."

"I do like steak," he confirmed, "but I think I'm in the mood for something different."

"Really?" I said, surprised.

"Yeah, I took a look at the menu while you were getting my root beer, and I think I'll have the grilled chicken, side of French fries." I jotted his order down, and he said, "I wonder what happened to that lady over there."

"Who?" I asked.

"The big lady Death brought in. I tend to wonder about folks—their stories, you know?"

"You can see her?" I asked.

"You can see a lot if you just look. I guess most people don't see things quite like I do."

"I guess not."

"Making music opened my mind. I know it might sound crazy, but I, myself, am music." I blinked, unsure of how to reply. "I was 19 or so, and one night I came home after a long night of jamming and drinking, laid in my bed, and found I couldn't sleep. Usually, I listened to my Cure CDs to help ease me into Sandman's land, but, on this occasion, I was too tore up to pick out something I wanted to hear. I was laying there, in the dark, and I heard how my breathing, my heartbeat, and even the blood circulating in my veins all played together harmoniously. I wasn't just making music—I *was* music."

"Wow," I said, genuinely impressed. "You're pretty young, how old were you when you died?"

"Twenty-seven."

"Do you know how you died?"

"I fancy I drank myself to death," he laughed. "I don't remember exactly. When Death called, I followed. I knew it was him, and I knew I was going on a journey."

"Odd," I commented.

"I've been singing songs about him for five years now—on almost every continent on this planet," he said. "Our paths have even crossed before, but that's another story. See, all my music is about either love or death. Love is something we can experience during a lifetime, but death… I've spent my entire life thinking and dreaming about Death, and, now that I'm here, I have a few questions."

"Questions?"

"Yeah, just a few things before I head wherever it is I'm heading. Can you answer some things for me? Or do I need to wait for the guy in the expensive suit?"

"I don't think you'll get him to talk. He doesn't say much, and, although he's fair, he's not what you'd call friendly. Me, I'll answer what I can, but, really, I'm no expert."

"I'd appreciate it," he smiled. Vanion was certainly good-looking.

I smiled back and turned for the kitchen. I saw Natalie hand the obese woman a cup of coffee before I pushed through the swinging doors—*chirp*.

"Hey, Flyswat. Where are you? I got an order?" I passed the drink station and then the dish room, entered the kitchen and looked around, but he wasn't anywhere in sight. "Come on, Flyswat. Where are you?"

I didn't want to go to the back, to the stockroom, but I didn't know what else to do.

I took a deep breath and started for the back.

Flyswat almost bumped into me he came around the corner so fast, and he had this funny look in his eyes.

"M-miss Brite. Did you need something?"

"Yeah…we got an…order. Where were you? I was in the stockroom not that long ago, and everything was put away. You haven't had a truck come in have you?"

"No, no. I was just, uh, just looking for something. In the back."

"Uh huh."

"So, we got one?"

"Yeah, a smart one, too. He's got a lot of questions about this place, and I guess I'm going to tell him what I know."

"All right. Is that the ticket?" I nodded and tore it from the pad, handing him Vanion's order. Flyswat looked it over and grinned, turning to the reach-in where he kept the raw meat. "It'll be up shortly."

"Thanks. Take your time, this guy is interesting." I turned and headed for the swinging doors. They *chirped* when I pushed it open, and I stopped, calling back, "Hey, Flyswat, can you oil this door? It's driving me crazy."

"No problem, Miss Brite," he called, and I *chirped* back out to the dining room.

I stopped in my tracks—Natalie was all over Vanion, kissing him and rubbing her hands all over his chest. She had him straddled in the booth, and he was working his hands up her shirt. I gasped— they were moments away from knowing each other in the biblical sense in front of everyone in the dining room. I'll admit, I was cavalier in my day, but what they were doing was obscene, whether they could be seen or not.

"HEY, HEY, HEY," I screamed. "WHAT ARE YOU TWO DOING? THIS IS A PUBLIC PLACE."
Natalie looked over her shoulder towards me, her hair falling in her face.

"Chill out, Valerie. Why don't you go back into the back and help Flyswat do whatever it is he does back there." She stuck her tongue out before resuming making out with Vanion.
The words burned me bad—I realized that working with this girl was hell, further punishment for all my slanted deeds in life. I knew my

face was red, and I turned, racing back through the swinging doors, *chirp, chirp.*

I paced back and fourth in front of the dishwashing machine, swearing under my breath. I could hear the sound of the French fries cooking in the back, and I heard the *sizzling* of the chicken breasts being laid on the grill.

I was so angry about what was happening in my dining room, I punched the side of the dishwasher. Pain shot through my entire arm, and I shook my hand in an unsuccessful attempt to brush it off. Flyswat rushed to my side, wearing a worried look. "What happened, Miss Brite?"

"I punched the darned dish machine," I said, rubbing my wounded fist.

"Are you OK?"

"Yeah, just stupid. That Natalie girl is going to be the death of me."

"Death of you?"

"Just an expression, Flyswat." I hated her as much as the itch in my throat. No one ever said being damned was going to be easy.

"Is everything all right out there?" He looked over my shoulder through the Plexiglas diamond. "Oh."

"Has this ever happened before?" He scratched his head and shrugged. I swallowed hard. "Mr. Dirge is going to flip."

"What do we do?" He was trying not to look back out through the diamond window, I caught him stealing little peeks.

"I'm not sure."

He looked back towards the kitchen and gasped, "My food." I smiled—he really does a good job here—unlike that trollop in the dining room. He picked up his spatula and quarter turned the chicken, finishing his perfect grill marks. Presentation is an important aspect of cooking, and all of Flyswat's food looks pretty when it hits the table.

I decided to give it up. There was no use in yelling at Natalie, he was going to do whatever she wanted to do—I had no control. I sighed and went into the kitchen to watch Flyswat finish the meal.

After marking the chicken, he flipped it over and grabbed one of the plates in the serving window. He ripped a piece of kale from bin on the expediting table, and placed it at twelve o'clock on the plate. He took a lemon wedge and nestled it in the kale, completing the garnish.

He went to the fryers and pulled out the basket holing the fries, dumping them under a bin warmed by heat lamps by the expediting table. He salted the fries with his own Cajun seasoning and then used scoop to place them on the right-hand side of the plate.

He scooped the plate up and took it over to the grill where he extracted the chicken with the spatula and served it beside the fries. The meal looked scrumptious, and I salivated at its toothsome glory, forgetting how thirsty I always am.

He set the plate in the pick-up window, and hit the bell, *bing*, shooting me a morose look. "Order up."

"I hope they're done out there," I said.

"I want no part of it," replied Flyswat, returning to his grill and picking up the grill brush.

"Here goes nothing." I grabbed the plate from the Pick-up window and headed towards the swinging doors. I turned my back and walked backwards through the swinging doors, *chirp, chirp*, holding my breath.

I almost didn't want to turn around, but, when I did, I found they had finished their carnal pursuits. An unkempt Natalie sat beside Vanion smoking a cigarette and stroking his arm. I was hot because she had betrayed me—there needs to be order in here, or Dirge will punish us all. Looking over, I saw the obese woman twiddling her thumbs and looking around, a sign of boredom and bad service. Smiling, I set the food before Vanion and shot Natalie a dirty look.

"You need to tend to your table," I said, not attempting to hide my anger.

"Whatever," Natalie said. She kissed Vanion on the cheek and *squeaked* out of the booth. She looked like she'd just had a roll in the hay, and it sickened me to think of the sub-par service she was doling out.

"Enjoy yourself?" I asked Vanion, who was cutting into his chicken.

"Yeah," he chuckled. "I can't go anywhere without meeting fans."

"So," I said, unable to conceal my disgust, "what did you want to know about this place?"

"Mmm. This is some of the finest bird I've ever had the fortune to taste."

"Well, it's going to be the last."

"I'm sorry to have inconvenienced you, miss. I couldn't help myself—a woman's touch is one of my favorite experiences...up there with listening to and playing music."

"Well, I hope it was worth it. What about those questions?"

"You're angry."

"Damn right, I am."

"I wasn't trying to offend."

"Not my problem. Now, what about those questions?"

"Look, I know it's probably been a long time since you've been with a man, but if you're jealous, don't be. I still have some fight in me if you need some affection."

"YOU BEAST."

He laughed. "I guess I'm an American satyr, darling. Eat, drink, and be merry, for now I have died."

"I hate to burst your ego, but I'm not interested," I lied, crossing my arms against my chest. "I fact, I thought you were a dreamboat until your actions showed me what a pig you are."

"Really?"

"You have no respect for women. You see them as disposable... things for you to use and throw away."

"Just met me, and ya think you have me figured out, huh?"

I nodded. "You claim to have experienced love while you dream of death, but I don't think you know the first thing about either one."

Vanion leaned back, resting his silverware on his plate. "Do you?"

"What?"

"Do you know anything about love or death?" he asked.

I could not hide the redness I felt in my face. "I know they're both not what anyone thinks they are."

Vanion leaned forward. "What if I told you I had the greatest love in the world, and after I lost her, nothing mattered?"

"Everyone has heartache," I said.

"Yes, lovers come and go. But, once in a lifetime, you meet The One. To have a chance with that person... If you lose The One, nothing matters after that. Life becomes a string of experiences, and I chose to chase pleasure. Many drinks and many women made me feel good. But know, to live with a lost heart—most everything loses meaning after that." He smiled and picked up his fork. "Still going to answer my questions?"

I waited a moment before answering. "Sure, I'll do what I can."

"All right," he said, drinking a sip of his root beer. "This isn't Hell, right? In Hell I wouldn't have scored a meal and a woman."

"I don't believe this is Hell, Vanion."

"Is this Heaven?"

"No, I don't think that it is. It's more like somewhere in-between."

"Purgatory?"

"No, just a diner," I said, lying a little. For him it's a stepping stone; for me, the worst job imaginable.

"When I look out the windows, all I see are stars," he said. "It's grander than any night sky I've ever known, and I've looked up all over the world."

"And?"

"And, I was wondering if we're in outer space—some sort of eighth-and-a-half dimension?"

"No, just a diner." I leaned closer and said, "Sometimes I like to think all those stars out there are other places just like this. Each one its own restaurant with souls passing through to wherever they go. It makes me feel not so lonely, you know?"

He looked at the infinite stars, at endless space, and smiled, taking another bite of chicken.

When he swallowed, he said, "Where does all this food come from?"

"It comes on a truck, like a normal restaurant."

"Where do you unload it at?"

"In the back, we have a door that opens up. The truck drivers ring a bell and our line cook opens up so they can unload."

"And these drivers?"

"Same as me," I told him. "Working off debts."

He ate a couple French fries (funny, no ketchup) and then said, "My family always told me I was going to Hell for the way I lived my life."

"Who said you're not going to Hell?"

"True," he smiled. "Good point." He leaned back and said, "Really, I don't believe in Hell."

"Yeah?" I asked.

"I'm Wiccan," he said. "It's a nature-based religion. We worship the moon and various other deities—both male and female. Everything has balance, and all energy maintains that balance. Yin and yang. You ask for something, you must give back."

"Seems to me you've taken quite a bit during your time."

"I've tried to do good. Make up for my excesses by helping communities and donating to youth groups and shelters. Heck, my will says a large section of my estate is to help save rainforests. Balance."

I couldn't decide if I liked Vanion or not. He was extremely good looking and kind, albeit narcissistic. There was a confidence in the way he held himself, a sort of vibe that said he was going to come on top no matter what the situation was. I found myself wishing Natalie hadn't tainted him—that it was me who had felt his touch.

We were all going to get into trouble for her actions, and I had nothing to do with it.

On top of it all, I was thirsty.

"What else?" The back of my throat burned. Although it wouldn't scratch the itch, I needed a glass of water, bad.

"What do you think happens to the people who walk through that door?" He took the last bite of his chicken and chewed slowly.

"Honestly?" He nodded. "I think it's different for everyone. I think some of the Christians who come through here go to Heaven, Buddhists find nirvana on the other side of that door, and Islamic folks find Allah. I think you find what you're looking for on the other side of that door."

He smiled. "Even if it is a person? Do you think it is possible to have a reunion out there?"

I did not know how to answer him. "What do Wiccans think happens to the soul after they pass on?"

"I think we all believe in something different. Me, personally, I believe in the First Law of Energy—that it can't be created or destroyed, it only changes shape. I think my energy will scatter and go into places that need it. I'll be everything all at once, a tree, a rock, a soaring eagle…music."

I decided I liked Vanion.

"I just hope someone remembers me."

"I think they will."

"My compliments to the chef."

"You didn't finish your fries."

He looked at the plate and then to me. "I'm full. And eager to see what's out there. Honestly, after I walk through that door and my energy scatters, I hope I find the arms of someone I lost. Someone I once bargained Death for." Before I could speak, he asked, "Do I owe anything?"

"No."

"At least let me sing you a song. You're right, I took a lot in my lifetime. It's the least I can do for your food and information."

"Fair enough," I said, blushing a little.

He closed his eyes and took a beep breath before he sang to me with a voice from an angel:

> "Petite beautiful gypsy girl
> Soft white skin, hair of curls
> Eyes reflecting silver moon
> Dance with me till you must go
>
> Fancy delicate gypsy dress
> Snake green folds, spider webs
> Filling night with haunted songs
> Dance with me till we find dawn
>
> Pretty porcelain gypsy hand
> Chipped black nails, want of man
> Lips opening upon warm throat
> Dance with me till I must go"

Vanion *squeaked* out of his seat. He gave me a warm hug. "Tell Natalie goodbye for me."

"I will."

He nodded and started for the exit, looking back once at the obese woman, still waiting for her order. He got to the EXIT and stopped, glancing towards me.

"See you later, Valerie. Second star to the right, straight on till dawn." He opened the door and stepped into the inky blackness. I swear, as he vanished into eternal night, the most haunting melody I've ever heard tickled my ears.

~FOR NOW~

Natalie and I had issues. She wasn't listening to any of my re-
uests and smoking whenever she could panhandle cigarettes from
ur guests. I try to keep a level head in every situation; however,
e had been grinding personalities from, well, from as long as we'd
nown each other. Sometimes, you just lose face.

The restaurant had just emptied. I was straightening out my last
irty table when I heard an absolute disaster come from the kitchen,
s if dishes had broken or pots had slammed into each other.

"FLYSWAT. WHAT'S GOING ON IN THERE?" I didn't hear
n answer, so I threw the damp towel I was using on the table, my
ork halfway finished. I was mad, he'd been disappearing so much
tely, and it was getting on my nerves. We're supposed to be a team,
nd when I can't count on a member of my team, I get ticked.

I went through the swinging doors, murder on my mind, and,
ven though Flyswat had oiled them and they no longer *chirped,* there
as no calming me down.

As soon as I reached the drink/salad stations, Natalie stopped me
1 my tracks.

"What's the problem, Val?" I wanted to slap her.

"What was that noise, Natalie? Sounded like a hurricane ripped
hrough here."

"I dropped some dishes. Just an accident, no big deal." I knew
he was lying, her eyes gave the deception away. We were coming to
point in our relationship where either she was going to straighten
p, or I was going to have a talk with Mr. Dirge.

Flyswat came around the corner, strange expression on his face,
nd he stopped when he saw me. "Something wrong, Miss Brite?"

"I heard a noise…is everything OK?"

"Yeah, everything's kiwi strawberries." I didn't quite understand
is lingo, but his body language lead me to believe that things were
osher. Lately, I'd found myself trusting him—not an emotion I give
nto easily.

Ping-a-tonk.

It was time to work, and the Law of Balance told me it was my table—Natalie had waited on the last—an Italian wanting a plate of spaghetti. Although it's not something on our menu, Flyswat was able to whip up a bowl, red sauce and all. I guess it was part of his private stash, or something.

I abandoned the noise and returned to the dinging room where Dirge was seating a middle-aged man wearing a camouflage jump sui and a bright orange vest at table 4. I put on my best smile and pulled out my order pad, reaching his table by the time Dirge was leaving the entrance. Mr. Dirge paused before he went back out, shooting me a look. I wondered if he knew what Natalie had done with that musician, and shivers tingled up and down my spine.

"How are you?" I asked my table.

"How'd I get here? I was in the woods...hunting..."

"Welcome to Café Elysium," I said. "What can we get you to drink?"

"I like Shirley Temples. Do you guys have those here?"

"You know, I think I can whip one up." The first customer who ordered a Shirley Temple from me had me stumped. It was a teenage girl who died from a fatal snakebite in her grandmother's back yard, and she had to explain how to prepare it.

"Thanks," he said, and I noticed a wet stain in the camouflage, possibly blood. I nodded and went to the swinging doors, almost bumping into Natalie on the other side.

"Excuse you, Natalie."

"You need to watch where you're going, Valerie. Other people work here besides you."

"HA, you call what you do here work?"

"What are you saying?"

"I'm saying you barely lift a finger. I had to practically force you to start taking orders, you wont prep salad dressings, you ignore your tables, you break the news to the guests as if their feelings don't matter, and, most of all, I don't like you, Natalie."

She lunged, pushing me into the salad station, the countertop's corner jabbing my skin. Pain shot through my body as I grabbed for her hair.

"FLYSWAT," I hollered into the kitchen before Natalie wrapped her fingers around my neck, choking me.

"He's not gonna come because he's not here." In her voice, a blend of elation and madness. "I'm gonna make you wish you never met me." She tightened her grip, hurting my neck. I've contemplated what would happen if I died here, but it seemed improbable.

I stomped her foot. She yelped, loosening her death grip enough for me to get my arms in between hers and remove her hands from my throat. Now that I'd regained my balance, I shoved her with every ounce of anger in my soul, knocking her to the floor.

I pounced on Natalie, both of us screaming, clawing, and hair pulling on the ground. Natalie opened the salad station door, knocking it against my forehead. I spun over, flipping her underneath me, and I pounded her chest and head with my fists. Natalie threw up her arms in an attempt to shield my blows, but I—in pugilist mode—hit harder and harder, hell bent on seeing if I could kill the woman underneath me.

It would not have been the first time I've taken a life.

"STOP, GIRLS, STOP. WHAT ARE YOU TWO DOING?" Flyswat was yanking me off her. I tried to pull free, but his hold was stronger than my tempest. Natalie stood up, her hair tangled and her make-up smeared. A rivulet of blood dripped from her nose, and she wiped it with the back of her hand, smearing the crimson across her cheek.

"I'm gonna kill you, Val."

I lunged, but Flyswat had me.

"Nobody's doing nothing." Flyswat never lost his hold. "Natalie, you're bleeding. You need to clean yourself up in the bathroom. Miss Brite, do you have any tables?"

"Yes," I said as Natalie slipped away towards the employee washroom. "Just one." *Ping-a-tonk.* "Two."

"I'll take care of them." He let me go. "You go to the customer bathroom and fix yourself up. After we clear the restaurant, we three are going to sit in the dining room and straighten things out."

"I'm not willing to straighten things out, Flyswat. That harlot has crossed the line. In fact, I'm telling Mr. Dirge what has been going on around here, and you know he's not going to be thrilled."

Flyswat's eyes widened. "Please don't bring him into this. We can fix this ourselves."

I took a deep breath. I didn't know if I wanted to fix things with Natalie—it just seemed like I was right and she was wrong. I knew my table was waiting for their drink, and there was another table behind the hunter I hadn't even greeted yet. I knew I looked horrendous, and I didn't want to infringe upon our service, so I gave in.

"All right, Flyswat. The guy in the camouflage wanted a Shirley Temple." Flyswat grinned. "You gonna take care of him?"

"You bet, Miss Brite. I'll treat them right, just like you."

"Thanks." I watched him pour grenadine over the fizzing Sprite and then toss it back and forth with another cup. I handed him a straw from my apron, and pushed the hair from my eyes.

"You go on out," he said. "I don't want you two getting back into it while I'm taking care of business."

I nodded and slipped through the swinging doors, hurrying as fast as I could to the back of the dining room to the public restrooms. I glanced at Flyswat, serving the hunter his Shirley Temple, and I hoped he did us right. I pushed open the pink ladies room's door, and gawked at my appearance. I looked as if I'd been rode hard—there were dark rings under my eyes, and my lower lip was swollen.

"Damn," I said to myself. "Valerie Brite, that witch has given you a fat lip." I couldn't help but laugh after that, and I turned on the water, splashing it on my face. My muscles were tense, and the insatiable burning in my throat was at its worse. I cupped my hands, filling them with water, and bringing it to my lips for a large gulp.

The water was cool on my lips, but as I poured it in, the fire did not cease. It got worse…

Looking back at myself, I saw a drop drip from my nose—several others clung to my eyelashes. I pulled of one of the rough hand towels from the dispenser next to the mirror and dried my face. I wish I had one of those fancy facial cloths this one generous woman kicked me over a grilled chicken salad—they make my skin feel revitalized.

I decided to hang out in the ladies room and count the green tiles. I normally despise wasting company minutes, but today was an exception. I'd tried everything with Natalie, and none of it seemed to be getting through. I dreaded the powwow Flyswat was planning, because getting that woman to do anything was an endeavor. Some folks just won't work with you.

I had counted up to 700 tiles when a little old woman (no doubt our other table) entered. She was wearing this white pajama gown with little blue flowers all over it. Fuzzy pink bathroom slippers shuffled across the floor. Covered in wrinkles, and she had a nest of kinky silver hair pulled back tight on her head. She walked in slow, stopping to look up at me.

"Hello, girl." Her crowfoot eyes were milky and gray, but they went right through me. Then her wrinkles scrunched up, he face flooded with a concerned look. "What happened, girl? You get in a brawl?"

I blushed and looked down. "Yes, ma'am."

"Darling," she said, "I'm ninety-three years old, and I'm gonna tell you, woman, life's too short to be bickering."

"It wasn't me," I argued. "It's all Natalie's faul—"

"Don't give me that lip, young lady. I bet you swung on her, didn't ya?"

"Yes, ma'am."

"What's a well-mannered lady like you doing a fool thing like fighting?" she asked. I shrugged. "When I was young, women didn't lower themselves like that—we had class."

"You've still got a lot to learn." She snorted and walked past me, disappearing into one of the stalls. I heard the latch click, and I decided it was time to leave the bathroom.

I felt wounded—not just from the fight, but something within.

I passed the hunter, who was dining on a hamburger and fries, and I saw Natalie sitting at table 23, rubbing her scarred wrists. Every instinct I owned begged me to avoid her, to hide in the loathsome stockroom until I felt better, but I couldn't do it. I knew I had to face Natalie and try to work things out.

I swore under my breath and headed over to table 23. I *squeaked* in across from Natalie—neither of us said anything or made eye contact. I looked across the room towards the old lady returning to her seat, and then I looked over towards the entrance—really, I was looking at everything but Natalie...I couldn't bring myself to do it.

Flyswat emerged from the kitchen, carrying a large salad and delivered it to the lady. I heard them speaking in hushed voices, but I couldn't make out what they were saying to each other. I hoped he was telling her gently, I wasn't sure if he'd ever done it before. I watched them talk a moment, and then Flyswat leaned down, letting the old lady embrace him. After he stood up, he shot me a little smile and bounced over to us, squeaking in next to me.

"Everything all right, Flyswat?" I asked.

"Yeah, we had that nice hunter who, from what I gathered, got shot by his buddy while they were stalking deer, and that sweet lady who passed away peacefully in her bed." I looked over and saw the hunter walk through the EXIT, the reflection of the diner's lights flashed across the glass panes.

I wished I could have been anywhere but sitting across from Natalie. She had no respect, and I didn't want to work another moment with her. I chewed the inside of my mouth, praying this wouldn't take too long.

"All right, girls," Flyswat said. "I can't take you two fighting all the time."

"She started it," Natalie whined.

I almost opened my mouth and started yelling, but Flyswat interrupted. "I don't care about any of that. What I care is that we finish , now." He turned to me and said, "Miss Brite, what's the problem? What can Natalie do to make things better?"

"Well," I said slowly, not wanting to lose my temper and make a scene, "I need her to respect my authority."

"You're not the boss of me. Who put you in charge?"

My mouth hung open, no one ever put me in charge. I always took charge of things because I figured no one else would. Flyswat was here when I arrived, but he always kept himself in the kitchen and out of dining room affairs. I didn't see myself as the boss. As far as that goes, I'd say Dirge was in charge, but maybe I was acting that way. Had I been too pushy wanting Natalie to do her job?

I wasn't sure anymore.

"No one said Miss Brite was in charge, Natalie," he said. "She has a real level head, and she's all about the job, so it's just understood that she is the manager here." I couldn't believe Flyswat referred to me as the manager. Bless that simpleton...

"She's always on my back, though," grumbled Natalie. "Miss Brite just wants you do the best job you can," he told her. "None of us want to upset Mr. Dirge. He has powers we can't begin to imagine, and I don't want to meddle with his temper."

Natalie nodded, and said, "Have you guys ever seen him get angry?"

Flyswat and I exchanged a glance, and I said, "When you first got here, you tried to go back through the entrance. Remember that night, the screaming the pain you felt?" She nodded, and I continued, "I have seen things from Mr. Dirge that make that look like a game of marbles."

She gasped. "Like what?"

"Let's just say we saw him take a customer who didn't want to go through the EXIT and make him wish he'd complied the first time we asked him."

"Really?" she asked, then chuckled, "What did Mr. Dirge do to him, turn him into a toad?"

"He put him in a place where he'll never find any peace," said Flyswat, and we both jerked our heads towards him. "A place where there is no distinction between shadow and light, pleasure and pain."

"I don't think he has that much power," Natalie chortled. "He's not God."

"No one said he was God, Natalie," I said. "But, mark my words Dirge is nothing to mess with. That's why you need to do your job, not complain, and try to keep a low profile."

Natalie snorted. "I'm not taking any orders from you, Valerie— you need to stay outta my way. If you think Mr. Dirge scares me, you've got another thing coming. He's nothing but a silly man in a high-dollar suit. You two tremble in front of him, but I could care less what he thinks of me—I'll spit in his face."

Ping-a-tonk.

The entrance swung open, and Dirge coasted in, alone. The look in his eyes…oh, the look in his dark eyes. He'd heard, or maybe sensed, Natalie's thoughtless remarks. He stopped at our table and motioned for Flyswat and myself to leave him with her. We both *squeaked* out, dashing for the swinging doors.

Flyswat and I went to the back of the kitchen. Panting, we locked eyes, and I saw fear in his. He looked over my shoulder towards the dining room.

"W-what do you think he's going to do with her?" Flyswat asked. I shrugged, my imagination blazing with images of her tossed into a pit filled with rusty barbwire and bloodthirsty asps. "S-she shouldn't h-have done t-that." I closed my eyes, trying not to think about it.

"I think we're OK. We were trying to help her. We tried to warn her. We didn't do anything wrong."

"Do you think he knows about her and that music guy?"

"I wouldn't be surprised, Flyswat. He knew that she was mud-slinging just then."

"Yeah, and she wasn't even talking loud."

I looked back at him and laughed a little. It must be so easy to be so ignorant. I wondered what he did to wind up as the chef in an afterlife hole-in-the-wall.

Uncountable time passed. For me, it seemed like a lifetime. Flyswat and I sat on our haunches on the kitchen's cold floor, saying nothing like wandering phantoms haunting a lost highway.

The swinging doors opened. Flyswat and I watched Natalie enter, her skin pale and her eyes worn, as if she'd been weeping.

"Natalie," exclaimed Flyswat, "you're alive."

"No," she quietly said. "No, I'm not."

"Aw," he laughed, "you know what I mean."

"What happened," I asked, longing to know. "What he'd do?"

"He gave me a warning," she said. "He told me I was messing up around here, and he wanted it to stop. You're the boss, and I'd better act as if I was a part of this team."

"What happens if you mess up?" Flyswat asked.

Natalie looked up at him and frowned. "He's going to put me in a place where there is no distinction between shadow and light, pleasure and pain." She looked as if she was beginning to cry again, and I rushed to her side, forgiving the friction among us. I put my arm around her and pulled her hair from her cheek. A glance back towards Flyswat, and I saw his head lowered towards his sneakers.

"Don't worry, Natalie," I assured. "It'll be all right."

"I hope so," she said.

I decided it was time to give up my anger towards her and try to really care about her. She'd hated herself enough to slash her wrists, and things have been hell ever since with the job and my attitude. We were a team, and we needed to get tight like one—not just for Dirge, but for all of our sakes.

"What can I do?" I asked her.

"What?" she said.

"What can I do to make things easier for you here?"

Flyswat smiled as Natalie exchanged looks with first him then me. When she saw my eyes, she knew I meant it. She offered a weak grin.

SPACE ODDITY

It wasn't coming upon the ghost ship that bothered the crew. We'd all worked salvages before, and the simple truth is that no matter how good your tech, too much can go wrong in space. Solar flares, micrometeoroids, dark matter, unmapped singularities, or simple metal fatigue leading to explosive decompression. We'd seen it all.

So, yeah, the ghost ship was no problem.

The problem was all the damned ghosts.

The first hint of trouble came during the shuttle over from the Celeste. The pilot and navigator were busy with instruments, so I was the only one to see the glow in the derelict's forward observation windows. The rest of the salvage crew was below decks prepping their gear, and as crew chief I was riding shotgun in the cockpit. I checked the scanner readings, but nothing registered. I didn't say anything to the crew. I told myself it was a reflection from our retro rockets. Seemed reasonable.

We forced the airlock and made our way into the dark corridors. Stardust had been a survey craft from a university research program, and records showed it had dropped off the grid three years ago. If it had been a cargo hauler, the owner would have come looking for it.

But as it was little more than a sight-seeing excursion, with little by way of cargo except whatever the grad students had brought along, the loss had been deemed not worth the cost of sending ships and crew this far out to search.

Like I said, problems in space were the norm in those days. Lost ships were expected.

We moved through the corridors in our EVA suits, tagging potential salvage items and collecting nametags from the mummified corpses we came across. There was no sign of damage, but all the electrical systems were fried. It looked like they'd flown through an electromagnetic pulse, possibly from a rogue star or a wormhole, and their ship had lost power. Before they could repair the problem, they'd lost life support.

Could be that death came even quicker, though. I noticed none of the dead wore an EVA suit, which you'd expect if someone was trying to outlast a failing environment. Could be the EMP had fried their brains too, and they never had to worry about freezing or suffocating.

Space is harsh, and death here is often sudden and unforeseen, but sometimes even that can be a blessing, as you'll see.

The Major had split us into quick-action squads before sending us over to the Stardust. We set to work getting the engines back on line and juicing the computers, and we brought any valuables aboard to be stowed in the Celeste's secure hold. The ship was barely space worthy after three years in the Ort cloud, but we were able to seal the command decks and repressurize them. We got basic maneuvering systems to respond, fired retros and brought the little surveyor alongside our cruiser. Magnelocks kept her close and inside our warp field, and the Major set us back on course for the way station at Alpha Centauri.

I'm sure someone else had a moment that day when they felt their short hairs rise, or heard voices from nowhere, or saw a tool moving across a deck of its own volition. But no one said anything.

They wrote it off as a trick of the intercom system, or a fluctua-
on in the inertial dampeners, or something like that. It wasn't until
1e full-body vaporous apparition manifested in the mess that night
1at we realized the ghosts had followed us back aboard our boat.

A bosun's mate came screaming out of her bunk, ran naked into
1e mess and vomited onto the deck. She said she had been assaulted
y an invisible octopus. None of us knew what to say. A few moved
ɔ assist her.

Just then, a tall man in a long coat walked through the wall and
ɔoked at us as if confused before opening his mouth in a soundless
cream and erupting into a geyser of smoke that seemed to seep into
he bulkheads.

An alarm sounded. The Major called from the bridge for all
ıands to assume emergency stations. We all scattered, even the
•osun's mate, who I saw later that night in her full uniform, seem-
ıg none the worse for the experience, if still a bit pale. I never heard
vhat had set the Major off, but I suspect it had something to do with
·ctoplasm.

There was a quick meeting of the command staff, and a quicker
lecision to jettison the Stardust. We popped the magnelocks and
vatched her drift out of our warp field, where the sudden decelera-
ion twisted her fuselage, causing the ship to disintegrate.

But we weren't free of the visitors. Something moved through
he engineering sector, disrupting the electrical systems and throwing
ɔur engines offline. Inertia dampeners ringed around the hull kept
ıs from coming apart like the Stardust, but we were left adrift in the
ınterstellar void, the darkness between star systems.

We never got the engines back. Life support held out for six days.
Most of the crew were already dead by then, either by their own hand
ɔr because of something the ghosts did to them.

I tried to get rid of them, but it was too late. I got the strongbox
illed with our salvage from their ship and shot it out an airlock. They
lidn't follow it. They had found something more valuable.

Major Tom launched in a lifeboat, the cowardly bastard. Left us there on our own as the lights failed and the air ran out and the cold creeped in. We were trapped in the dark with the ghosts for so long. Years and years and years. So lonely.

So lonely.

I'm really glad you found us. Don't be afraid. It won't be long now.

(With apologies to the Thin White Duke)

TONY SIMMONS

FRIEND TO DARKNESS

I have never been a friend to darkness. Afraid of it, like other people, I guess, but more afraid than most. When I was a boy, my fear
took a typical form: the occasional sleep-robbing terror that some
monstrous form lurked in my closet. Not so much under my bed because I always checked from a safe distance with a flashlight before I
ever climbed in for the night. Walking or biking by dark even a short
distance from a friend's house set my hair on end and had me looking
over my shoulder every few seconds. So gripped in fear that I nearly
slammed into a couple of parked cars. I must have looked ridiculous
to anyone who chanced to look out their door or window.

Anyway, we're supposed to put away childish things after a certain
age. Okay, so I did. At least on the surface. Still, I harbored some
real fright. Doesn't everybody?

In the Navy, night sentry duty on a bridge over a black band of
water spooked me. During the four hours I was so hyper-attuned to
any movement or sound that I was a profoundly sharp sentry. The
truth is that I could think of nothing else other than my bizarre,
macabre, grisly impending death so that a demolition specialist could

have been applying C4 to the bridge beneath my feet and I would scarcely have known.

Other things like that. Till it came to this, taking out the trash at night, a grown man with a family. Can you imagine?

So take out the trash during the daytime, what's the big deal?

Easy for you to say. There come times when you just have to take out the trash at night or have it stink up the whole house, you know? You think you've got it all, the bathrooms, the cat litter box, the clean-up from dinner, all nicely contained while the twilight wanes, so you tote it out to the large green trash container, winding across the yard, then between the large, nearly touching Confederate rose bushes—trees really. Here, tucked out of sight because Lord knows we don't want to offend the neighbors or anybody with our trash container. So here it is in the gloom, shadowed by the over-hanging oak tree, shielded by a brick wall on one side, a path down into our meager little wood. No threat, still light enough to see well. So, there, it's done, the trash bag dumped, and me making my way back across the lawn to the door. Done.

Then it's an hour or two later. The wife decides to clean out the refrigerator, two of the cats cough up kibbled orange masses, and the litter box has a fresh bloom of uncovered cat crap—almost a con-spiracy to build an odorous deposit that must go outside.

So I'm a grown man, what the hell! I can do this. I bag it all up, grab a flashlight, and go out into the dark, just as I've learned to do. Nothing ever happens. My hair stands on end, I make haste, shine the flashlight into the dark, sweep the beam into the woods, quickly dump the bag in the container, and then in my false bravado way, I whisper, "Bring in on, fuckers! Come and get some of this!"

I make my way back through the space between the Confederate rose trees, planning a backward jab with the flashlight, enough of a blow to smash in the teeth of some growling fiend, and I practice the sharp backward elbow thrust, laying low any imagined attacker, no matter how fast it might move.

I do this a couple of times a week. It remains a tense moment, but I do this and I get used to it. After all, it's what men are supposed to be able to do. Nobody I know ever talks about this sort of thing, so I just do my job—a man's job—fighting through the terrors of darkness.

Ever since men roamed away from their campfires, maybe because their bladders or bowels were full and it just couldn't wait, they dared venture into darkness. They did this often enough that they knew they could get away with it, taking along a spear or stone-blade knife just in case.

Nothing happens. The dark isn't nearly as scary as we're tempted to believe, right? We—I—just have this primordial fear of the dark and enough rational mind and manly devil-may-care daring-do to go out into it ever so often.

Tonight was just another night like that, another trash load that simply had to go out, my feeling a twinge of dread at the prospect, and yet, so what?

Out I go, trash bag in hand, not even taking a flashlight this time, the taunt rising to my tongue, "Go ahead, bring it on. I'll destroy you." A flash of adrenaline.

So the bag snags on a branch. "Miserable sleazy-assed bastard, son-of-a-bitch," I hiss. "Goddamn it."

Some of the trash spills out, and I can barely see to jam it back in the hole in the bag, and something gets on my hand, smelling to high heaven. It smells like something dying. "Fuck!"

That's when I sense something else, and the old feeling of hair on my neck standing straight up returns full force. I swear something's there, nearby, but then I always think something murderous and monstrous is nearby on these little trips.

"Whatever you fucking are, you can go straight to hell," I whisper.

I'm almost finished gathering up the spillage and dumping it into the trashcan, when I hear a steady voice, soft, but not really a whisper, just steady, assured, "Perhaps you'd like to join me."

I jump and swing around, looking for something, anything, in the gloom. Nothing there but the lightened shape of a tree trunk, some filtered light from the distant streetlight.

"What the fuck," I say, breathing hard suddenly.

"So . . .," says the voice again, "finally we meet."

Out of the dark emerges a shape, then two others, not so much walking as floating . . . emerging. Faint faces, a man, a woman, a . . . something. He is the proverbial vampire—no dumb cloak but white teeth, incisors, a witch's peak forehead and hairline, heartless eyes emitting their own light.

The woman, a black-lipped sylph, an alabaster face with something moving above her head. This is the dark and dangerous sex partner of my Id. I feel a thrill and a repulsion at the same time. A flash of white thigh appears at the slit in her robe.

And this other creature is . . . I don't know what, darker, harder to see, but I think he has horns, small nubs of horn above the dark skin of his forehead. Some low sound comes out of him—or it.

Sure, I'm scared shitless, but I'm fascinated, too. I'm not even sure there is anything there and instead I'm imagining all this. I'm daring myself not to run. This night will pass like any other.

The man, the vampire, speaks.

"You have invoked our names night after night. And then you've seen fit to provoke us." The vampire backs the sneer from his upper lip, casting a look at the horned creature, who'd yet to say a word, but who continues to birth a gurgle from deep in his throat. Now, a toad-skinned gorgon appears just behind the other three, he enthusiastically huffing what I gather is an affirmation.

The sylph with her twisted strands of hair writhing as though alive—in most every other way suicidally beautiful, mounds of breast moving with each of her breaths—looks slant-eyed at me, raising a high-arching eyebrow beneath a head tressed with black snakes. "Otherwise known as the *Invoke and Provoke Clause*," she says with a voice of murderous velvet.

Then she adds with a careful legalistic precision, "Whereby said
erson summoned the undersigned being or beings into existence by
epeated thought construct or actual spoken word, and whereby said
erson then imaginatively presumed to defeat the undersigned being
r beings in mock combat, the undersigned then reserve the right to
ontest such defamation and humiliation on the corporeal plane in
1e presence of said person." I once played pool in a bar and went
ome with a woman like this.

"I'm sorry, I, uh, really didn't mean anything," I say.

"Ah, and how do you think that makes us feel?" says the sylph,
that you did this so casually and in such an off-handed manner?

The vampire shifts his weight fluidly, albeit impatiently.

Then the devil rumbles, not so much speaks as puts these ideas
1 the air: "You recently cheated on your wife, and you promised
ever again. You were paid for work you didn't do. You stole. You
arbored resentments and hatred—these especially heart-chilling.
'here's more."

They know everything. They see into my own black spaces.
'hey've been waiting till it—till I—was dark enough.

"The question is . . . do you want a way out?" The vampire's
carlet red eyes gleam at me.

I nod vigorously before I speak. "Yes, of course. Anything."

The sweet-voiced sylph's eyes narrow into calculating slits.
'There's that word anything again. He did say anything, didn't he?"

"Indeed he did," replies the vampire, the distant streetlight glint-
1g off his impossibly white teeth. "It is . . . do as we ask, or else
our wife and daughters—and then you—will take days to die."

Finally, the devil-like creature speaks as though from a deep fis-
ure in the earth. "I see your girls hanging from hooks as their skin
eels away like wallpaper." He makes these pealing flickering motions
7ith his fingers, showing long black nails.

I cringe and my breath catches.

They then close their circle around me, pinning me against one
f the trees, and I listen in horror as one by one they whisper a list

of dark despicable acts they will require of me. And the choice has already been made. Within my own circle of darkness that I have approached warily for years, I know I am theirs.

LYNN WALLACE

WHERE SHADOWS CREPT

amie watched Brian plug wires extending from his digital Panasonic camcorder into the Sony VCR beneath a 42" flat screen television. Brian pushed the power button on the lower right-hand side, and the screen came to life with a warm blue glow. He looked over at Jamie and smiled.

"Is this really going to work?" she asked, arms crossed. Her boyfriend's infernal meddling often bored her, but his hobbies made him happy, so she tolerated whatever silly project he pursued. She found him cute while tinkering with his toys, irresistible even. That same triumphant look won her heart when they met over an underground game of Texas Hold'em at a mutual friend's house. Brian was on fire that night, winning almost every hand, shooting her dangerous and exultant looks. That charm landed them in the same Safe Ride cab to her house that night.

"Of course it's going to work—I've followed the experiment exactly like the ghost hunters on television." He opened the camcorder's side viewfinder.

"I guess TV never lies." Jamie tossed her curly black hair. She hated how the loose ends would jab her blue eyes, vowing one day to go shaved. Maybe that would draw back her lover's attention, a new hairstyle. It seemed like eons since he looked at her like a gift begging for unwrapping.

Brian shot her a silly look, sticking out his tongue, and flipped the camcorder's red switch with his thumb. A tight angle shot of the living room rug replaced the blue screen, and loud feedback squelched an ally cat serenade. Jamie dropped a pair of 3D glasses, cupping her hand over her ears as Brian scrambled to mute the television. With a sheepish smirk, Brian regained his composure and sat up.

"I forgot I was sitting kind of close. Sorry."

Jamie shrugged. "What happens next?"

"Well, you point the camera towards the TV, put on the glasses, and...and wait."

"And they will come?"

"It worked on the show."

For six months, Brian devoured programs involving hunting ghosts, deciding he too could track them. To Jamie's angst, he sent three hundred dollars to a web site, purchasing an electromagnetic field meter, a small, square device for measuring magnetic anomalies ghosts supposedly create. They spent the next two months walking all over Bay County, Brian pouring over the LED display and Jamie following, tight-lipped, hopelessly searching for paranormal activity. The meter failed to indicate any outré presence and Brian attributed this to 'boring Panama City life', promising a venture to New Orleans or Savannah where the ghosts really boogie. Now he was trying to record EVP, or Electronic Voice Phenomenon, furthering his communion with the dead.

"Honey, will you turn off the light?" he asked, locking the camera atop a tripod in front of the TV. Jamie sighed, hitting the switch on the living room's back wall. His trailer was small but cozy. Thanks to an inheritance, it was paid for, allowing Brian the luxury of nice things. Jamie hoped that one day he would spend some of that amenity on her. More than what lurked in his pocket, Jamie wanted alone time together.

Brian waved her over, and she sat Indian-style on the rug. As she rubbed his shoulders, he aimed the camera towards the TV, and the screen went from shaky, *Blair Witch* camerawork to a dazzling display of light—a maddening, silent static.

"What's happening?" she asked.

"By pointing the camera towards the screen, I've created an endless loop of nothing. It's sort of like opening a doorway to the next world, using the camera as a key. Remember those photos in the mall, the ones with pictures hidden within pictures after you relax your eyes?"

Jamie nodded, unblinking. She spent hours staring at those damned things with little payoff, and she hoped whatever skill needed to gaze into the nether region didn't apply here.

"If you do the same thing when the TV is set up like this, I believe you will see and communicate with the dead. Scientists have been experimenting with EVP with cool results."

She watched the angry pixels illuminate Brian's face and forced a smile. He looked so happy, so content, his brown eyes sparkled like Christmas snow. Jamie, not willing to convey her disappointment, swallowed hard and rested her palm on his designer blue jeans. They used to spend a lot of time together, walking along the beach and hunting down rare comic books, but lately, he was so…distracted.

"I'm going to record what we see, so we have proof after we make contact. Those skeptics are gonna go crazy after they get a hold of us." Brian licked his lips and Jamie noticed they were beginning to chap. As a result of his nervous habit they would split, and Jamie would have to play doctor, piling on the lip gloss and nursing them back to health. She loved the way he would lay there, scrunching up his eyes as she applied the ointment—so intimate.

They silently sat, watching the electronic salt and pepper crawl across the screen. After a few moments, Jamie began tapping her long red nails on one of the tripod's silver legs. Brian looked over at her, squinting.

"Do you mind?"

"Sorry." Her face warmed. "When are we going to see them?"

"Um, I'm not sure." He leaned in closer to the screen. Jamie sensed his whole body tense up. Brian snapped his fingers. "*Oh, we forgot the glasses.*"

He chuckled and extended an open hand; Jamie slapped the red and blue specks he bought at a comic book store from a curly-haired kid with thick glasses into it. He looked her up and down a moment. He rolled his eyes, adorned the glasses, and gazed into the bustling dots. Several long moments passed.

"Damn it, Brian." She stood up. "This is stupid. I can't believe I'm subjecting myself to this childish nonsense. We're twenty-eight years old, Brian. People our age are getting married, have real jobs… starting families. What am I doing? I'm watching nothing on the TV with my line-cook boyfriend on a Friday night."

"Hey." Brian was unable to mask the hurt on his face.

"Do you know what Sally and Paul are doing tonight? Do you?" Brian turned his 3-D glasses to the rug, shaking his head.

"They're driving to Atlanta for a Nick Cave concert at the Tabernacle and a romantic evening in some fancy hotel. I bet they even eat at the Marietta Diner. I love it there, Brian."

"Do you know how much those tickets cost?"

"That's not the point, Brian. What I'm saying is that they're doing things together."

"We, uh, do things together. What do you call this?"

"We've been together for almost a year, and you won't move in with me. Every time we do something you have to include your mother, and I hate, hate, hate comic book shops. I don't find looking for ghosts romantic. In fact, it's sick. You want to chat with dead people, Brian, but I'm alive—I'm here. I have needs, and I don't mean going to haunted bed and breakfasts. I don't believe in ghosts, Brian."

Brian gasped. "I—I thought you liked ghosts."

"It's all…crap. You know what? I'm outta here. When you decide to grow up, call me." Jamie stormed out, slamming the front

oor. Brian heard her stomp down the shaky steps outside and slam
er car door. Her engine cranking soon followed, and she peeled out
f his driveway.

Brian sighed, returning his attention to the screen...

The next morning, Jamie awoke in her one bedroom apartment
egretting her behavior. She had not meant to blow up like that.
rian did not deserve that. He was a nice guy, sincere to her. She
eally did love him. She just wished he would pay more attention to
er, as much as she paid to him. When stepping back, he was into
nteresting ideas; he would just get carried away with them, that's all.

After a simple oatmeal breakfast (apples and cinnamon, her fa-
orite), she called the small trailer Brian owned off North Lagoon.

The phone rang seven times before a shaky voice answered.
Hello?"

Jamie didn't recognize her boyfriend's tone. "Brian?"

"Yeah?"

"Are you, OK? I'm sorry how I acted last night, but, Christ, I
st—I just want to do something, just us, ya know. Without the
hosts."

"I'm sorry, Jamie, but it happened last night." His words lacked
mbre, alarming Jamie.

"What happened? What do you mean?"

"I made contact...with the other side."

"Other side?"

"Them—or, at least, someone from over there talked to me.
aught me a better way to communicate. I have to try."

"And you recorded the whole thing, huh?" She couldn't help the
arcasm, but she expected a little more from the man she loved.

"I—I forgot to hit the button on the VCR."

"IT FIGURES. I thought I was a little rough last night, but I
uess I wasn't harsh enough. I can't believe you would lie to keep me
rom being angry—that's so typical. 'Forgot to hit the button'—do
ou think I'm stupid?"

"Listen, Jamie, this is serious. I was sitting there after you left and the static—the static began...taking shape. It became a face, and I saw its lips move. I couldn't hear what it was saying because I muted the TV, remember?"

"Yes," she replied.

"So, I turned up the sound and, through the hiss, I heard it speak."

He fell silent a moment and she could hear him licking his lips. Whatever it was that did happen, it had gotten to him. Worry nibbled at her.

"It said I invaded where shadows crept."

"What does that mean?"

"I'm not sure, but then it said I could see more."

"Are you sure you were talking to a ghost? What if you were just picking up some cell phone call or a CB transmission? How do you know you were talking to a ghost?"

"Because it mentioned my Aunt Ethel."

Jamie fell silent. Brian's Aunt Ethel practically raised him and, after dying three years ago, she left him the trailer where he now resided. Jamie never met her, but Brian still hurt over her passing. He had her picture in several places in the living room, and every time conversation wandered in her direction, Brian would tear up and change the subject.

"What did it say about her?"

"It said I could see her again if I built a psycomantrium or a catoptromancy chamber."

"A what?"

"A scrying room."

"Strike two," Jamie laughed. "What is scrying?"

"You've seen the pictures with the wizard looking into his crystal ball?" Brian asked.

"Sure, Wal-Mart has puzzles with Nostradamus looking in a crystal ball and writing his prophecies. Some even glow-in-the-dark."

"Nostradamus foretold the future with a shallow pan of water
and ink drops but, you get the picture. He was divining the future
through a method called scrying. Magicians and fortunetellers have
scryed for centuries, and they've used crystal balls, water, and mirrors
to do it. It goes back to practices in ancient Greece and the Oracle
at Delphi. Whenever you use mirrors to divine the future, it's called
Catoptromancy, and a room for this is called a psychomantrium."

"How do you know all this stuff?"

"I looked it up on the Internet after talking to the TV ghost."

She sighed. "I should have known."

"Anyway, the information I was getting on psychomantriums was
a little different that what the TV ghost was telling me."

"This ought to be interesting," snorted Jamie. "How was that?"

"The web sites explain the psychomantrium as a candlelit room
with one mirror while the TV ghost described an eight-mirror setup."

"Don't tell me, you're going to build the damned thing." There
was more lip licking, and Jamie imagined Brian's mouth bleeding
from the stress. "You are, aren't you?"

"I have to—this is why I got into ghosts in the first place. To
find my aunt."

"That's sick, Brian. She is dead and nothing you do can bring her
back. You can miss her, that's fine, but I'm here, Brian. Let her go."

"I have to build it, Jamie. When you're ready to accept things the
way they are, you can come over. I'll be here...watching."

The line went dead. Jamie returned the phone to the hook. She
loved Brian, but he needed to grow up. She was ready to give herself
to him, and he responded by wallowing in arrested development.
Telling herself Brian needed to sweat it out, she vowed not to call
him for a while.

She was able to hold out three days before heading over to Brian's
trailer in her gray (the owner's manual called it gunmetal) Kia Spectra.
Jamie pulled up next to his white Chevy, noticing a several black trash
bags at the curb. She walked the three shaky, wooden steps to the
front door and knocked. There was no reply, so she tried the knob.

To her surprise, the door swung open. Brian cherished his thrift store finds and comic books, he never left the door unlocked. She looked into the trailer's darkness.

"Brian, are you in there?" After several long silent minutes, she entered, shutting the door behind her.

Inside, everything appeared as if she left it: camcorder perched before the television, stacks of anime and horror movies beside the DVD player, dishes done in the kitchen, and Spiderman posters on every wall. The computer's moon screensaver still went through its phases, and the nightlight in the hall leading to his bedroom burned soft green. She looked for some sign of disarray but found no detour from the norm. Worry festered inside of her.

She wondered if he was asleep and made her way past the glass coffee table where the latest issue of Wizard magazine and an empty green tea bottle rested. Two folded beach chairs and a cooler stuffed with Panama City Beach koozies, a beer bong, and towels from when they used to take coastline walks were tucked beside a bookshelf stocked with all the classic nerd tomes, from H. P. Lovecraft and Wiccan grimoires to *Hitchhiker's Guide to the Galaxy* and *Starship Troopers*.

The bathroom door was ajar and, again, everything was in its place.

She opened the door to Brian's bedroom, flipped on the light, and gawked—everything was different. His windows and walls, once lined with Laura Croft and X Men posters, were draped with thick black velvet sheets, forbidding light to penetrate the room. Gone were the waterbed and boxes of comic books she both loved and hated, and in their place was eight, full-sized oval mirrors arranged facing each other in an octagon—one of the mirrors opened like a door into the Stonehenge circle. Within the circle was a black stool. Jamie stepped in, noticed a large white candle lying on its side before the stool, and knew instantly how the psychomantrium operated. She suspected something had appeared to Brian the other night and realized what the trash bags out front contained. He was prone to whims, true, but for him to toss out all of his comic books could only mean one thing: Brian was telling the truth about the face in the static.

His absence gnawed Jamie; something happened and it didn't feel...right.

She entered the apparition booth, and a billion other Jamies entered at the same time. She didn't want to look at them, fearing she would lose herself in the jumble. She knelt down and picked up the candle, noticing a Newby's Too matchbook by one of the stool's legs. Grabbing them, she exited the psychomantrium and walked to the bedroom's egress. She sighed and tucked the candle into her left armpit. Striking a match and lighting the candle's charred wick, she turned off the bedroom light and headed for the mirrors, her breathing intensifying.

She entered and the candle's flame became multiplied a thousand-fold, becoming its own galaxy. Her blue eyes reflected an eerie, staring cluster. She balanced the candle on the stool and turned, completing the octagon enclosure by drawing in the eighth mirror. She turned and looked into infinity. Uncountable Jamies stared back. Taking a deep breath, she sat on the stool and gazed into the abyss. *Funny thing about mirrors*, she thought, *not only can they reflect, they can reflect themselves.* She understood why magicians utilized them for their invocations, their phantasmal needs. Mirrors were magic.

Time passed. She was unable to determine exactly how much, but that was all part of it. A longing to close her eyes nagged, but she could not look away and break the spell. Focusing on the closest reflection, she concentrated on her features, her dark skin and cerulean eyes. Silver earrings flickered from time to time, supernovas in the dim night. Her vision became weary as her attention began to drift from the closest reflection to the next and then to the next. Soon, she was lost in the chamber's labyrinth.

The colors began to bend and bleed, and she could no longer determine where she was. Every turn of the head magnified the kaleidoscope, and her heartbeat pounded in her ears. She wanted to flee but needed to understand what happened to Brian. Next, around her thirteenth reflection, where the shadows crept, she saw him.

In the curls of her dark hair, Brian was looking at the candlelit universe, licking his lips. His mouth moved as if he were speaking. Yet, Jamie couldn't hear anything other than her own heartbeat. She moved her mouth to speak but it changed the reflections, momentarily blurring Brian. She froze, not wanting to lose him forever.

Helplessness... She had not planned for this. How could she reach her love, her friend? What would she tell his mother if she ever escaped the psychomantrium's hellish grip? More importantly, how would she escape this nightmare?

It was then she noticed her—the old woman behind her. It wasn't the aunt Jamie had seen in pictures Brian proudly displayed around the living room, but someone, something else. Jamie, intent on finding Brian, was so distracted by herself she never saw the crone approach, and in a blink, she was right behind her, as if she were there all along. Her wrinkles and crows feet. Her pulled-back gray hair. Her thin round eyes staring at Jamie, staring through Jamie.

Jamie looked around finding her reflection no longer dominated the psychomantrium's vortex. Now the old woman was ubiquitous. Jamie was nothing more than a shadow in one of the old woman's wrinkles, and Brian was gone all together. She screamed, lunging forward into the madness.

The music of breaking glass.

Then…nothing.

Fumbling in the dark, Jamie struck a match to find herself in Brian's darkened bedroom. She had jumped into the chamber's wall, knocking over and shattering three of the mirrors. Smoke wafted from the extinguished candle on the floor as hot wax seeped from its crown. The match burned Jamie's finger and she shook it out.

Another match and she saw the fallen mirrors' glass fragments catching the flickering flame. The dancing light flashed traces of Brian, herself, and the spectral old woman—fading out—until there

as only a match, burning the finger of Jamie, a woman standing
one and believing in ghosts.

NTHONY S. BUONI

CONTRIBUTORS

ANTHONY S. BUONI is a musician, writer, and DJ in Panama City Beach, Florida who publishes the art and lit zine, Meow. A bartender at La Vela, Anthony enjoys gardening with his son, Fallon, film, and road trips. In addition to future volumes of "Between There," Anthony has several novels planned ranging in genres from horror to counterculture.

W. ADAM BURDESHAW is currently a student living and working in his hometown of Panama City, Florida. "Whiteblood" is his first work of fiction published in a tangible medium. He is currently in the process of rewriting his first novel in the adventure/fantasy genre, and hopes to have it ready for submission by the end of the year.

BRITTANY LAMOUREUX is a writer from Panama City, Fl. and a graduate of GCCC. She enjoys writing screenplays and short stories.

JONI LeCOMPTE is a student at Ashford University, working towards a bachelor's degree in health care administration. She is a current member of the Alpha Sigma Lambda national honor society. Joni is a writer of short stories and poetry and has published several poems in the periodical zine, Meow. She also occasionally writes song lyrics for her fiancé, Randy's music. Joni loves to read and has no particular genre she prefers. There are simply too many good stories out in the universe to keep to just one.

NATHAN SIMMONS is a recent graduate from the Theatre department at the University of West Florida. In addition to his passion for

cting, he tries to find time to write poetry, lyrics, and plays. He is a
published playwright and has another script on the way.

TONY SIMMONS is the author of the novel "Welcome to the
Dawning of a New Century," and the short story collection "The
Best of Days." His book "Dazed and Raving in the Undercurrents"
collects many of his award-winning columns for The Panama City
News Herald, where he is the online content editor.

TOBY UNION writes erotic horror and exploitation tales speckled
with a twist of social commentary. The book, "The Absinthe Butter-
ly," marks the first installment to his "Insect Trilogy," an illustrated,
pornographic descent into the depraved world of alcoholism and
bars. He is currently working on the second installment, "The Chartreuse Moth."

LYNN WALLACE writes fiction, screenplays, and poetry. He teaches
at Gulf Coast State College.

CONRAD YOUNG uses art as a weapon. He writes out of Panama
City, FL, where he is currently taking all comers. He also enjoys
spending time with his daughter, Olive, and fronting the band, Pig
Chicken Suicide.

CPSIA information can be obtained at www.ICGtesting.com
Printed in the USA
LVOW121418231011

251697LV00002B/5/P